Cuckoos on the

Conrad Jones

A Child Protection Team Novel

1

Red Dragon Publishing LTD

ISBN: 978-1739406608 Cuckoos on the Mersey

This book is a work of fiction. Any resemblance between these fictional characters and actual persons, living or dead, is purely coincidental.

RED DRAGON BOOKS

PREFACE; I'm dedicating this book to my partner and the amazing people she works with in child protection.

Cuckoos is a new series inspired by the work that the child protection teams across the country carry out, seven days a week. During covid, my partner and her colleagues were forced to work from home. The social workers were still out there, protecting children and vulnerable families. They were driving to designated car parks to pick up PPE, so that they could still visit the most vulnerable children. Lockdown meant that children were not going to school, the most vulnerable were even more so, as teachers weren't seeing them, and that layer of protection was removed. Domestic violence increased as families were forced to be at home 24/7 and alcohol and drugs related incidents skyrocketed. When we were clapping on our front doorsteps for the NHS, the child protection teams were flat out too and still are today. We should be banging the big bass drum for every child they save from harm.

The work that the child protection teams do is nothing short of incredible, but we often only hear about the mistakes that are made. They are a forgotten emergency service, up there with ambulance, fire and police. When they are called upon, they respond with professionalism and urgency to match any other service. The children they save will go on to have children of their own and their legacy will echo through time for generations to come. Future generations will have children of their own because of what they did yesterday, today and will do tomorrow. You are heroes in our midst, each and every one of you.

Glossary of terms
CE Child Exploitation
PR Parental Responsibility
DV Domestic Violence
WP Witness Protection
PVPU Protecting Vulnerable Persons Unit
C and F Child and Family report.
EDD expected delivery date.
Strat. Strategy plan

Chapter 1. Day one; Mummy.

I*go to sleep and imagine that you're there with me...*
    4.30pm

Calvin was sitting on the rug because it was slightly warmer than the bare floorboards and he was less likely to get anymore splinters in his feet. His mother had plucked the last one out with her tweezers, which had been painful. He had complained for weeks that it was sore and becoming red and painful, but it was only when it had become infected and yellow goo was coming out of it that she did something about it. His shoe rubbed the sore and made him limp a little and his teachers at nursery had asked what was wrong with him. Of course, Calvin said nothing was wrong, just like his mum had told him to, but they wouldn't leave it at that.

They took him to the nurse, who said it was infected and she asked why his mum hadn't taken him to see a doctor and Calvin didn't know the answer to her questions. His mum had told him not mention the injury in school or the 'fucking social worker witches' would be back, banging on the door, telling her how to parent her own children, insinuating what a bad mother she was. Whenever the witches visited, she would rant for hours.

She did like to rant a lot. Fucking this and fucking that; it was his mum's special word. Well, if it wasn't her special word, it was definitely her favourite word.

Fucking was a bad word, his teacher said but his mum used it all the time, especially to the neighbours. They said she was a bad parent too. Tony Knobhead, that was what his mum called him, who lived next door, often patted Calvin on the head and told him he felt sorry for him having a mother like that. Calvin didn't think his mother was anything but a good mum, but he loved her and didn't know any different. He loved her unconditionally. Even when she drank dirty beer, which was often.

When she drank dirty beer with her men friends, she was different. He didn't like the men who came to their house, luckily most of them ignored him anyway. They were always trying to get rid of him and Coco.

'Go and play in your room, kids.'

Or,

'I just want to talk to your mum on our own for a while.'

Or,

'Fuck off, you little brat.'

He was a very nasty man. One of them gave him a pound to go in the garden to play, but it started raining and Calvin and Coco came back in. He kept the pound though and bought some sweets for him and Coco. Some of his mum's friends tried to boss him around but he didn't take any notice and pretended not to hear them. They were all called Uncle something or another and they all drank beer and smoked weeds, although why anyone would want to smoke weeds was confusing. Smoking weeds made everyone hungry and also made the house stink.

Calvin hated the smell and Coco said it made her feel sick. Smoking weeds and drinking beer made his mum behave as if Calvin and his sister Coco weren't there anymore. When she was drinking, she smoked more cigarettes and swore more and danced more and it made her happy for a while, but eventually she would want to punch everyone, especially the neighbours.

Tony Knobhead from next door was friendly with his mum most of the time but they often fell out. He would come banging on the door if the music was too loud. His wife, Sandra Knobhead hated his mum, and they didn't speak at all. His mum had called Sandra a fat C-word and Sandra hadn't spoken to her since. The C-word was especially bad, apparently. Mum said she saved it for special occasions.

Although she could be fun, when she was drinking, she neglected them, and Calvin and his sister Coco would get hungry. They were hungry now, and he had tried to tell her that they were hungry, but his mother wasn't answering him. She was sleeping on the settee, and he couldn't wake her up.

He was wary of disturbing her when she was sleeping because she could be nasty when she was woken. The last time he shook her, she woke with a start and had slapped him in the face with the back of her hand and split his lip. There was blood on his jumper, and she said that she was sorry and hadn't done it on purpose. She said that she had been having a bad dream. He had tried to be brave and not cry but it had hurt. There was a bruise on his cheek and a cut on his top lip, so he had to tell the teachers at school that he had fallen during a game of football in the back garden. Of course, they hadn't believed him, and he had been sent to the nurse again and she asked lots of questions.

Later that day, the 'fucking social worker witches' had come knocking again and Calvin and Coco had hidden behind the coffee table, while their mum hid upstairs. They went away eventually but they always come back with the police.

It was two days later when they came again and asked about his football accident. Not that he could play football in the back garden anyway because it was covered in dog shit. There wasn't an inch available to play on and he was scared of the dog. It was nasty and barked all the time day and night. It wasn't their dog but one of the uncles paid his mum to look after him. He was Uncle Mike and he never smiled.

Uncle Mike was scary and had skulls tattooed all over his arms and he smoked weeds all the time and smelled funny. He came and took the dog away sometimes. Mum said it was to see a bitch. Calvin wasn't sure why. Bitch was a bad word, his teacher said but not when talking about a dog. It was an ugly dog with big teeth and a big head and a squashy nose as if it had run into a wall, like in the cartoons. It had run inside the house one day and knocked Calvin over and he banged his head on the table. That was another bruise he had to lie about at school, and they didn't believe him that time either. It seemed like his teachers didn't believe a word he said about home. Calvin didn't like the dog especially because he couldn't play out in the garden anymore and he loved to play.

He couldn't play out at the front of the house either because his mum said the estate was full of perverts, like Tony Knobhead next door. Calvin wasn't sure that was his real name or who the other perverts were but if she said they were there, they must be. The social worker witches had told his mum that she had to clean up the garden and get rid of the dog, so her children had somewhere safe to play.

She said she would but when they left, she shouted, 'fuck off!' really loudly at the door and stuck two fingers up as they drove away. His mum said there was more chance of King Charles clearing up the shit from the garden than her doing it. Coco had laughed so hard, she nearly wet herself.

That was weeks ago, and King Charles had not turned up and the dog was still there snarling at everyone who walked past, and the garden was still covered in shit.

'Cal, I'm hungry,' Coco moaned. She was kneeling next to the settee waiting for their mum to wake up. Her nose was running again, and she wiped it with her sleeve. She had blonde hair tied up in two bunches. Her intense blue eyes were slightly bigger than her brother's.

'Me too,' Calvin said. He was blonde too and they were almost identical to look at, apart from the bunches. 'I'm starvin Marvin.'

Coco chuckled. 'I'm starvin Marvin too. Who is Marvin anyway?'

'He's a guy that is always starvin,' Calvin explained as best he could because he had no idea who Marvin was, but it made Coco chuckle.

'I'm fed up with being starvin Marvin and it's getting dark. Can we put the big light on?'

'There's no money in the meter,' Calvin said, shrugging.

'Why not?'

'Mum said the meter is a thieving bastard and has taken all her money again,' Calvin whispered.

'That's naughty,' Coco said putting her hand over her mouth and giggling.

'Don't say that word when mum is awake,' Calvin whispered in her ear. 'Mum will know it was me who said it.'

'I won't,' Coco said, shaking her head. 'I'm so hungry. Can we make beans on toast ourselves?'

'No. There's no gas either,' Calvin said, stroking her hair. 'We'll have to wake mum up to put money in the meters so she can make some dinner.'

'Okay, go on then,' Coco said, hugging her bear. Teddy was her constant companion. 'You wake her up, Cal.'

'No. You wake her up,' Cal said, lowering his voice. 'She slapped me last time.'

'She pinched me on the leg, last time,' Coco whispered, shaking her head and hiding behind Teddy. 'My leg was purple and sore.'

A knock on the door startled them. Coco ducked down and peered around the couch. She looked at her brother for instructions. He stood up and went to the window, peering through the blinds. A friendly face appeared, her smile warm and infectious. It was Jo Lilly, one of the fucking social worker witches. Jo was the boss of the other social workers, and a nice lady and Calvin didn't know why his mum didn't like her. She was always kind and came to see him at school sometimes. He had to tell her lies a lot, but she always knew when he was lying and she always said it was okay because his mum had told him to lie, so it didn't count. She would tell his mum that she knew what was really going on and that there was absolutely no point in telling the kids to tell lies. His mum would get angry with the social workers, and he didn't like that.

'Oh, you know what's really going on, do you? Blah, blah, blah. Aren't you so fucking clever that is hurts,' his mum had said one time. 'Why don't you go and talk to someone who is interested in what you think?'

He remembered because Jo Lilly had shaken her head and winked at Calvin. He worried that his mum would shout at him because he wasn't good at lying to his teachers, but she never did. Another knock at the window startled him from his thoughts.

'Hello Calvin,' Jo Lilly said, waving through the glass. 'Where is your mum?'

'She's sleeping on the settee,' Calvin said.

'Wake her up,' Jo said.

'She won't wake up. I think she's really sleepy today,' Calvin said, whispering at the window. 'I've tried shaking her but she's not waking up.'

'Okay. Open the door and I'll wake her up,' Jo said. She pointed to the front door. 'Come on. I bet you're hungry, aren't you?'

'Yes,' Calvin nodded. The emptiness of his stomach spurred him into action. His mother had warned him never to open the door to the witches, but his obedience was trumped by hunger. He ran to the door and opened it. Jo stepped in, stooping to give him a hug. A tall man was behind her. Calvin didn't recognise him. 'Who is he?' Calvin asked. 'I think my mum will go mad at me for opening the door.'

'Don't you worry about it. This is Phil,' Jo said, stepping past him towards the settee. 'Phil is a social worker like me.'

'But you're the boss?' Calvin said, smiling.

'I am the boss of all the witches,' Jo said. She ruffled Coco's blond hair. 'Hello lovely girl, how are you today?' she asked.

'I'm hungry and so is Teddy,' Coco said.

'That's not good. What does Teddy want to eat?'

'Nuggets with ketchup.'

'That's my favourite,' Jo said. 'It's getting dark in here.' She flicked the light switch. 'No money in the meter again?' she asked Calvin. Calvin nodded and felt a bit ashamed but wasn't sure why. 'Angela, wake up!'

'You must be Calvin,' Phil said, smiling. He was a giant. Calvin nodded but didn't speak.

'Angela,' Jo said, shaking his mum's shoulder. 'Angela, can you hear me?' she said louder. 'Angela. Wake up for me.'

'Can you take Coco and Calvin into the kitchen for a minute please,' Jo said to the tall man. Jo looked concerned.

'Come on little man,' Phil said, guiding him gently. 'Coco, come with us for a moment. Let's see what you've got to eat in the fridge.'

'There's nothing in there except beer,' Coco said, shaking her head. 'We had pizza this morning, but we ate it all up.'

'I like pizza too,' Phil said.

Calvin was watching Jo. He sensed that all was not as it should be. He watched as Jo turned his mum onto her side. At first, he thought she was awake. Her eyes were open, but they were not the same as usual. She was staring at nothing. There was sick like porridge on her chin. Jo looked at the tall man and shook her head. She took out her phone and walked out of the front door. Calvin heard her say ambulance and police. He pulled away from the tall man and ran to his mum, stopping before he reached her. She stared into space, looking through him not at him. He touched her face and it felt odd. Calvin didn't know much about much, but he knew right there and then that his mum wasn't there anymore.

Chapter 2. My name is Leo.

N *ever coming down, no more, no more, no more...*

ACROSS THE ROAD FROM Angela's house, Leo Tomkins was feeling the tide go out. He was sixteen and had been taking ketamine and pregabalin for over two years. Withdrawal was the darkest of dark pits to be in, yet he visited it daily; It felt as if his body was being sucked dry from the inside. His intestines had a mind of their own and contracted and expanded painfully. The cramps were coming and going, and he felt like he needed to go to the toilet to pee but when he tried to go, there was nothing but a burning sensation in his waterworks. It was eye-wateringly painful. Water infections were ruining his life, but they were one of the side effects of long-term ketamine abuse. He had taken the last of his supply the day before and there were no more drugs in the flat. The drugs had worn off and the glow had faded, being replaced by a torturous vacuum. The experience of withdrawal was something non-users could never comprehend. It was unbearable and there was nothing but the ache for more drugs and an emptiness, which couldn't be filled. There was no sleep, no eating, no peace.

The pregabalin helped sooth the nerve pain caused by withdrawal, but nothing stopped it completely, except more ketamine. His girlfriend, Abi had gone to buy some more, except they had no money, which meant she would need to ask for credit again. Asking for credit from any dealer was a slippery slope but needs must, and the need was overwhelming.

He was looking through the window, hoping Abi would be walking up the path but there was no sign of her. He'd seen a car pull up at the house opposite his flat and two people got out, one male and one female. He recognised them as social workers. The man was called Phil and he was very tall and gangly; Phil had been the only social worker he had clicked with in all his years as a looked after child. The woman was called Jo, Phil's boss and he had talked to her many times over the years. She was the manager of the social workers he had, and she was a good one. They actually cared what happened to Leo. He wondered what Phil was doing there. If he hadn't felt so shit, he would have gone to say hello.

Leo watched the social workers knocking on the door, but no one answered, so they knocked on the window and peered inside. It was Angela Deacon's house and one of her kids opened the door and let them inside. They were often knocking on her door, sometimes she answered and sometimes she didn't. Angela was an alright lady and he liked her, but she partied hard and didn't do herself any favours. Abi liked her and she was a good judge of character. They would sit in the kitchen drinking tea and putting the world to right. Angela was full of advice for Abi, don't do this and don't do that. If she had listened to her own advice, she would be a lot better off. The number one message she had for Abi, was not to get pregnant. Angela blamed having children too young as the root of all her problems and she was probably right. Half the estate was young women bringing up kids on their own. It was a sign of the times. The Instagram generation was sexualised from an early age, where lips were enhanced, wrinkles smoothed, and people met on social media and fucked without considering their future. Young mums with several children from different fathers were the norm. Co-parenting was as common as a cold. He felt sorry for Angela with two little ones clinging to her hemline and no partner to help with the bills.

Angela was under scrutiny from social services because they had concerns about her children's welfare, something he knew all about. His own safety had been threatened as a child and he was brought up under the protection of social services for most of his young life. With no family members alive, they would be there for him until he turned eighteen. To all intents and purposes, Knowsley borough council were his parents, and would be until he became an adult.

Leo had been born into a domestic nightmare. His mother and father, Carol and Harold, were both alcoholics with amphetamine addictions. They smoked cigarettes rather than buying food and argued like two people who hated one another. There was no love in the home and food and affection were absent. His mother had her moments, but they were few and far between; he had no happy memories of his father. Leo was too young to realise what was going on when his father was sent down for a serious assault on his mother, but he felt the loss regardless. She was beaten on a regular basis but on that particular occasion, he had broken her jaw and fractured her skull, and she ended up in the intensive care unit. The police stepped in and prosecuted Harold. If it had been left to Carol, he would have got away with it again and again. This time, there was nowhere to hide, and he went down.

Harold was a serial abuser with a violent streak. He beat Carol regularly, drunk or sober and when she wasn't prepared to meet his sexual needs, the kids were the targets of his affections. When he was sent to prison, Carol and her children were no longer terrified of him. The dark cloud of his presence was gone. Social workers supported Carol and one by one, her children disclosed their abuse at the hands of their father. The police listened to the harrowing evidence, and Harold was charged with a number of sexual abuse offences and his prison sentence was increased by ten years.

None of the extended family visited him, most didn't even know which prison he was in. He was labelled a nonce and forgotten.

A year later, they were informed that Harold had been put into a wheelchair following an altercation with another inmate, who had picked him up and thrown him over the landing, breaking his back in three places. Leo remembered his mother saying it was karma and karma was a bitch. He hadn't understood at the time, but it made sense later on.

Carol Tomkins had a new lease of life for a while, and she tackled her addictions head on with the help of her social workers. The children were happy too and were bathed and dressed in clean clothes every day and had regular hot meals cooked by their mother. Leo and his older siblings, Harry and Sarah were safe, went to school, made friends and enjoyed some normality for the first time. Everything was perfect and the memories of their father faded.

Carol was walking her children to school on a wet and windy Tuesday, having dropped Leo at his entrance to the primary school, she was taking Harry and Sarah to their entrance further down the street, when a drunk driver mounted the pavement and ploughed into them, crushing them between his van and the iron railings. Leo's mother lived for six days before she succumbed to her injuries, but his siblings were killed outright. Leo was in his classroom when a social worker came to see him, and she explained that his mum was in hospital and that he wouldn't be going home that day. He didn't realise he would never go home again.

After a spell in foster care, Leo was taken into the care of his paternal grandmother at the age of six and he stayed with her until the bruises started to appear. His teachers noticed that he had become withdrawn and moody. The bruises were investigated and found to be non-accidental. The timelines showed that it could only have been her partner who was hurting Leo. His grandmother's partner resented Leo being with them, and the financial burden that he brought to them, and he demonstrated his anger with his fists.

He was charged with assault on a minor and jailed for eighteen months. Social services had to protect Leo, so his grandmother was told that Leo could not be near her partner, and she had a choice to make. She chose her partner and Leo went into care again. After losing his mother and father, brother and sister, Leo had attachment issues and being removed from his grandmother was devastating. She refused to have contact, stating it was kinder to break all ties. Leo was distraught. There was no consoling him and he never really recovered from the losses he had endured. He cried for his grandmother for weeks, refused to eat and would wake up screaming. Leo Tomkins was traumatised.

In care, Leo didn't have an easy time of it. Intellectually, he was challenged, struggled with reading and writing and retaining information. His ears protruded and he had a lazy eye, which made him prone to being the butt of cruel jokes at school and he was bullied relentlessly. As he approached his teenage years, Leo was an angry, abandoned child. He was lonely and unloved and vulnerable. That was when he met George.

One of the older boys in the home had bought himself a new pair of Reebok trainers, much to the envy of the rest of the house. The residential care workers in charge of the home were suspicious of where he had come up with the money to buy them. He told them that he had got himself a paper round at a corner shop on Bluebell Lane. Of course, the care workers checked out his story and the owner, George, confirmed that he was working for him, delivering newspapers, magazines and sweets. Leo went to the shop the following day and asked George if he had any more jobs going spare. George was a ruddy faced man in his fifties, wide at the shoulders and narrow at the waist with the nose of a pugilist. He was a warm and friendly man with a big smile and a gravelly laugh, and he befriended Leo immediately. They chatted over a bag of salt and vinegar crisps and a mars bar, washed down with a Pepsi max. George asked him lots of questions and seemed to be delighted that Leo was in care and living at the home. He asked all about his past and shook his head when Leo told him about his father going to jail and his sibling's and mother's tragic death. George told him that he had been very unlucky, and he would help him to get a leg up.

An hour later, Leo was cycling through Page Moss towards Knotty Ash with a package in his backpack. Inside was an order for Mrs Jacobs, who apparently liked mints and jellybeans and ordered them in kilos. She lived just off Prescot Road, near the hospital. Leo had knocked on the door and her grandson had answered, just as George had said he would. He gave the package of sweets to the man and in return, he gave Leo an envelope, which he put straight into his backpack, and he took it back to George. George had told him never to look inside a package and Leo never did.

George paid him twenty-pounds for a thirty-minute round trip and told him that he could loan the bicycle until he could buy another one for him. He said a bicycle came with the job. Leo had never owned a bicycle of his own, so he was very excited. George patted him on the head and made him feel like he had done something good and done it well. He said he could pick a chocolate bar of his choice and to be there after school the next day as he had another delivery for him.

Leo felt like it was Christmas and of course, he was there the next day, keen and willing. Over the following weeks and months, he met some of the other delivery boys, who were all from the local area, some were from his school and two lived in his home. He also met George's son, Barry. Barry was in his thirties and drove a black Range Rover with tinted windows and a banging sound system. Leo liked his clothes, all top designer stuff, Stone Island, CP Company and Armani. Barry was the epitome of cool.

The other delivery boys were older than Leo and they looked out for him at school. Suddenly, he had friends and the bullying stopped. One of the bullies who had picked on him got a bloody nose and split lip for laughing at his ears. Leo felt like he belonged with George's boys, and they would hang out together in the park after work and the older boys introduced him to cannabis. Not long after his first spliff, he was experimenting with whizz and cocaine. George's boys had a bond and George paid them well for what they did. Sometimes they would all gather in the flat above the shop to watch football or boxing and George would buy takeaways, Chinese or Indian or Leo's favourite, doner kebabs. It was George Madern who gave him his first taste of ket and over the next few years, his world nosedived.

Chapter 3. Sam and the witch.

*H*ow *can you just walk away from me, when all I can do is watch you leave? Cause we've shared the laughter and the pain, and even shared the tears...*

SAM HEARD THE AMBULANCE arrive and watched through the window as the paramedics parked up and rushed up the path with their equipment. He thought Angela must have had a ding-dong with one of her many suitors again. She used her sexuality to lure men and then milked them for whatever she could get, booze, cigarettes and money, and takeaways for the kids. Some of them turned nasty when they realised, she wasn't prepared to have sex with them.

She had told Sam that she didn't sleep with any of them, which was a dangerous game to play. She was a liability to herself and society in general. She had a radar for locating bad boys and she was a sucker for anyone with more ink than skin, especially if they had access to class A drugs. There had been a steady stream of absolute wrong ones, none of them left her with anything more than bruises.

She said she didn't sleep around but she had been caught pregnant three times. The first child had been taken from her by social services and she was doing a brilliant job of losing the other two, Calvin and Coco. Sam felt sorry for them, the poor little buggers. They were good kids but didn't stand a chance while their mother was entertaining anyone with a couple of grams on them. The parties were relentless, noisy and violent and the neighbours were constantly complaining to the police and the council. Angela was in a state of permanent conflict with her neighbours and the authorities, who she blamed for all her troubles.

When she was sober, she did her best, but the sober times were few and far between and her best was nowhere near good enough. The kids were resilient, but their lives were chaotic. They always looked like they needed a bath and a good dinner and social services had engaged to protect them. Angela hated social services with a passion, and she felt that they were persecuting her. Sam had talked to her until he was blue in the face trying to reason with her and get her to accept that they were protecting her children, nothing more but she couldn't see it.

Sam and Angela had a strong bond. Sam had started life in similar circumstances to Angela, both removed from their birth mothers and placed into the care of the local authority. After leaving school he had struggled to remain on the rails but had managed to adapt and thrive. He knew Angela was different to him. When she asked him why he thought she was different, he would tell her it was because she was fucked up in the head. They always laughed about it. Her perspective of life was askew to the norm, whatever that was.

She was a care leaver like him; that's where they had met. They were wary of everyone and very vulnerable. When they had first met, after their initial cautious interactions, they had clicked and from then onwards, were best friends. They became inseparable and creating mischief was their talent. Their teenage years were memorable and full of laughter.

At the end of their school years, reality hit hard. They had both been chewed up and spat out by a system that was drowning beneath a deluge of addiction, child exploitation and domestic violence. Brexit and Covid-19 had shaken the United Kingdom to its core. Society was in danger of imploding and the gap between the haves and have-nots was widening.

Social services were struggling to cope. There were too many children in danger and not enough placements available. He had lost count of the number of social workers they had through those years. It felt like they would build a rapport with someone and then they were gone, replaced by another stressed out social worker who was struggling to cope with their caseload. He couldn't remember all their names, some of them were okay and some of them didn't really give a shit. It was easy to spot the good ones, who cared. Really cared. And it was just as easy to spot the box-tickers who went through the motions but did nothing to enhance their development.

He didn't envy them. They were fighting a losing battle. It was obvious even as children that working in child protection was a high-pressure career and burnout was common. The attrition rate was high, and the constant turnover of qualified practitioners led to drift and delay on active cases and vulnerable children sometimes weren't seen as often as they should be.

Sometimes, months went by before Sam and Angela were visited. It was easy to see how some children fell through the net. As a care leaver, he could see disasters were just waiting to happen. When disaster hit, the press jumped all over it and exposed the weaknesses in the system, appointing blame wherever they could.

Sam knew it was unfair to tar everyone with the same brush, while ignoring the incredible work that went on behind the scenes three hundred sixty-five days a year. Most of the time, the kids in their care home were healthy, happy and safe but they were always seen by society as different. He could see people's expression change when he told them he was a care leaver. It made people uncomfortable.

He learned early on that society doesn't want to see or hear about the neglect and abuse of its children because it's a sensitive subject. The truth is, they are someone else's problem. Until disaster strikes and then the finger pointing begins and everyone has an opinion.

Sam was grateful for the chance the care system had given to him, Angela not so much.

Angela knew the system and she played it. She engaged as much as she needed to and no more than that and ducked her social workers whenever possible. The kids had become expert at hiding behind furniture when there was an unexpected knock on the door.

Covid had compounded her situation because social workers couldn't gain access to the most vulnerable families if the virus was present. If they said they had covid in their family, there was no access and Angela had covid at least once a month for nearly two years.

Sam knew that the authorities were full of best intentions and promised hope but were massively underfunded and understaffed. When he left the system, he tried to make something of his life, but it was hard to break free from the shackles of being poorly educated, abandoned and underprivileged. He had struggled at school and dodged most of the last few years. Dyslexia had been diagnosed when he was thirteen but by that time, he was so far behind that he couldn't catch up. The other kids called him thick and stupid. Some called him a retard, which hurt, so he stopped going.

Sam knew society was prejudice, like it or not, and everything seemed to be harder without qualifications and the support of a family behind him. Sam struggled to begin with but had settled down and was making progress at work. He had started out as a picker in a warehouse but had trained and qualified to driving a forklift truck. It didn't pay a fortune, but it was much better than being on the dole and there was always a demand for forklift drivers.

On the other hand, Angela simply couldn't cope in the real world. Being an independent adult was alien to her and she couldn't adjust. She said it was ridiculous to work all week at a job she hated and have fuck all to show for it when the bills were paid. What was the point?

Angela couldn't grasp the concept of working five days a week and still being skint at the end of it. It just didn't compute for her. Her availability to work longer hours was dictated by her children's nursery and primary education and childcare wasn't affordable for people like Angela. She became disillusioned and flitted from one shit job to another until she gave up altogether. It was easier not to work, sign on and get pissed and high all day. She sold a bit of weed here and there which supplemented her benefits and funded her own habits and she was better off than if she was working. She was in the poverty trap with no easy way out and her children were trapped with her. Unfortunately, like all children, they had no say in the matter.

Sam tried to support her as best he could. 'It was her life,' she said whenever he tried to talk to her about her lifestyle and choice of company. And he couldn't argue with her. There had been many occasions when he could have told the boss to stick his job up his arse and gone to the pub but there were no answers to his problems in the bottom of a pint glass and he had seen too many people drowning in alcoholic remorse day after day. It was a quick fix but long term, it didn't make them happy. The demon drink would get its hooks into them, so that when they sipped from their glass, alcohol sucked from their soul. It was a drug just the same as any other, except that it's accepted and legal but just as addictive and destructive. He had seen far more people die from alcohol and tobacco than drugs.

When Sam and Angela had time together, they talked sometimes into the early hours of the morning about how their lives had been shaped by their parents' failings. They were soulmates and comfortable sharing their feelings. The truth was that he loved her but had never told her how he felt. Sam was skinny and a little effeminate and Angela was attracted to meatheads and machomen. She trusted Sam and he never abused her trust by asking for more than her friendship. Then she fell in love.

She had met Barry Madern when she was fifteen and Madern was in his twenties. Sam could see how Madern had mesmerised her. She was smitten by him, and he treated her like a dog, and Sam was nothing more than a broken-hearted spectator, who picked up the pieces each time she was broken.

He was well-known as 'Mad Madern' because he had a penchant for biting anyone who came to blows with him. One challenger lost his thumb, which Madern had bitten off and spat down a grid, making its recovery and reattachment impossible. Several combatants had lost their noses and earlobes. He was a psychopath but a handsome one, covered in tattoos and Angela fell, hook, line, and sinker in love with him.

She had told Sam that her biggest regret was being with Barry and getting pregnant the first time at such a young age, but it hadn't bothered her enough to stop her getting pregnant again. Twice.

Angela had been placed into care as a six-year-old, taken from a mother with alcohol and heroin addictions. She had no idea who her father was, and it was unlikely her mother could remember. Her mother didn't put up a fight to keep Angela and she never tried to find her later in life. When social services removed Angela's first child, Tom, the wheel had turned full circle.

Sam was rolling a cigarette when one of the ambulance crew came out of her house, followed closely by two people he knew were social workers and the kids. No sign of Angela. The garden path dissected two scruffy patches of lawn. The grass was knee-length and there was a discarded armchair on one side of the path and a washing machine with a missing door on the other.

Calvin was clearly distressed, and a tall man was carrying Coco. She looked confused and was reaching for her brother, tears streaking her face. A vehicle pulled up and the tall man put the children into the back seat. There was a brief conversation and the man climbed into the front seat and the vehicle drove away, leaving the female social worker. Angela still wasn't there, which wasn't a good sign. Sam was concerned for her wellbeing and slipped on his trainers.

He left his flat and walked across the road to find out what was happening. The female social worker was on her mobile as he approached. She was an attractive woman with dark hair and bright blue eyes. Sam walked towards her, but she turned her back and walked away. He overheard her saying that there were no grandparents or immediate family to place the children with. That didn't sound good. Why would they be placing the children anywhere, unless something was wrong with Angela?

Sam allowed curiosity to get the better of him and walked up the path. The front door was open and as he neared, he could see someone on the settee. Someone?

Who else could it be but Angela? There was no way she would have stayed calm and remained in her house, while someone took her kids away. She would have been screaming like a banshee on the street. It had to be her. Then he saw her ankle, a tattooed chain and crucifix showing from beneath a sheet. Angela was lying on the settee, covered with a sheet.

At least, he had to assume it was her. He felt his guts clench as if squeezed by a giant hand. Whatever her failings were, the world was a better place with her in it. His eyes filled with tears as the memories of their turbulent teen years rolled back to him. It had been them against the world and he had loved her in silence, treasuring what time they had spent together but never expressing his feelings. Now she was gone, and he wished he had told her how he'd felt when he'd had the chance. It was too late.

'Excuse me. You can't go in there,' Jo called, walking up the path. He could smell Chanel Mademoiselle. 'Please don't go inside.'

'I'm not going to go inside, chill out,' Sam said, sniffling. 'Angela is my friend.'

'I have to keep people out.' Jo could see that Sam was upset. 'I'm sorry to shout but the police will be here soon.' Sam stepped away from the door. 'So, you know Angela?'

'We are good friends. I live across the road,' Sam said, feeling sick. 'I'm Sam. Angela and I were in care together. We go back a long way.'

'I'm sorry, Sam but Angela is dead,' Jo said.

'I gathered,' Sam said, gesturing to the front door. 'I saw the ambulance arrive. They couldn't save her?'

'She was dead when we arrived,' Jo said. 'It was too late.'

'What happened to her?'

'It's too early to say.'

'What will happen to Calvin and Coco?' Sam asked.

'We will apply for a police protection order, which means we can keep them safe for seventy-two hours before we need a court order,' Jo said. 'They're safe. Don't worry. We'll take good care of them.'

'What do you think happened to her?' Sam asked.

'I can't say.'

'Can't or won't?'

'Can't. I really don't know.'

'You must have some idea?' Sam said, frustrated.

'I don't, unfortunately. It would be pure speculation,' Jo answered. She sounded genuine and sympathetic. 'Until the post-mortem report is done, your guess is as good as mine.' Sam nodded that he understood. He was clearly distressed. 'I'm sorry for your loss. I liked Angela. I'm part of her social worker team.'

'One of the witches,' Sam said, nodding with a wry smile. He wiped a tear from his eye. Jo managed a narrow smile but there was sadness etched into her expression. 'That's what she called your lot.'

'She called me much worse to my face,' Jo said.

'I bet she did,' Sam said, nodding. 'She had a way with swearwords.'

'She did. Angela could turn the air blue when she was on one,' Jo said, shrugging. 'Witch was one of the milder insults, to be honest.' Sam smiled and sniffled, tears flowing freely now. 'Being a witch would imply I have a magic wand of some kind but unfortunately, I don't have one.' She shrugged. 'On days like this, I wish I did.'

Chapter 4. Abi and her mother, Marion.

*K*indness in your eyes, I guess you heard me cry, you smiled at me like Jesus to a child...

Abi was waiting in her mother's front room, watching the clock which didn't appear to be moving. She knew it was working but it didn't feel like it. Leo was clucking and he desperately needed some ket to straighten him out. They were both users of the drug, Abi occasionally but Leo was hooked, badly hooked. She had seen his health deteriorating drastically recently. He had the shakes twenty-four-seven and was becoming incontinent, which was a massive turn off. His constant water infections were affecting their sex life, which was almost non-existent now. Abi was seventeen and horny and while she loved Leo, things had gone from bad to worse. He had promised to come off the ket, but it was almost impossible while he was being manipulated by the dealers he worked for and their associates. He was like a puppet on a string, dancing to their tunes.

There was misplaced sense of loyalty because Leo was grateful to George Madern, who had treated him as if he mattered. Unfortunately, George Madern had taken ill, sold his shop and retired from the business, leaving his son to take over and Leo and his friends were part of the takeover. Barry Madern had dozens of employees and Leo was told he was now working directly for the Tickle brothers, Simon and Ged. They were treating Leo like he was their slave. They bullied him into doing the most ridiculous journeys with wraps of ketamine and cocaine inserted up his anus. Cocaine and Ket mixed was known as Calvin Klein on the street, or CK. CK was a powerful combination and the demand for it was high. The

Tickle brothers were using Leo and other addicts as mules to supply their county lines business in North Wales.

They were giving Leo enough ket to stop him from refusing to carry their drugs but not enough that he could walk away. He needed their drugs because he couldn't afford his habit. They had him in their grasp and there was no easy way out of the situation. Abi understood his dilemma and it broke her heart to see him squirming and unhappy. He felt worthless.

The week before, they had taken him to one of their cuckooed houses on the estate and made him insert a cling-film wrapped sausage containing fifty wraps of CK up his arse before taking him to Lime Street station and putting him on train to Rhyl. There was a delay at Chester and Leo got the cramps really bad. He panicked and had to shit into a Tesco carrier bag, so as not to lose the consignment. Then he had to recover the drugs from the bag and rinse them in the handwashing sinks, much to the disgust of other rail travellers. It was the most disgusting thing that he had ever had to do.

When he arrived at Rhyl, the men he was delivering to were suspicious that the drugs were not inside him. It was a valid concern. They were concerned that the consignment had been compromised and that Leo may have cut the product en route and kept some for himself. He was beaten up and he thought they were going to stab him and had been so scared, he had broken down and begged them to let him go. The men called the Tickle brothers, and they convinced their customers to let Leo go, unharmed.

He had to walk three miles back to Rhyl station, by which time he was clucking, and he was broke. He had to jump the train and a bus from Liverpool, and it was the journey from hell.

That night Leo had come home angry, exhausted and scared to death because the Tickle brothers said Barry Madern was pissed off with him. That meant he was going to be disciplined and that could be anything from a good hiding to being thrown into the Mersey tied to a concrete block. The entire incident traumatised him and he cried himself to sleep that night. It broke her heart to see him so frightened and upset. Abi loved him but something had to change. They couldn't go on as they were.

She heard the back door being opened and her mother talking to a male. Abi went into the kitchen to see who it was. A man in his twenties wearing a dark tracksuit and new trainers was leaning against the sink. He had a pockmarked face and cropped hair. There were sovereign rings on his fingers, and he was sporting a heavy gold chain around his neck. He didn't look happy to see Abi.

'Who is this?' he asked, frowning.

'My daughter, Abi. This is Kenny,' Marion said. 'Relax. Say hello to Kenny, Abi.'

'Hi,' Abi said, feeling his eyes on her.

'Do you want a brew?' Marion asked.

'I'll have a tea,' Kenny said, still staring at Abi. 'You look like your mother, poor fucker.'

'Less of that, thank you!' Marion said, laughing.

'Only joking. Your mum is a MILF, aren't you, Marion?'

'Give it a rest,' Marion said, blushing.

'Nice to meet you, Abi. How old are you?' he asked.

'She's seventeen and she's my daughter,' Marion said. Marion was approaching forty but looked older than her years. She had blond hair shaped into a long bob, which framed her pretty face. Cigarettes and alcohol had aged her, but she was still very attractive. Her jeans clung to her curves and her body was gym toned. 'Wind your neck in, or we'll be falling out.'

'There's no harm in looking at a pretty woman, Marion,' Kenny said. Marion shook her head.

'There is when she's, my daughter. Have a bit of respect.'

'I apologise if I've offended you. I'm just a red-blooded male,' Kenny said, smiling. Marion ignored him. 'Enough of the chit-chat. Are we okay talking business in front of Abi?'

Marion looked at Abi and she nodded. 'She knows I am not an angel and have a business sideline going on.'

'Sideline?' Kenny repeated, grinning. 'I like it. How much do you want this time?'

'The same as usual,' Marion said, reaching into the cupboard beneath the sink. She took out a box of Bold laundry pods and removed the base, revealing a bundle of notes, sorted into fives, tens and twenties. 'There's two grand there. Count it if you want to.'

'No need, Marion. Thank you, nice doing business with you,' Kenny said, taking the money and sticking it into his boxer shorts. He handed Marion a large bag of wraps and she took a tube of scouring powder from the cupboard. She twisted the top off and hid the bag inside the tube. It was a squeeze, but it fitted. Marion put the scouring powder beneath the sink with the box of laundry pods and closed the door.

'She's a very smart lady, your mother.'

'Thank you. Always a pleasure, Kenny.' She gave him a mug of tea and he sipped it. He studied Abi and she blushed. 'I need something else.' Kenny raised his eyebrows. 'Abi wants some ket, if you have any on you.'

'Ket?' Kenny said, whistling. 'That's nasty shit. You should stay away from that, young lady.'

'It's all nasty shit and it's not for her. Have you got any or not?' Marion asked, stony-faced.

'I may have,' Kenny said, winking. 'Kenny has got all sorts of goodies for people he likes and luckily for you, I like you.'

'Good. She needs a bit of a favour.'

'Does she, now?' Kenny asked. 'And what is the favour?'

'She needs a couple of grams on tick until next week,' Marion said.

'Mum! That's so embarrassing,' Abi snapped. 'Can't you buy it for me, and I'll pay you next week?'

'Yes, if it was for you, but it's not for you, lovely,' Marion said. 'It's for the useless fucker you live with and what are you going to pay me back with, brass buttons because he doesn't have any money this week and he won't have any next week?'

'I'll pay you back,' Abi moaned.

'Your mum is right,' Kenny said. 'Never buy an addict his drugs, because you'll never get the money back.'

'He gets his social this week and he's owed money from work,' Abi protested.

'Work?' Marion snorted. 'That's a joke.'

'This is so embarrassing. Mum, please!'

'Leo must be over his tab limit with the Tickle brothers, or you wouldn't be here asking me to front up for him,' Marion said, shaking her head. 'He's a waste of space. I've told you a thousand times to ditch him.' Marion lit a cigarette and puffed it deeply. 'I'm not funding a habit he can't afford. Not today and not ever.'

'Who is your boyfriend?' Kenny asked, face darkening.

'Leo Tomkins,' Marion answered for her.

'Ah, little fellah with a wonky eye?'

'That's him,' Marion said, inhaling.

'I know him and if he's already in debt to the Tickles, I can't give you any credit, as much as I would like to.' Kenny shrugged. 'We all work for the same company, if you see what I mean.'

'No. I don't see what you mean,' Abi said, sarcastically.

'They all work for Barry Madern,' Marion said to Abi. 'Leo should know that Kenny works for him too, and he shouldn't have put you in this position in the first place. He's a waste of space.'

'We can only let someone have so much on credit or things get out of hand and people get hurt, if you know what I mean but we could come to an arrangement between me and you,' Kenny winked. He gestured to his groin. 'Sort me out and I'll sort you out with some ket.'

'Mum! Did you hear what he just said to me?' Abi whined. Her face was purple with embarrassment. 'I can't believe you're doing this to me. I feel like dying. This is too much.'

'I'm not doing anything, lovely,' Marion said, sadly. 'Your boyfriend is dragging you down into the gutter. Can't you see that?'

'It's up to you,' Kenny said. 'I have some ket on me. You don't have any money. A quick fuck over the table and the drugs are yours.'

'Don't push it, Kenny,' Marion said. 'I'm teaching her a valuable lesson but don't go overboard.'

'I'm just telling Abi how it works when a pretty girl can't pay,' Kenny said, shrugging. 'Your mum is talking sense. This is what happens. I fuck you and you get the drugs.'

'I'd rather die,' Abi said, shaking her head.

'How about a blowjob?'

'Fuck off,' Abi said. 'You're disgusting.'

'That's enough, Kenny,' Marion said, angrily. 'Listen to me, Abi. This is where you're going to end up if you keep trying to feed his habit. You have no money and all you have to offer a dealer is between your legs.'

'Thank you so much, mother!' Abi said, shaking her head. 'At no point in my life am I going to touch a man to pay for drugs. Not in a million years!'

'You will be amazed how many women have said that to me in the past and ended up begging me to fuck them for a gram,' Kenny said. 'Your mum is right, get rid of him.'

'I'm not going to end up screwing you or anyone else,' Abi said, folding her arms. 'Keep your ket. I don't want it that badly!'

'Good to hear. I think I've proved my point. Give me two grams.' Marion got a different tub out of the cupboard above the sink. It was marked coffee. She took the top level out to reveal a hollow full of twenties. She counted out the money and handed it to Kenny. He handed her the ket. 'Thank you.'

'The offer still stands,' Kenny said, winking at Abi. 'We could have a bit of fun another time and your prick of a boyfriend gets his fix?'

'Go away, Kenny,' Marion said, frowning. 'Enough is enough.'

'See you next week,' Kenny said, opening the door. 'Nice to meet you, Abi. And if you stay with Leo Tompkins, I'll see you soon, I reckon.'

He closed the door and there was an uncomfortable silence in the room. Abi was horrified and a little frightened. The experience had hit home how desperate she was.

'Can't you see where you're heading if you stay with that little junkie?' Marion asked, stubbing out her cigarette. 'You need to leave him.'

'I can't leave him, mum,' Abi said.

'You can do what you like, whenever you like,' Marion said. 'This is your life. Leo has his own.'

'It's not that simple, mum,' Abi said, tears rolling down her cheeks. 'I'm pregnant.'

Chapter 5. Protecting Vulnerable People Units.

Now the drugs don't work, they just make you worse, but I know I'll see your face again... Jane Bennet parked her car with two wheels on the pavement and she noticed huddles of neighbours standing in their gardens, no doubt curious about what was going on. She was a detective inspector with the Merseyside police. She was a member of the Protecting Vulnerable People Unit and no stranger to this part of the city. It was historically a deprived area where employment was low, and crime was high. Some of the families they encountered were third generation long-term unemployed.

There were two marked patrol cars at the scene already, and uniformed officers were present to stop nosey neighbours and the press from getting too close. She took off her seatbelt and glanced in the mirror. The thirty-five-year-old woman looking back at her could have been ten years older. She blamed her wrinkles on the job and an unhealthy addiction to sunbeds as a teenager. There were deep creases at the corners of her eyes and her forehead was etched with frown lines. Botox was something she had tried to avoid but she was on a collision course with it. Father Time was a relentless taskmaster and each year the lines multiplied and became deeper. All the wrinkle cream on the planet couldn't help. She scraped her long brown hair into a ponytail and fastened it. Her passenger was reading her phone.

'I've got a text update. These things do my head in.'

'What absolutely obvious gems of wisdom have they sent?' Jane asked, smiling.

'It says that social services have asked for a PPO for the children, and it's been granted. And that the deceased is still in situ,' detective sergeant Gill Alan said, reading the text while she opened the door. 'Why do they send these stupid messages? She's unlikely to get up and go out. She's deceased, for fuck's sake. That's why we're here, because she's deceased.'

'The deceased?' Jane said. 'They mean Angela Deacon.' Jane tutted, opening her door. 'Angela is still in her home. She's still Angela and she's far too young to be dead.'

'She was a character. I worked with social services on her case a few years back,' Gill said, opening the boot. She took out two forensic suits and passed one to the DI. 'They removed her first child. It was a difficult one to work on. She wasn't a bad mum, she just made bad choices in men.'

'I glanced at her file. The father was part of an OCG, right?' Jane asked.

'Yes indeed. Barry Madern,' Gill said.

'Barry Madern. I didn't read that. You're kidding me?' Gill shook her head. 'The lovely Mad Madern,' Jane said, rolling her eyes. 'Why are women attracted to blokes like that?'

'Bad boy syndrome. It's beyond my comprehension,' Gill said. 'One of my friends is seeing a guy who has a collection of machetes on his living room wall and three Japanese sword stands in his bedroom and a baseball bat with nails through the end of it, next to his bed.'

'Do you think he watches a lot of zombie films?' Jane asked.

'He's clearly scared of something.'

'I wonder if he sleeps well,' Jane shook her head in disbelief.

'I prefer my men not to own any weapons and be able to hold a conversation that isn't about how hard they are, how hard their mates are or UFC.'

'You and me both. I didn't realise Madern was involved with Angela.'

'It was a long time ago.'

'What a twunt that guy is. I'm surprised he hasn't been shot or locked up.'

'Fingers crossed, eh. He's a first-class wanker. He was ten years older than Angela, but she was madly in love with the bastard, and she fell pregnant at sixteen. Before the baby was born, he was battering her black and blue. From the moment she left hospital, Angela and the baby were seen to be bruised numerous times. Eventually, a health visitor reported unexplained injuries to the baby's ear. The doctor said the bruises looked like pinch marks and were non-accidental. Social services were involved, and the timelines proved that only Madern had the opportunity to inflict the injuries.'

'He pinched the baby's ear hard enough to bruise. What a guy,' Jane said, shaking her head. 'What goes through their minds?'

'Who knows. Anyway, Angela was told that Madern wasn't allowed any contact with the child, but she wouldn't stop letting the fucker into the house. She was given plenty of chances, but she was besotted with him. They went to court and the judge granted removal of the child.'

'And what happened to her child?' Jane asked.

'A plan of adoption. At least he will have a chance of a good life in a safe family,' Gill said.

'Kids having kids,' Jane said. 'Whatever she's done, she's too young to be put in a box.' They struggled into their suits and walked towards the house.

'Hey, pigs,' a teenager riding a BMX called to them. He was wearing a black tracksuit, black trainers and black puffer jacket, topped with a black baseball cap. His friends were dressed in similar attire, and it was difficult to tell one from another. 'Is Angela Deacon dead?'

'If she's dead, can we have her weed?' another called. The teenagers laughed.

'Is she dead, or what?' another shouted. He snorted like a pig. 'Is she dead?'

'No. She's having a fancy-dress party,' Jane answered without turning to look at him.

'And you've come as a pig?'

'I can see you've come as a scruffy fucker. Nice costume.' Jane flicked him the finger. His friends laughed at him.

'Fuck you, pig!' the boy stuttered, red-faced. He rode off away from the cordon, chased by his friends who were peddling after him and calling him a scruffy fucker. She could hear them jeering and laughing as they rode away. Jane reckoned that nickname would stick for a while, which was comforting.

The detectives walked up the path and stepped into the house. It smelled musky. A mixture of cigarettes, stale beer and unwashed laundry. Portable lights had been set up inside the gloomy living room.

'No electric?' Jane asked a uniformed officer. He shrugged and gestured to the social worker, who was talking to a detective. 'Hello Jo. I didn't see you there. Is Angela one of yours?'

'Yes,' Jo said. 'Unfortunately, she is. I'm just making a statement and grabbing some things for the children.'

'Did you find her?' Jane asked.

'Yes. We were carrying out a surprise visit and the kids had to let us in. They had tried to wake her up, but she was gone. There's no money in the meter so, we suggested uniform brought some lights in.' Jo gestured to a female detective who was coming out of the kitchen. 'I put the call in, and uniform arrived quickly followed by Laura.'

'Were you the first here, Laura?' Jane asked a detective she recognised from the Matrix unit. She frowned, confused by her presence. 'You were here sharpish.'

'I was indeed.' Laura nodded and looked at her phone.

'What are Matrix doing here?'

'The address is flagged as part of an ongoing investigation,' Laura replied, showing her the alert on her screen.

'What type of investigation?' Jane asked.

'There's an OCG linked to this address.'

'An OCG linked to Angela Deacon?' Jo asked, shocked. Laura nodded. 'Is this to do with Barry Madern because we thought he was ancient history?'

'Yes. Barry Madern is high on our list and this address is linked to him. We've been on him for nearly two years now. It's just a matter of time before we lift him and his outfit,' Laura explained. 'This is a sudden unexpected death at a marked address, so here we are to see if there's anything we can add to the case against him.' She turned to Gill. 'As Jane hasn't introduced me, I'm DI Lunt by the way. You can call me Laura.'

'I'm Gill. We thought Madern was subject to an injunction from years ago?' Gill said. Laura looked confused.

'An injunction for what?' she asked.

'He had a kid with Angela, a boy called Tom, but he was removed and placed in care and there was an injunction preventing him approaching Angela or this address.'

'Since when do the likes of Madern take any notice of an injunction?' Laura said, shaking her head. 'Madern thinks he's above the law. Injunction or no injunction, our sources tell us he's a frequent visitor here and we have camera footage of him parking up and walking here.'

'You're joking?' Jo said, shocked. 'We had no idea he was still around.'

'According to our surveillance, he regularly parks his vehicle a few streets away, climbs over the fence to the rear, and uses the back door. But he only comes after dark.'

'Obviously, social services didn't know anything about this?' Jane asked, Jo.

'Absolutely not. I haven't heard his name mentioned in connection with Angela for years. We wouldn't have allowed him anywhere near the children. He poses too much of a threat.' She paused. 'You said he only comes at night?' Jo asked.

'Yes. In the early hours of the morning, apparently,' Laura said, nodding. 'I'm not surprised social services didn't know they were still in a relationship, he's like a ghost most of the time.'

'It's a big surprise to me.' Jo frowned. 'We don't camp out in the back garden, and we don't do visits in the early hours of the morning. People lie to us, I'm sure we all know how that works.'

'It's one thing we all have to take for granted,' Jane said, nodding. 'People lie to us most of the time.'

'How often has he been seen visiting?' Jo asked.

'A couple of times this year,' Laura said.

'A couple of times this year?' Jo said, shaking her head. 'So, it's not like he's here all the time and they're living together under the radar.'

'No but he does visit; hence the address is of interest to us,' Laura said, dismissively.

'I'm not surprised at all. She was always besotted with him,' Gill said, trying to calm the situation. 'Sounds like she never moved on and hid their relationship from everyone. None of us are mind readers.'

'I'm not suggesting social services haven't done their job properly,' Laura said, retreating. 'I was just speaking aloud. I meant no offence.'

'No offence taken,' Jo said, lying. Her expression gave her true feelings away; she had no poker face. If she was pissed off, it showed. 'But if you had communicated what you knew about his connection to this address with us, we would have reacted accordingly because of the children.'

'We don't disclose our surveillance for obvious reasons,' Laura said, apologetically. 'We deal with some very serious criminals, and they have eyes and ears in places they shouldn't have. They pay good money for information, police officers, social workers, lawyers, and judges, no one is beyond reproach. We can't take anyone's honesty for granted and we trust no one when we're dealing with an OCG.'

'I see,' Jo said. 'Thankfully, we operate in a world full of unicorns and rainbows where we can trust everyone.' She smiled to let her know it was a joke because she didn't have the stomach for an argument. The detective didn't rise to it.

'Barry Madern aside, what do we know about what happened to Angela?' Jane asked, changing tack.

'I found her on the settee. Her kids thought she was asleep, and they couldn't wake her up. I checked her and she was warm but unresponsive. We called an ambulance and carried out CPR but when they arrived, they said it was too late and she was gone.'

'Did they indicate a possible cause of death?' Jane asked.

'No. She had been sick, but her airways were clear,' Jo explained. 'They said there was no obvious cause.' She pointed to the stairs. 'Uniform took a quick look around the house and there was a locked bedroom upstairs but no sign of the key. We had to make sure there were no other children in there, so they broke it down and found a desk with a substantial amount of bagged powder and two sets of scales on it. We haven't touched anything in there.'

'I've taken a look at it. Could be cocaine but it's more likely ketamine,' Laura said.

'So, she was dealing ket?' Jane asked.

'I doubt it.' Laura gestured to the sparsely furnished house. 'She sold a bit of weed to the local scrotes but nothing major. Look at the state of this place. There are no designer brands in her wardrobe. Her clothes are from Primark, her furniture is old, and she has no carpets downstairs. If she was dealing, she would have some money for electric.'

'I agree. She was always running out of electric and gas,' Jo said. 'The kitchen cupboards are empty. She didn't have the bus fare to take the kids to the doctor or dentist sometimes. Angela wasn't dealing class-A drugs.'

'But someone was using her bedroom to bag up and store ketamine,' Jane said, sighing. She looked out of the back window and saw an American Bulldog patrolling the fence, barking continuously. 'That is a seriously expensive pet.'

'That's a money-making machine,' Jo said. 'They're not pets, anymore. They're fashion accessories. Angela told us she was minding the animal for a friend called John, who was paying her to look after it. We told her it needed to go but she clearly didn't get rid of it. It was one of the reasons we were visiting unannounced today.'

'Her friend with the dog, is John who?' Laura asked, suddenly interested.

'Let me think. I'm sure his surname is Trent,' Jo said. 'We ran some checks because he was visiting the home when the children were present. He is a carpenter from Maghull, married with two children.'

'A carpenter and a lot more than that. Trent is a known associate of Madern. We know Madern is connected to a website selling designer dogs. They're bringing in five-grand a pup nowadays,' Laura said. 'The more I look around here, the more it looks like Madern had his hooks into Angela in more ways than one.'

'It certainly looks suspicious,' Jane agreed.

'If Angela had a soft spot for Madern, she would have been easy to manipulate. I think Angela Deacon was cuckooed.'

'She was being manipulated by Madern?' Jane asked.

'I think so.'

'And now she's dead,' Jo added.

'Is there anything to link him to the drugs you found upstairs?' Gill asked.

'Not yet but there might be. CSI are on the way,' Laura said. 'We might get lucky but I'm not holding my breath.'

'I need to get going, and find somewhere for the children to stay,' Jo said. 'I'll leave you guys to do what you do best.' She turned to the DI. 'Let me know what comes up, Jane, I'm worried about this link to Madern.'

'I'll keep you in the loop but why the concern?'

'Because Angela never disclosed who fathered her children and after what I've just heard, I'm beginning to think it might be the same guy who fathered her first.' Jane rolled her eyes. 'Midnight visits and drugs in the house, adds up to Barry Madern and he may be the father. We need to make sure the bastard doesn't get access to those children.'

'Is it likely he would try?'

'He contested the removal of his son and became hostile to the social workers and police officers on the case,' Jo said. 'Threats were made, and a car was burnt out. One of the officers was attacked in a pub in the city centre but no one was ever charged. He's a walking warzone. I need to be sure he can't go anywhere near them.'

Chapter 6. The Child Protection Teams. 7pm.

I'll protect you from the hooded claw, keep the vampires from your door...
Calvin and Coco were at Nutgrove Villa, the headquarters of the Knowsley children's services in Huyton Village. It was one of the management hubs for the Knowsley area of Merseyside. The children were eating chicken nuggets, fries and drinking Fanta orange. They were unaware of what exactly had happened to their mother. They had asked but the social workers thought it better to delay the truth. It was deemed to be in their interest. Jo had told them their mother wasn't well at all and had gone to hospital, although Calvin didn't believe her. He was keeping his thoughts to himself because Coco had stopped crying, which was all that mattered to Calvin right now. His sister crying was a major problem for him. He felt like he had to stop her if he possibly could.

She loved nuggets and was eating them as if she hadn't eaten properly for days. There were three dips in front of her, ketchup, barbeque and curry sauce. She plumped for barbeque and showed the nugget to Teddy. He was sitting on the desk next to her Fanta. He must have given his approval as she bit off half the nugget and chewed it enthusiastically.

Phil, the giant social worker had bought them food from McDonalds, which catapulted him to their favourite man of the moment, but he couldn't tell them where they were going to sleep that night. Apparently, home wasn't an option.

'Are you two okay there?' Jo checked the children. They both nodded, their mouths full. Coco smiled. She made a thumbs-up sign and they reciprocated.

Once she knew they were okay, she went to her service manager to bring her up to speed about Angela Deacon. The sudden death was a disturbing twist in an already complex case. The police were on the scene as far as Angela's suspicious death was concerned; placing the children was her priority.

'Have you got five minutes?' Jo asked, knocking on the open door of her service manager. Her direct manager was in her sixties and had the air of a headmistress, strict but deeply caring. She had been in the profession for thirty years and seen it all.

'Yes. Of course. I can't believe that you've stumbled into this situation. What a mess,' Hayley Banks said. 'Come in and sit down. It must have been a terrible shock for you.'

'It was, to be honest,' Jo said. 'I wasn't expecting to find her dead.'

'Are you feeling, okay?'

'I'm a little shaken but I'll get over it,' Jo said. 'She could be difficult, but I liked Angela. I thought we were getting somewhere with her. It just feels like such a waste.'

'Is she your first death?' Hayley asked. She had a way of making people want to open up. Her voice was soothing but assertive and her eyes were always searching for information. Jo knew they were part of the skillset that had taken her to the service manager position. Analysing human beings was an important part of the job from the ground up and the good social workers were experts at it.

'No, Angela is my second,' Jo said.

'Oh,' Hayley said, surprised.

'My first was while I was on placement from university. He was a vulnerable adult in his fifties, and they think he may have been dead for two weeks and nobody had noticed. It was very sad, but that placement pushed me towards working with children rather than adults.'

'Aah, old people dying alone is so sad. I'm sure that stayed with you,' Hayley said. Jo nodded. 'My first was a baby. Mum had gone to the pub to buy cigarettes and ended up staying for a couple of drinks. A couple of drinks turned into too many and she ended up intoxicated.'

'Oh no!' Jo said, listening.

'She was an epileptic and had a fit in the pub and was taken to the Royal. No one knew about the child until the next day and by then, it was too late.' Jo nodded and grimaced. The death of a child was traumatic enough, but the needless death of a child was heart breaking. 'Mum was charged with neglect and reckless endangerment, and she hung herself a year later. That was in the nineties, and it still haunts me to this day. Two needless deaths for the price of one,'

'I sometimes wonder if I made the right decision to take my degree and become a social worker. There are easier ways to make a living, that's for sure,' Jo said, thoughtfully. She smiled. 'And there are many times when I question why I have stayed in the job for so long.'

'I'll tell you why you stay. Because you make a difference, Jo,' Hayley said, sagely.

'Do you believe that?' Jo asked. 'When the cases keep stacking up and we feel swamped, I sometimes wonder if we make any difference at all.'

'I know it to be true. You make decisions every day that save children and their families from dangerous situations.' Hayley smiled and nodded. 'Those children will grow up in safety and have children of their own and so will their children. Your legacy will echo for generations after you have gone from this earth.'

'Wow. That's something we should all be told at the end of a shitty day. Thank you,' Jo said.

'Someone said that to me once, at the end of a really shitty day,' Hayley said, nodding. 'I save it for special occasions and particularly shitty days like this.'

'It has been shitty but that means a lot to me.'

'People like you are worth your weight in gold. Thank you for staying in the job,' Hayley said. She steepled her fingers together. 'Back to the case in hand. This can be handed over, you know?'

'What do you mean?'

'The Emergency Duty Team are sourcing emergency accommodation. If you hadn't found her when you did, this would be placed with the MASH team or EDT, and you could be at home in bed.'

'I can't hand them over to the duty team, Hayley,' Jo said, shaking her head. 'I know these kids and they know me.'

'Okay. What foster options do EDT say we have?'

'Two options at the moment but one foster parent doesn't take siblings and the other doesn't accept children under six,' Jo said. She could see Hayley weighing up the options. Her mind ran like clockwork.

'So, technically, we could place them?' Hayley said. 'Separately.'

'They have been through enough and I'm not separating them.'

'I didn't say we should separate them, just that we can.' Hayley said, shaking her head. 'Just that it's an option.'

'You know I'm not going to separate them.'

'It's only one night and you've had a nasty shock.'

'No. I'll wait until EDT find a suitable home for them. If we separate them now, they'll be traumatised, especially Coco. She's like a trumpet where her brother is concerned. I can't do that to them.'

'Limpet,' Hayley said, laughing.

'What did I say?' Jo asked, chuckling. Her laugh was contagious.

'Trumpet.'

'A classic Jo-ism,' Jo said, laughing. 'I do it all the time. Especially when I'm tired.'

'Jo,' Phil called from his desk. He pointed to the phone. 'EDT have found parents in Southport willing to take both children.'

'Excellent,' Jo said, standing up. 'There is the call I was waiting for. I'll take them to Southport and ring you on the way home.'

'I'm not going anywhere for a few hours and if I'm at home, I'll be online,' Hayley said, taking off her glasses. 'Feel free to call me.'

'If it's late, I'll leave it until tomorrow,' Jo said, knowing full well that Hayley was online until midnight, every night. She knew that because she was greeted by a raft of emails every morning, sent late into the evening. Her mobile rang and she checked the caller. It was a switchboard. 'I need to take this, sorry.'

'No problem,' Hayley said.

'Jo Lilly speaking,' she answered. She knew it would be the police. There was a brief conversation, and her face became ashen. She ended the call with a huge sigh. 'Fucking hell,' she muttered, shaking her head.

'What is it?' Hayley asked.

'That was Jane Bennet from the PVPU,' Jo said, frowning. 'Angela Deacon has multiple broken ribs and severe bruising to her thighs and pelvic region. They think she was raped before she died. They're escalating the investigation to a homicide.'

Chapter 7. The Matrix teams. More than meets the eye.

All along, you were a phony girl, you sit behind the mask and control your world...

A Detective Lunt was thinking about leaving the scene when the CSI officers made a discovery upstairs. The initial examination of the body had changed the course of the investigation and she could smell blood in the water around Barry Madern. The murder of his ex-girlfriend, if she was an ex at all, at an address they could prove he visited, was like gold dust for the investigation into his illegal activities. If he was still her partner in any respect, he was immediately top of the suspect list and would be questioned by Matrix. Any opportunity to bring him in and make him sweat was a bonus. It could be used to shake his tree to see what else fell out.

'Detective Lunt?' a CSI called to her.

'That's me. What's been found?'

'We've found something that you need to see in the small bedroom.'

'Thank you,' Laura said.

She made her way up the stairs. The walls needed a lick of paint, but the steps and risers were varnished with a matt oak colour, which was hardly marked at all. It looked relatively new. Angela Deacon didn't strike her as the DIY queen. She glanced into the children's bedrooms, and they were clean and well kept. Angela's bedroom was tidy apart from two pillows which were on the floor in random positions. The bedding appeared to be clean, and the room smelled fresh, which made the dark stain on the quilt look out of place. It looked like dried blood. She moved to the bathroom and looked at the window ledge above the sink and opened the medicine cupboard. Three toothbrushes, one adult and two juniors, no sign of an adult male in there. The bath and towels were clean. Upstairs was in decent condition in contrast to the scruffy living room and kitchen. Laura found the CSI officer in the spare room.

'Hello Dawn.'

'Hello Laura,' she said, without looking up. 'I hear this could be a murder enquiry now?'

'I've heard the same, but it's not been confirmed yet.'

'So, who is SIO on this?'

'I think it will fall with MIT, so they will have to appoint the SIO.'

'Is this becoming a hot potato type of thing that no one wants to grab hold of?'

'It's a suspicious death at an address with links to an OCG,' Laura said, shrugging. 'Things are going to get messy very quickly.'

'As they often do.'

'Have you processed her bedroom yet?' Laura asked, already knowing the answer.

'Not yet,' Dawn replied. 'There's blood on the quilt but we haven't looked underneath at the bedding yet.'

'What about the bedside cabinets and drawers?'

'Not yet but feel free to take a look,' she said, shrugging. 'What are you looking for?' Laura shrugged and smiled. 'Fine. Take a look but be quick and make sure you wear gloves.'

'Okay thanks, I will.'

'Sorry to ask the obvious but I'm sick of processing prints that belong to police officers that should know better.'

'I understand,' Laura said. 'What have you found in here?'

'The bad news is there are no prints on the packets of powder, but we may be able to pick something up from the scales at the lab,' she said. 'That's the bad news but the good news is behind here. I think you'll want to see this.' She slid the desk from the wall to reveal a rectangular patch of relatively fresh paint. 'See here. This plaster feels reasonably new and there's still efflorescence on the surface.'

'Of course, there is,' Laura smiled. 'Efflore-what?'

'Efflorescence. See the chalky deposits on the surface?' Laura nodded. 'The natural salts and minerals dissolve in the water, which makes its way to the surface, where it evaporates, leaving these mineral deposits behind. It's part of the drying process so, it's certainly, only six months or so old.'

'And it was plastered by Mr Magoo,' Laura said. 'This isn't a tradesman's work.'

'I agree,' Dawn said, nodding.

'Why would it be replastered and hidden from view behind a desk unless someone doesn't want anyone to know it's there.' Laura looked along the skirting board. 'That is very interesting indeed,' she said, touching the wall.

'And the floorboards here are loose,' Dawn said, pointing. 'They have been cut short and fitted together. Do you want me to lift them.'

'Absolutely. Yes please.'

The CSI took a thin bladed tool and slid it between the floorboards, lifting one side. She removed the next board and allowed the detective to look beneath them. There were two bricks of powder between the rafters and a bundle of black material.

'Do you want me to lift it?' Dawn asked.

'Yes. It looks like a firearm to me,' Laura said. She nodded and lifted it, unwrapping the material. A Smith and Wesson revolver was in one side and a marine flare gun in the other. Several rounds of ammunition were in a plastic bag and three cartridges for the flare gun were wrapped in clingfilm. 'Bag the firearms but dust the powder bricks for prints and leave them where they are.' Dawn nodded reaching for some evidence bags. 'Whoever put the powder under there will want it back. And if they've buried something in that wall, it's valuable and they will come to recover it. When they do, we'll be waiting for them.'

'I'll need authorisation to leave it here,' Dawn said, looking concerned. 'If that goes missing, I'm in deep shit.'

'I'll have it sent to you,' Laura said. 'I need to make a few calls to get eyes on this place tonight.'

Chapter 8. An Unwilling Participant.

D*on't make me feel any colder, time is like a clock of my heart...*

SAM WAS SITTING IN his armchair watching what was going on across the road. Things had become increasingly busy as the hours ticked by. More people in protective suits had arrived and more uniformed police and detectives were there too. The psycho dog was taken away by handlers, who had muzzled it and bundled it into the back of a van, and he thought that was telling. Angela and her kids hated that dog, but she needed the money and agreed to look after it.

Sam could see the police conducting a fingertip search of the garden to the rear. His window overlooked only part of the back garden, so he could see everything in one corner but not the rest. He had a bad feeling about it. There was no way this number of law enforcement officers would be there if Angela had died accidently or taken her own life. The sheer number of crime scene officers at the house suggested foul play. That meant that someone else was involved in her death. The thought of her being hurt made him feel sick. It was bad enough that she was dead. If he knew that she had suffered, he would struggle to cope with that thought running around his head.

As he watched people coming and going, a black hatchback slowed down as it passed several times and the occupants appeared to be focused on Angela's house. It turned right at the end of the road and then reappeared again, circling the block repeatedly. It stopped near the front of Sam's building. The passenger lowered his window and spoke to some onlookers, but they just shrugged and shook their heads. Two men approached the car, one of them was his next-door neighbour, who lived in the flat below him and he was a fucking nightmare. He was a bag-head called Les. Les was a serial burglar, hated and despised by most people on the estate but he was tolerated because he was related to Barry Madern. He spent more time in prison than he did at liberty, and he was a nasty bastard.

Sam avoided him like the plague and was polite when he did bump into him but Les always sneered at him and called him a faggot beneath his breath, when he had walked past. Sam never responded to him and pretended he didn't hear him, but it riled him, and he wished that he was physically more intimidating. Angela and Sam had gone to a boxing club for a few years, and they were both capable boxers, but Sam didn't look like he was able to defend himself and sometimes became the target of abuse. Les wasn't a particularly tough guy, but he was protected by his family and Sam couldn't compete in that world. There was no point in attracting the attention of nutters. It was safer to say nothing and be offended in silence.

Sam stood up and stepped back from the window, making himself difficult to see from the street. Across the road to his left, he could see young Leo in his window, watching proceedings. Leo was a nice kid, and his girlfriend Abi was a lovely girl. They were a nice couple, although Leo hung around with some dangerous characters. Les had seen the Tickle brothers going into his flat several times. They were connected to Barry Madern and were bad news. Sam had seen one of the brothers slap Leo across the face and push him to the floor, where they kicked him several times. They were laughing and joking but Leo wasn't. They were bad news and best avoided.

Sam felt like he was a voyeur, his breath was shallow as he watched Les talking to the occupants of the hatchback; Les turned around and looked up at his window. He pointed at Sam's flat. Sam felt like he had been punched in the guts and ducked away from the glass. Who was in the car and why would Les be pointing out his flat to them? The last thing he wanted was the local chavs on his case. Les was a prick.

The passenger leaned his head out of the window and stared up at Sam's flat. Les took out his phone and scrolled on the screen. Sam was startled when his mobile buzzed in his pocket. He looked at the screen and his heart nearly stopped.

Les downstairs. Flashed on his screen.

Sam suddenly remembered taking his number when he was moving in. Les had been friendly that day and said he could get fridges and televisions cheap. Sam obviously didn't know he was a burglar then and he had forgotten they swapped numbers. He stared at his phone, wishing it would stop ringing but it didn't. After what felt like an age, it stopped but seconds later, it rang again. A text message arrived from a different number.

Answer your phone or we'll knock on your door.

Sam didn't recognise the number, but he could see the passenger in the hatchback using his mobile.

Fuck, fuck, fuck. Sam was shaking as he answered the call. The man in the hatchback was glaring up at his window.

'Hello.'

'Sam, it's Les from downstairs,' Les said.

'Hello Les,' Sam said. 'What do you want?'

'My mate needs to talk to you.'

'What about?' He saw the phone being passed into the car.

'Hello Sam, lad,' the voice said. The accent was heavily scouse. 'Can you hear me?'

'Yes.'

'Les said you're mates with Angela across the road.'

'Yes,' Sam said.

'What's going on with all the bussies here, lad?'

'Angela is dead,' Sam said. 'That's all I know.'

'Are you sure that's all you know?'

'Yes.'

'That's strange because Les said you were talking to the Dibble by her front door?'

'I wasn't talking to the police,' Sam said, stuttering. He always stuttered when he was nervous. 'I was talking to the social worker who found her.' The voice stayed quiet. 'She's not the Dibble, honestly.'

'A social worker found her?'

'Yes.'

'How do you know she was a social worker?'

'She told me she was a social worker.'

'You do know what happens to people who talk to the Dibble around here, don't you?'

'I haven't spoken to them.' Sam insisted. He felt like he could strangle Les. 'She was a social worker, not the police.'

'Snitches get stitches, understand, lad?'

'Yes. I understand that.'

'Good. I hope you do understand,' the voice threatened, calmly. 'How did she die, lad?'

'The social worker didn't know how she died,' Sam said. 'She found her on the settee.'

'But you saw her dead?'

'Yes. She was on the settee, covered with a sheet but I don't know what she died of.'

'I need you to find out for me,' the voice said.

'What?'

'You were her friend,' the voice said. 'Ask questions until you get answers.'

'I have no idea what you mean. Ask who questions?' Sam asked, stressing.

'I don't give a fuck who you ask. Just ask around the police and CSI and find out how she died,' the voice said. 'I sent you a text message. Use that number to contact me when you find out how she died.' Sam was speechless. 'Do you understand me because I don't want to say it again?'

'Yes. I understand.'

'Do it and do it quickly. Don't make me call you, understand?'

'Yes.'

'Good lad. I'm not a patient man, so make it snappy.'

Sam stared at the blank screen for what felt like hours, wondering what his next step would be.

Chapter 9. Leo. Helpless and Alone.

Only know you've been high when you're feeling low, only hate the road when you're missing home, only know you love her when you let her go...and you let her go...

LEO WAS WATCHING THE police operation across the road to take his mind off the pain. He was aching all over and shivering when he saw Marion parking her car outside his flat, underneath the streetlight. Anxiety gripped him. He couldn't cope with Marion at the best of times, and this was the worst of times. Abi was in the passenger seat and even though it was dark, he could see that she was crying. This was all he needed, a massive comedown and Abi crying about whatever she was crying about, and her mother there to rub his face in it. Abi cried at adverts and cartoons, she cried for the sake of crying. Sometimes, she didn't know why she was crying. Fucking brilliant.

Marion scared the bejesus out of Leo. She was so sharp and quick-witted, sarcastic and cruelly funny at times. Her mind worked so quickly, Leo couldn't keep up with her and she knew it. He knew that Marion hated him, and he had told her that he knew. She said that she didn't hate him, she hated Abi being with him, which amounted to the same thing really. He eyed them both as they climbed out of the car and walked up the path. Marion had a face like thunder and Abi looked like she had been crying for a month. They were walking with purpose, like they were on a mission, and he reckoned that he was their objective. They ganged up on him sometimes and that did his head in. Abi could peck his head all by herself, she didn't need back up. Her mother was the nuclear option. They often conspired and discussed what they were going to say before they confronted him with whatever the issue of the week was. Some of his rollockings were so well rehearsed that they made his head spin and the impact stayed with him for weeks. He wondered what they had been saying about him today.

Let's go and tell Leo what a twat he is...just because he is a twat..

He could hear them in his mind conspiring to ruin his day. Leo sighed and turned away from the window, hugging himself. The pain he was suffering was a million times worse than anything Marion could bring on him.

She vilified him for his ketamine use and banged on about him getting clean and going straight, getting a job, so he could treat Abi like a princess. Abi thought she was a princess anyway and acted like a spoilt brat if she didn't get her way. Leo knew he was punching above his weight, everybody did, and if he was honest, he knew she deserved better than he could offer. Leo wanted to make her life wonderful, buying her whatever she needed and loving her with all his heart, but he knew it was all just a pipedream.

He was sixteen, with no qualifications, no training or skills and zero chance of landing employment which paid the bills and rent. His social payments were twice what he could earn legitimately. The way rents and utilities were going up, he couldn't understand how most people coped.

He heard the front door open, whispering between them and then Abi and Marion walked into the living room bringing a frosty atmosphere with them.

'It's cold in here,' Marion said, her face like thunder. 'Why is the heating not on?'

'Hello Marion, how are you doing?' Leo asked, sarcastically. 'It's always nice to see you.'

'Shut up, Leo, you moron,' Marion said, shaking her head. 'Why is the heating not on?'

'The boiler eats the gas at a ridiculous rate, and we've been struggling for money lately,' Leo said, shivering. 'I would love it to be like a greenhouse in here, but this is how it is.'

'If you're struggling for money, what have you been doing all day, apart from fuck all?' Marion said, shaking her head.

'Apart from fuck all, fuck all,' Leo replied, raising his middle finger. 'I can't be doing with your mother in my face right now, Abi. Can't you tell her I'm not in?'

'Why do you turn everything into a joke?' Abi said. 'It's not a joke.'

'Do I look like I'm laughing?' Leo replied. His hands were opening and closing, trying to get rid of the pins and needles in his fingers.

'Have you made Abi anything for tea tonight while she was out begging for the shite you put up your nose?' Marion asked.

'I was going to put a casserole into the slow cooker but then I realised, we don't have one.'

'Seriously, Leo,' Marion said. 'Is there anything to eat in the flat?'

Leo ignored her but the question stung. He hadn't made anything because withdrawal is the only thing he was concerned about. Food and drink were irrelevant. There was nothing in the kitchen cupboards anyway.

'Did you get some ket?' Leo asked Abi. Abi slumped in the armchair and sobbed into a tissue. She couldn't look him in the eye. 'Why is she so upset?'

'Why don't you ask her, genius?' Marion said, rolling her eyes.

Leo went to Abi and knelt beside her, holding her. 'It doesn't matter if you couldn't get any. I can cope until we get paid from the social. I'll get a couple of hundred from the Tickles too.'

'But you owe them money,' Abi said, wiping her eyes. 'There will be nothing left again.'

'They'll have more work for me soon. Don't cry, little starling. Everything will be alright.'

'Little starling?' Marion repeated in her pissed off voice. 'You make me puke.'

'It rhymes with darling and that's what we call each other when you're not here poking your nose into our lives,' Leo said. 'We do love each other, you know.'

'So, this morning you said, 'can you go and beg a dealer for some ket for me because we are skint and I can't even buy my own drugs, little starling.' How romantic.'

Leo wanted to scream but remained calm. Marion took out her cigarettes.

'While we are talking about being romantic, she had to ask Kenny Fulshaw for a tab for your drugs.'

'I know Kenny,' Leo said. 'Why did you go to Kenny Fulshaw?'

'We bumped into him,' Marion lied. 'Kenny works for Barry Madern the same way your bosses do, so when Abi asked for a tab, he knew the Tickles won't give you anymore drugs on tick, so he won't either.' Marion lit a cigarette.

'So, he said no?' Leo asked. He was aching for the drugs.

'Kenny said he couldn't give her a tab, but he would give her the gear for a fuck over the kitchen table or a blowjob.'

'What?' Leo stuttered. 'She didn't...'

'No, she didn't,' Marion said, blowing smoke from her nose like a human dragoness. 'No thanks to you. If she stays here in a relationship with you, that's all she has to look forward to because you shove every penny you have up your nose.' Leo felt like he had been winded. He simply couldn't think of anything to say to defend himself. 'Have you got nothing to say, like sorry I have put you in this position, little starling?' Marion said, sarcastically. Leo didn't reply. He stared at Marion and wished she would fuck off and die.

'No, nothing to say?' Marion asked. Leo looked at her in the eye but couldn't find the words. 'You're a waste of space. I cannot for the life of me understand why a pretty girl like Abi is with a loser like you.'

'Why are you here?' Leo asked, confused. 'I know you hate me and you're clearly on a mission to break my balls, but this is over the top even for you. So, what is going on?'

'Tell him,' Marion said to Abi.

'Mum!' Abi moaned. 'Stop it, please.'

'Tell him.'

'Not like this, mum,' Abi said.

'Tell me what?' Leo asked, confused.

'She's pregnant,' Marion said. 'And before you ask, you're the father, much to my dismay.'

'Pregnant?' Leo said, stunned.

'Yes, pregnant, up the duff, in the club, bun in the oven, expecting, having a baby,' Marion said, sarcastically. 'Do you get it, yet?'

'Why didn't you tell me?' Leo asked, squeezing Abi. Her crying became more intense. 'It's not the end of the world. I don't understand why you're so upset.'

'She's upset because she's living with a junkie, with no prospects, no money and no ambition and she's pregnant, which means that if she stays with you, her child is as fucked as you are before it's even born.'

'Give me a break, Marion,' Leo sighed. 'Can't you just fuck off now you've told me?'

'I couldn't give a shit about you, Leo,' Marion said. 'But she's my daughter and the baby is my grandchild and they will not live like this while I have breath in my body.'

'I'll get off the ket,' Leo said. Marion shook her head. 'I'll get a job and we'll be the best parents ever. Don't you worry, Abi. I love you all the world and I'll love our child to Pluto and back.' Abi looked up and shook her head, wiping mascara from her eyes. Leo could see the steel in her eyes. Something had changed. 'We'll be fine, Abi. Just give us one more chance. We'll be fine.'

'We won't be fine, marlin,' Abi said, touching his face. 'You're not well and I can't bring a baby into this. We have no money, no food and no electric.'

'What are you saying?' Leo whispered. 'Don't leave me, Abi. I love you.'

'I love you too, Leo but I can't carry on like this,' Abi said, sniffling. 'I can't live like this. I'm weary of it all.'

'Abi is going to come and live with me while she's pregnant,' Marion said. Leo shook his head and opened his mouth to object. 'Here is your ket, Leo.' Marion put it on the coffee table between them. Leo wanted to snatch it up but restrained himself. 'Listen to me, Leo. There is a pound left in the meter, no food for tonight or tomorrow in the kitchen and you already owe the Tickle brothers the money you will be paid this week. So, because she is pregnant, Abi is going to pack some essentials and come home with me. She will be warm, and she can eat well for her and the baby. You can come and see her when you get off the ket.'

'I fucking hate you,' Leo muttered.

'I'm sure you do, and the feeling is mutual. You might understand when you have a child of your own to worry about,' Marion said, calmly. Abi stood up and walked out of the room. He could hear her sobbing while she was packing, and it broke his heart. 'You can make a start of proving yourself to Abi by coming to mine tomorrow with that ket still untouched.' Leo looked at the packets and the wonderful powder inside them and his spirit froze. The pain was so bad. He needed the powder more than anything in the world right now and she knew it. Marion knew he was too weak to resist it. Leo wanted to tell her to stick it up her chuff, but he couldn't, because he needed it. Marion put her fingers on the packets and slid them away from him. 'I can take them with me if you like and I'll tell Abi you're making a start to get off the gear?'

Leo didn't speak but he felt tears rolling down his cheeks. He felt helpless and completely unable to help himself.

'No, I didn't think so, somehow.' Marion stood up and left the living room, closing the door behind her. Leo heard them leaving, the front door closing, and he curled up in a ball on the carpet and cried harder than he imagined was possible.

Chapter 10. Sam.

The victims we know so well...

SAM FELT ANXIOUS AND angry that he was being threatened by someone he didn't know. On the face of it, the threat was nothing more than a strange voice on the phone and a text message from the ether but the reality of it was that he had to take it seriously; the threat to him was real. It was something much more sinister than it appeared at first glance. This was all because of Les and his big mouth, pointing him out to his friends in the hatchback. A different person could be tempted to ignore their demands and hope for the best, but Sam knew better. Les is related to Barry Madern so, Sam had to assume the men in the hatchback were connected to Madern too. That meant the men in that hatchback didn't make idle threats, so he had no choice but to comply with their demands.

Madern had people beaten to a pulp, shot, stabbed and set on fire, some disappeared completely. Sam and Angela had been talking about it the week before and they had counted four users from the area, who had recently vanished and never been heard of again. They may be in prison; they may be in a different city begging on the streets, or they could be at the bottom of the Mersey feeding the fish because they owed money. There was no choice but to do as they had ordered. Simple.

Fuck, fuck, fuck.

Sam didn't want anything to do with them. Madern and his rivals were like dark clouds hanging over the city. They operated in the shadows of the underworld, but they also moved amongst the normal people unseen; they were intelligent and articulate, smiling assassins and their menace was felt throughout society, worldwide.

Liverpool had become a gleaming tourist destination, steeped in history, buzzing nightlife and an infinite music scene but beneath the glittery surface were the organised crime gangs who controlled the streets. The history of the city attracted tourists from home and abroad. The Eurovision Song Contest had further raised the city's profile worldwide. All year around, the hotels were full, the shops were busy and the bars and restaurants thriving. The atmosphere was electric and while the city was generating economic opportunities for legitimate business on a level never seen before, so were the gangs who ran the supply of cocaine, ketamine, prostitutes and protection rackets. The black market had never been bigger, cocaine and ketamine were being taken as openly as tobacco and alcohol and the financial gains were humungous. Rival gangs operated in a fragile framework of tolerance for each other's turf. Keeping the peace was essential to living long enough to spend the money they made. There were plenty of opportunities to make millions and enough for everyone, as long as no lines were crossed, and boundaries were respected. If the rules were broken, rough justice was brutally administered, and shootings were frequent. Stabbings and punishment beatings were so common, they often went unreported. The gang networks were spread through the city like a spiders' web and the affluent leafy suburbs and sprawling housing estates alike, were all pieces of someone's turf. Rich or poor, the boundaries were the same, and cocaine use was as rife in high society as it is elsewhere. Wealth was no protection from the gangs if you crossed them.

Sam's estate was a mixture of housing association and council tenants with an increasing number of homeowners in the mix. The postcode meant it was part of Madern's empire and if Madern and his cronies said jump, then you jumped as high and for as long as they told you to. The inner city was a jungle and Sam was way down the food chain. Asking a few questions about how Angela had died couldn't hurt anyone, could it? He had no choice anyway, so it was best to bite the bullet rather than become the target for one.

Sam put the kettle on and rummaged for his thermos flask. He'd last seen it when Angela ran out of money the week before and her electric meter was empty. He had given her some candles and made her a flask of hot chocolate and toast for the kids to take to bed. She had brought it back the next day, washed and dried with a big kiss on his cheek for his efforts. He knew she had loved him, just not in the way he would have liked. Everything he had done for Angela had been done with love. He wished he could have just one more minute with her, so he could tell her that he was in love with her.

The thermos was behind the soup cooker, which made sense as he had used it the day before. He took it out and removed the lid, smelling the inside to make sure it was clean. He knew it was but sniffing things in the kitchen was a habit. He couldn't put his finger on when it started, but he had been thirsty in the night and drunk sour milk from the bottle while in care and it had made him wretch for hours. After that, he sniffed the milk before he drank. Maybe that was the trigger.

Sam poured boiling water into the flask and then made coffee in it, adding milk last. He tucked a packet of sweeteners into his pocket and put his parka on. His baseball cap was on the hook, but he thought it would make him look Chavie, so he left it where it was. Sam peered through his front window and tried to identify a target to home in on. He could see a couple of plastic police officers being used to man the cordon. Crime scene tape flickered in the breeze and formed the imaginary line that the public couldn't cross. The part-timers, and some volunteers seemed to get the shitty end of the stick whenever there was an incident on the estate. Sam had never seen them patrolling the estate on foot. The police were not well liked, and the part-timers would probably be verbally abused, threatened and intimidated and without the power of arrest, it would be foolish to deploy them alone. Dangerous even.

Sam wrapped a scarf around his neck and grabbed some disposable cups that had been there since Christmas. He took a deep breath and headed for the front door. Anger simmered beneath the cool façade he projected. He didn't want to be at the bidding of local thugs, criminals who revelled in being criminals, wearing it like a badge of honour. They swaggered around like rockstars, wearing designer gear and Swiss watches. He wanted to tell them to fuck off and ask questions about Angela themselves, but it wasn't worth provoking them. It wouldn't take long and then the job was done.

Sam walked down the concrete stairwell, which always had the unwholesome odour of piss and stale beer. No matter how often the communal areas were cleaned, the stink returned. It didn't help that several of the tenants in the block were piss-pots and didn't know what day it was by the time they got home from the pub. He had seen them so drunk that they couldn't get the key in the lock and desperate for the toilet, they would piss where they stood. There were often pools of piss by their doormats. Removing the odour would require removing those tenants.

He reached the bottom of the stairs and scurried past Les's front door, not wanting to talk to the prick. If he had kept his mouth shut, Sam wouldn't be in this predicament. He was almost at the main entrance when he heard a door open behind him.

'Hey,' Les shouted. Sam thought about ignoring him but decided it would be less trouble to be polite and humour him.

'Hiya Les,' Sam said, turning. Les was wearing a pair of baggy grey shorts, scratching his bollocks through the material. Sam loathed him. 'Everything okay?'

'The guy you spoke to earlier on the phone is my cousin, Smithy,' Les said, proudly. 'Have you heard of him?'

'There are quite a few people called Smithy around, Les,' Sam said, shrugging. 'It's a common surname.'

'He's called Derek Smith.'

'I can't say it means anything to me,' Sam said.

'Everyone who knows him calls him shotgun Degsy,' Les said, proudly. 'How cool it that, shotgun Degsy?'

'Great,' Sam said, nodding. He refused to ask why his cousin was called by that moniker. 'Very cool.'

'They call him shotgun Degsy because he did ten years for robbing an armoured van.' Les explained, anyway. Sam didn't respond. 'He's a fucking legend around here.'

'I see,' Sam said, shrugging. He didn't give a shit who he was but couldn't say that. If shotgun Degsy was indeed an armoured car robber, he was clearly a shit one as he got caught and did ten years. 'I can't say that I've heard about him, but he seemed to think I have been talking to the police.'

'And what?' Les sneered.

'Because you told him you had seen me talking to the police on Angela's path,' Sam said. 'I wasn't talking to the police. She was a social worker.'

'She looked like Dibble to me. I didn't know that she wasn't,' Les said, shrugging.

'That's right, you didn't know that, so why say it?' Sam asked, blushing red with anger. 'You know what people around here think of grasses and you have dropped me in the shit.'

'Like I said, she looked like the Dibble to me,' Les said. 'I was just saying what I saw.'

'This isn't Catchphrase, Les, you prick.'

'Watch your mouth.' Les pointed. 'I thought she was Dibble.'

'But she wasn't and that's very important to your relatives, Les.'

'Yes, you've said, several times.' Les shrugged, dismissively. 'Do you know what happened to the slapper across the road, yet?' Les asked, sneering. 'Smithy wants to know, and you had better not piss him off.'

'If you mean Angela, no, not yet. I'm on my way to ask what happened,' Sam said, biting his tongue. 'And she wasn't a slapper.'

'There were always blokes around there,' Les said. 'What do you think she was doing, playing Cluedo with them?'

'She was lonely sometimes. She smoked weed and drank too much with them,' Sam said. 'They were friends.'

'You would say that, wouldn't you, being on the other bus,' Les snorted. 'What would you know about shagging girls, anyway?'

'I'm not gay, Les.'

'You would say that,' Les scoffed. 'Bent as a nine-pound note you are!'

'I haven't seen you bringing women back to your flat,' Sam said, frowning. 'Not ever.'

'What?'

'I have never seen a single female come to your flat in all the time I have lived upstairs, plus you have spent years of your life in prison with only other men to have sex with.' Sam shrugged and pointed his finger. 'Are you on the same bus as me?'

'Fuck off,' Les stammered. He blushed. 'I'm not into blokes like you, bummer.'

'For fuck's sake. Grow up, Les,' Sam said, shaking his head.

'I'm into women, not like you! Queer.'

'Good for you,' Sam said. 'I can see women, women everywhere except anywhere near you. They're not exactly queueing up at your front door, are they?'

'I don't give a fuck what you say, your mate was a first-class slag,' Les said, blushing angrily. 'I bet she sucked like a Hoover.'

'She had male friends, Les,' Sam said, sighing. He paused long enough to confuse Les. 'Hold on a minute. I've heard your sister has quite a few men around her house and at regular intervals too, as if they have appointments. She's busy from morning till night.'

'Shut your mouth,' Les said, turning a weird shade of red.

'The difference between Angela and your sister is that your sister does fuck her visitors, and she charges, doesn't she?' Les looked like he had been slapped. 'How much does she charge for a blow job nowadays?'

'I'll fucking batter you,' Les growled but he looked worried.

'You couldn't batter a fish, Les,' Sam said, shaking his head. 'You're all mouth and no action.' Les turned purple but stayed in his doorway. 'Angela was a lovely woman, and she was too young to die. Have a bit of respect, you prick.'

'You need to be careful what you say to me, little faggot,' Les said, spittle flying from his lips.

'Or what, Les?' Sam asked, fuming inside. 'Are you going to tell your cousin that I said your sister is on the game because I think he knows. Every fucker on this estate knows.' Les couldn't find the words to answer. 'Angela wasn't a prostitute. If she had been, she would have had money. It's not a problem to me what your sister does, Les. None of us are perfect. I'm just trying to mind my own business. You should try it. Fucking prick.'

'I'll have you done in, you queer. Just you wait and see if I don't,' Les slammed his front door closed.

'I'm quivering in my boots,' Sam said to no one. 'Enjoy the rest of your evening.'

Sam turned and opened the entrance door. The night air hit him, cool and chilling but a welcome respite from the air inside the stairwell. He half expected Les to attack him from behind, but the man was a coward who hid behind his relatives. Sam had decided that Les was a cardboard cut-out, all front with no substance to back him up. He tucked the flask under his arm and put his hands into his pockets and headed for the uniformed officers at the cordon. They were chatting and stamping their feet against the chill. One of them spotted Sam approaching. They eyed him suspiciously.

'Evening officers,' Sam said, gesturing to his flat window. 'I live up there and I've been watching what is going on.'

'So, you live across the road. Did you know her?' the female officer asked.

'Yes. Angela was a good friend of mine and I'm devastated,' Sam said. The officers nodded and gave him a sympathetic look. 'Anyway, you guys look like you're freezing cold and losing the will to live?'

'You're not wrong there,' the female PCSO said, shaking her head. 'It's too cold to be standing in the street. Anyone with any sense is tucked up at home watching Netflix with a glass of wine.'

'I can't help with the wine, but I've got a flask of hot coffee and two cups that you can have,' Sam said, offering the cups. The male officer looked suspicious. 'I haven't pissed in it or dosed it with laxatives, honestly.' The officer laughed and took the cup. Sam took the top off the flask and filled their cups. 'Do you take sugar?' he said, shaking the sweeteners.

'I'll have one,' the male officer said, sipping the coffee. He grimaced. 'Actually, better make it two.'

'I like it strong,' Sam said, putting another sweetener into his cup.

'I can tell,' the officer said, smiling. He tasted it. 'That's better.'

'You said that you were friends with the victim?' the female officer said.

Victim.

'How did you find out about her death?' the male officer asked.

'I was there when the social workers found her,' Sam lied. 'It was a terrible shock. Never seen anything like that. Broke my heart.'

Victim. She said Angela was a victim.

'Had you known her for long?'

'Yes. We were in care together for years and ended up being placed nearby each other when we left, then we both moved onto this estate a few years back,' Sam said, plunging his hands into his pockets. The cold was starting to bite. 'She had three children, well two that she had with her when she died. She was a handful, but she never meant anyone any harm.' Sam shrugged. 'Apart from her neighbours. She didn't get on with them,' he added. 'She didn't deserve to die like that.'

'No one does,' the female officer said. 'In my opinion, rapists should be castrated and hung from a lamppost. Bastards.'

Rapist.

'I couldn't agree more,' Sam said, trying not to burst into tears.

Rapist. Rapist. Rapist.

'I'll leave you the flask. Just pop it by the entrance door of the flats when you're done. I'll grab it later.'

'Thank you for the coffee,' the female officer said, frowning. 'Are you okay?'

'It's been a shock, that's all,' Sam said. 'I'm cold and I need a large wine and my bed.' He held up his hand. 'Enjoy the coffee.'

Sam felt his lip quivering as he walked back to the flats. The thought of his beautiful Angela being raped, knocked him sideways. Stinging hot tears ran down his cheeks for the second time that day.

Chapter 11. Home Sweet Home.

*I*t's been a hard day's night and I've been working like a dog...

JO LILLY ARRIVED HOME just before nine-thirty, turned off the engine and sat for a few minutes to gather her thoughts. There were tough days and there were tougher days, but this had been one of the toughest that she could remember. She had settled Calvin and Coco Deacon with the emergency foster parents and the Emergency Duty Team would take over the case for now. The drive back from Southport was a blur. It had been a long time since she had been on a visit.

Jo was the manager of assessment team Alpha, which meant she had seven social workers in her team, each with an ideal caseload of over twenty children each. Ideal is not reality and the numbers climbed to thirty-plus during crisis periods when social worker numbers dipped. There were seven assessment teams identical to Jo's with equivalent case numbers. Their cases were as varied as the people they protected, ranging from one extreme to another but each had its own unique complexities. There was no let-up in the caseloads coming into the service via the Duty Teams, and MASH who service cases at their inception before passing them over to the assessment teams to work to a conclusion. Balancing the numbers each social worker carried was a never-ending task. This was one of five boroughs which made up the Merseyside social services.

It was like a relentless conveyor belt of misery that ran constantly, day and night, increasing its load year on year. There never seemed to be any lights at the end of the child protection tunnel. Jo said, if there is a light at the end of the tunnel, it's a train coming our way.

The Angela Deacon case had fallen into her lap because the allocated social worker had phoned in sick with stress, again, and the visit was out of the required timescale. Her other social workers were swamped with pre-proceedings and court appearances, covering parent contacts and the vital administration required. The duty teams, who normally covered the assessment teams when they were overwhelmed, had been wiped out with another wave of covid and vomiting sickness, so Jo had to put on her social worker hat to complete the visit within time. On another normal day, she would have been in the office, not at the coalface knocking on Angela Deacon's door.

Jo took a deep breath and got out of the VW. She walked up the path and the Arlo doorbell illuminated. Her phone beeped, alerting her that someone was approaching her front door.

'Thank you, doorbell. I know someone is at the door, because it's me,' she said. She opened it and stepped inside. 'You're supposed to be smart.'

'Hello, you,' her partner Lenny called from the living room. 'Are you talking to the doorbell again?'

'It's supposed to be a smart doorbell, so why doesn't it recognise us?' Jo complained, kicking off her shoes in the hallway. 'If it was smart, it would save its battery power, knowing we live here.'

'I'm sure some of them do have facial recognition,' Lenny said, 'But those models weren't in the promotional offer when you bought the alarm system, but you couldn't part with your money fast enough.'

'We bought the alarm system together, and we got the doorbell for free,' Jo said, peering around the doorframe, smiling. 'It was the free doorbell that swung the deal.'

'The deal was swung as soon as you let them in the front door. I said we would think about it, but you overruled me, saying we were missing out on a bargain,' Lenny said. He stood up and hugged her, kissing her cheek.

'It was a bargain.' Jo feigned to be shocked and kissed his neck. 'How can you say that? The doorbell was free, what more could we ask for?'

'No, they told you it was free if you signed up there and then,' Lenny said. 'It was definitely in the price already but you're a salesman's dream customer. Do you want a glass of wine?'

'Yes please. A big one,' Jo said, 'Which wine did you order?'

'Don't read the label and just pretend it's the expensive one,' Lenny said, hiding the bottle. 'It's South African, your favourite.'

'But there are nice South African wines and there are shite ones too,' Jo sighed.

'This is a nice one.'

'Then why are you hiding the bottle?'

'Because it's a surprise.'

'Is it shit?' Jo asked.

'No, taste it before you call it shit,' Lenny said. He handed the glass to her. She sipped it and smiled.

'Is it Villa Maria?' she asked, grinning.

'Yep,' Lenny said. 'ASDA are doing twenty-five percent off if you buy six bottles or more.'

'How many did you order?'

'Twelve.'

'Get in there!'

'They won't let you buy any more than that, so I ordered twelve.'

'I love you,' Jo said, slurping the wine. 'How was your day?'

'Good. I sold the Porsche Boxster and the Subaru, and I bought an F-type Jaguar and a fully loaded Range Rover from Terry Mac,' Lenny said, pouring himself a glass of Rioja. 'I think he's struggling because he was almost giving them away. I paid him half what they're worth.' He sipped his wine. 'I won't ask if you had a good day, because it's gone nine o'clock, so I know it was shit. How shit was your day?'

'The shittest for a while,' Jo said, plonking herself down on the settee. 'I told you I would have to do a visit for Tamsin Harris, didn't I?'

'Tamsin, 'here is another sicknote?"

'Yes her,' Jo said, nodding. 'She was supposed to go and see a young mum on a surprise visit, so I arranged to do it. It should have been a simple knock on the door and two questions, 'Have you got rid of the dog that you're looking after and tidied up the shit from the garden so the kids can play out?'

'Sounds simple enough,' Lenny said.

'The kids had to open the door because mum was on the settee and wouldn't wake up,' Jo sipped her wine.

'Was she drunk?' Lenny asked.

'Nope. She was dead.'

'Fucking hell,' Lenny said, concerned. 'I wasn't expecting that. How did she die?'

'We're not one hundred percent sure but we think she was raped and murdered,' Jo said. A tear rolled down her cheek. Lenny put his arm around her. 'Sometimes this job gets to me, sorry.'

'Don't apologise, Jo,' Lenny said, stroking her hair. 'I don't know how you and your teams do it day in and day out. I know it's always difficult but that must have been a shock. Do they know who did it?'

'The police are all over it now,' Jo said. 'The kids are at a placement in Southport for now. That's why I'm so late.' Jo paused, deep in her own thoughts. 'This poor woman has been through the system herself. She's a care leaver and she was doing well until she met an older man. He really screwed her up.'

'How old was he?'

'Twenties but she was fifteen and she was pregnant at sixteen. He was a bastard to her, and we removed her first child a few years back because the father was a known dealer, and he was hurting her and the baby. The court issued a restraining order against him, but she wouldn't stop letting him in the house, so she lost her son. It's all so sad and unnecessary. We were protecting her child from his father because he's a dangerous criminal, but she didn't listen.'

'You can only do your best, but sometimes your best isn't good enough.'

'I know but she was clearly influenced by this man and people will do what they want to at the end of the day.'

'There's no helping some people,' Lenny said. 'It's hard to comprehend a father hurting his baby. What a prize prick he must have been.'

'There are no words for him. He's well-known in town; he's called Barry Madern,' Jo said. 'Have you heard of him?'

'Barry Madern from Huyton?' Jo nodded. 'Mad Madern, they call him!' Lenny said, almost choking on his wine. 'Everyone knows Madern, especially in the motor trade.'

'Why in the motor trade?' Jo asked, frowning. 'I don't understand.'

'Drug dealers buy and sell cars all the time because their cars get marked by the police or rival gangs and they have to swap them regularly,' Lenny said. 'I've heard stories about dealers putting trackers on rival's vehicles to find out where they're hiding their money and gear, and then they go and steal it. Of course, they can't report their drugs or drug money being stolen to the police.'

'An occupational hazard, I suppose,' Jo said. 'We do hear of it happening. Tell me about his vehicles.'

'Madern has a raft of companies, security guards, taxis, construction and they all need motors. I know a few traders who part exchange vehicles from his companies and make a fortune because he's not bothered about the price. They all need wheels to operate, so they pay the asking price, no questions asked.'

'Do you know him?' Jo asked.

'No,' Lenny said, shaking his head. 'I know of him, and I've seen him at auctions on the odd occasion. He has a reputation in the trade.'

'What kind of reputation?'

'A bad one. He threatened to shoot Scotch Jonny in the kneecaps because a van he bought blew the head-gasket, six months after he bought it.' Lenny shrugged. 'He's irrational, apparently. It turned out the driver hadn't put oil in it for months.'

'That will be where the problem was,' Jo said. 'I'm not a mechanic but no oil is not good.'

'This is the interesting bit; the van was allegedly hijacked and found burnt out in Leeds and the driver had both legs broken but couldn't remember a thing about who attacked him.'

'How did it get to Leeds with a blown head-gasket?' Jo asked.

'One of the mysteries of the universe,' Lenny said. 'He still blamed Scotch Jonny. His windows were put through, and his car was set on fire on his driveway at home.'

'You're joking,' Jo said, shocked. 'How frightening would that be?'

'Terrifying. Scotch Jonny closed shop and retired not long after. He moved to Wales somewhere. Madern and his cronies are nutters. I wouldn't touch his business with a barge pole.'

'Keep it that way,' Jo said. 'He's bad news by the sound of it'

'Why did you bring up his name?' Lenny asked. 'What has he got to do with this if his kid was removed years ago, I mean.'

'The police have had surveillance in the area and Madern has been seen visiting the house a few times, climbing over the back fence in the early hours of the morning.'

'That sounds like more than a catchup to me,' Lenny said.

'Exactly. It appears they were still in a relationship, even if it was sporadic. That means there is a possibility that he may be the father of the other two children but, we don't know for sure yet,' Jo said, but the hairs on the back of her neck were tingling. 'Fingers crossed he isn't, but she never disclosed who their fathers are and now we can't ask her.'

Chapter 12. Sam.

If you leave me now, you'll take away the biggest part of me...

SAM WENT BACK INTO the flats and jogged up the stairs, his legs heavy like lead. He felt drained of energy and emotionally numb. Angela had been raped and he hadn't been able to help her. Sam had warned her that some of her male associates were chasing more than a few drinks and a conversation. She was a very attractive woman and most of her male friends were trying to get into her pants. It was obvious to everyone but Angela. A few of them had fallen out with her, labelling her as a prick-tease. Maybe one of them had decided he was going to take what he wanted, raped her and panicked. His head was spinning around and around in ever decreasing circles. Anything was possible and nothing made sense. What if, what if, what if?

Sam went into his flat and locked the door behind him. He slid the dead bolt over too, just to be on the safe side. Today's events had left him feeling vulnerable. He took off his coat and hung it up and then went into the kitchen and opened a tin of lager. He drank from it greedily and walked into his living room, sitting down heavily in his armchair. A desperate sadness was creeping through his very being. Life without Angela would be unbearable. She had been his soul mate. It had been them against the world for so long that he couldn't remember life before Angela.

Sam took out his phone and opened the message from Smithy. Shotgun Degsy. What planet were these people from? He thought about what he was going to say, choosing the words carefully. He typed the text message slowly.

The uniformed officers at the cordon said Angela was raped but they don't know the actual cause of death. I hope this helps. Sam.

He pressed send and waited. Less than thirty seconds later his screen was flashing with the same number. His heart sank as he answered the call.

'Is this Sam?' a different voice asked.

'Yes.'

'Who did you speak to?' the voice asked, angrily.

'I spoke to two of the uniformed officers manning the cordon,' Sam said. 'They said that Angela was a victim and that she had been raped.'

'How did she die?' the voice asked.

'They didn't know that, and they said the postmortem would answer that question,' Sam lied. The man remained quiet, but Sam could hear him breathing. 'Hello?'

'How well did you know her?' the voice asked.

'I've known her for years. We were in care together,' Sam said.

'Did you fuck her?'

'What?'

'You heard me,' the voice said. 'Did you ever fuck her?'

'No. We were friends.'

'That's the correct answer,' the voice said. 'Do you have a key to her house?'

'No,' Sam lied.

'Did she hide a spare anywhere outside?'

'Not that I know of,' Sam said. He waited for the next question, but none came. 'If that's all I can help you with, I'm tired and I need to get my head down. I've got work in the morning.'

'You're telling me the truth about the spare key, aren't you?'

'Yes,' Sam sighed, boring of the man and his threatening manner. 'I have never had a key to her house.'

'Do any of her neighbours have a key?'

'I don't know for sure, but she didn't get on with any of them for more than five minutes at a time,' Sam said. 'If you need to get into her house, your friend Les is the best burglar around here. He doesn't need a key to get into anywhere.'

'That's a very good point, Sam,' the man said, calmly. 'Clever lad. Keep my number in your phone. I might need to talk to you again.'

'Why would you need to talk to me?' Sam asked, annoyed.

'You could be useful. So, I might need to talk to you and if you like having your teeth in your head, you will keep this number in your phone. If you block this number or don't answer, I will come through your front door and pull your teeth out one at a time. Do you understand me?'

'Yes.'

'Good lad. Now, go and get your head down and keep this conversation to yourself.'

The call ended and Sam closed his eyes. It sounded like whoever he was, he needed to get into Angela's house. Sam had a key, but he wasn't going to disclose that. He took out his keyring and slid Angela's key from the clasp, sliding it underneath a table lamp next to him. It could stay there until he could dispose of it far away from his flat. He could take it on the bus to work and drop it down a grid. If they needed to get into Angela's house urgently, they would need a burglar. He thought about the man calling Les next and putting pressure on him to break into a crime scene. Les would be shitting himself. That made him smile inside. It was the only positive he could take from the day.

Chapter 13. Easy Money.

I *work all night, I work all day but still the bills I have to pay...*

MARION CHECKED HER watch. It was just before six o'clock and Abi was still asleep. She said that she hadn't had a full night's sleep for months, because Leo twitched, had nightmares and wet the bed on occasions. The deeper the addiction became, the worse the side effects were. Abi needed to sleep for seven hours minimum, or she was tired the next day. She had been like that since she was a little girl. Marion thought back to Abi's childhood and smiled at the memories, although she felt a tinge of sadness too, and even a slight sense of loss.

That little girl had been such a joy from her first day on the planet. She was so bright, crawling and talking earlier than most and she was reading books before she started school. Marion had such high hopes for her but all that was dashed on the rocks of life, when her father left them for another man, and she developed anxiety and an eating disorder. She changed from such a happy being to a fragile nervous wreck, scared of her own shadow. There was a paradigm shift in her personality. She went from a confident child to vulnerable teenager who hid herself in her room and self-harmed. Her upper arms and thighs were striped with scars from cutting. There were some dark times when she was researching suicide and Marion was distraught. She simply couldn't understand why Abi was so unhappy that she could consider killing herself. It was heartbreaking and came hand in hand with an overwhelming feeling of failure. Failure, as a mother, failure as a wife and failure as a human being.

Abi was at the lowest point in her short life, and that's why Marion believed she became attracted to Leo Tompkins. He was a teenager with a tragic background and was damaged and emotionally vulnerable too. Marion could see their vulnerability acted like a magnet and they made each other feel safe, at first but that had changed now. There was a third aspect to their love story. Ketamine. Leo was in love with Abi and ket, but he could only truly love one and the other would always play second fiddle. Abi had endured their relationship in the vain hope that Leo would be strong enough to quit the drugs completely. It wasn't going to happen. Marion had to step in and take her daughter out of the situation.

Marion went into the kitchen and retrieved her consignment of cocaine, placing it into an empty tube of scouring powder. She wasn't a dealer in the real sense of the word. She saw herself as a middleman. The connection between a supply and a demand. Each month she bought and sold two thousand pounds worth of powder. She doubled her money in one transaction, minimum risk, maximum profit. She put the tube into a rucksack next to a selection of other cleaning supplies. And fastened it.

Marion put on her work coat, which had Kleeni-Queen printed on the back and left breast pocket. The logo was a crown on a pink van. She left her house and went to her car, putting the bag in the boot. The street was quiet, illuminated by the yellow haze of streetlights. She lived in Allerton at the end of the famous Penny Lane. The staff at the trendy bistro across the road were locking up and sounded like they had been drinking the profits. Marion smiled and waved at them, and they cheered in unison as they walked away.

A double-decker bus went by the top of the road on its way to Liverpool city centre. It was empty but would be standing room only by the time it reached its destination. Marion drove away from the city, the few miles to Woolton, an affluent suburb where her two main clients lived. Her first stop was the Goodstone residence.

David Goodstone was a partner at a busy dentist on Rodney Street, although he was all but retired now. His practice had a great view of the Anglican cathedral and was surrounded by private medical practitioners of all sorts. Doctors, aesthetic surgeons, plastic surgeons, dentists, Botox providers, all wanted to be on Rodney Street. That was where the money was.

His home was a six-bedroom house with an indoor swimming pool, tennis courts, snooker room and cinema area. The Goodstone family were exceptionally rich three generations before David was born and clever investments had grown their fortune. They were beyond millionaires.

Marion reached the security gates and entered the code into the keypad. They whirred into motion and opened. She drove up a tree-lined driveway and turned left onto the service road which led to the rear of the house. There were three vehicles already parked up and her staff were standing in a huddle smoking. She pulled up and climbed out, walking to the boot to fetch her bag.

'Good morning, everyone,' Marion said. 'Is everyone well and feeling up to the task?'

'I'm as ready as I'll ever be,' one of the men answered. His badge was printed with Pat. 'What do rich people say when they tickle their kids?'

'I'm going to regret this, but go on, tell us, Pat.'

'Gucci, Gucci, Gucci.'

'They get worse,' Marion said.

'On a serious note, can I clean all the mirrors today as it's something I could see myself doing?' Pat said, chuckling.

'Fuck off, Pat,' one of the women said, groaning. 'It's too early, mate.'

'If you can't laugh, what can you do?' Pat protested. 'My mate's window cleaner dropped dead last week. Very sad.' No one spoke. 'My mate has contacted his spirit using a squeegee board.'

'Can you stop him?'

'He's doing my head in.'

'I'm phoning in sick if he's here next week.'

'Okay, okay,' Marion said, laughing. 'Give it a rest, Pat.'

'Miserable buggers, the lot of you,' Pat moaned.

'I want you all to work in the same areas as last week, please,' Marion said. 'Mr Goodstone has asked if we can bleach the changing cubicles in the swimming pool as one of his grandchildren has a verruca and he thinks he caught it from the tiles.'

'I'm in the pool area,' Mal said, shuffling his feet. 'I'll make sure it smells of bleach for a week.'

'Good man,' Marion said. She headed for the back door. 'The sooner we start, the sooner we finish. Let's get cracking.' The cleaners set off with as much enthusiasm as could be expected at such an early hour. Marion opened the basement door and stepped inside the boiler room. A steep staircase climbed up to the kitchen and the smell of bacon cooking reached her before she opened the door. The odour of toast was more subtle but just as mouthwatering. She could hear the radio playing, tuned to City FM.

'It smells so good in this kitchen,' Marion said as she closed the door behind her. 'Morning, Bernie.'

'Good morning, lovely,' Bernie said, frying eggs in an iron pan that looked as old as the house. 'Would you like a bacon and egg sandwich and a mug of tea or are you dieting again?'

'That was last month. I've moved on and decided diets are shite.'

'I couldn't agree more,' Bernie said.

'I would love one, please,' Marion said. 'I'm just going to speak to young mister Goodstone before he leaves for work.'

'Okay, I'll plate one up for you,' Bernie said. 'It will be here for you when you are ready.'

'I'll be two minutes.'

Marion walked through the kitchen and along a corridor which was carpeted with thick Axminster. The walls were decorated with oil paintings, depicting great sea battles from the Elizabethan era and beyond. The images were dark and brooding, the frames guilted and ornate. It was like walking through a museum gallery.

David senior often bragged that there were Goodstones fighting at the battle of Trafalger in 1805. He claimed one of his ancestors was aboard the HMS Victory during the battle against the French and Spanish armada. Marion didn't care but pretended to be interested whenever he went on with himself, which was most of the time. His fixation with his family tree was beyond boring as fuck but she could suffer him for the money she earned from the family.

Marion reached the gymnasium and David junior was finishing a set of bench presses. He sat up and smiled at her through the glass. Marion waved and opened the door. David was twenty-one, overweight and receding already. His father had the worst combover she had seen, and David was following suit. David was sweating profusely and looked as if his blood pressure was through the roof. His sister, Rebecca was jogging on a treadmill with her headphones on. Her Lycra gym gear was being tested at the seams and her rolls of fat were jiggling from side to side as she ran. She never said hello and was a total snob when it came to the hired help. They were beneath her and she barely acknowledged their existence.

'Good morning, David,' Marion said. 'How are you?'

'Very well, thank you, Marion,' he said, wiping sweat from his forehead. He looked her up and down and smiled. 'You look lovely today.' He winked. Marion cringed inside. 'Very lovely indeed.'

'I look like I've just got out of bed and come to work on autopilot, so save the bullshit flattery, please,' Marion said, hand on hips. Rebecca glanced at her. 'Morning Rebecca.' Rebecca didn't respond. 'I don't know why I bother trying. At least your sister is consistently rude and never lets me down.'

'She hates everyone.'

'Even you?'

'Especially me. Don't take it personally.' He smiled and Marion could see flecks of cigar skin between his teeth. She felt queasy. 'You do look fit, today,' David said, winking again. 'I would do you right now, definitely.'

'Wow, how lovely. Is that supposed to charm me because it won't, and I'm 'definitely' not interested in what you would or wouldn't do.'

'Come on, lighten up,' David moaned. 'I'll take you to heaven and back again.'

'I'm getting very bored quickly.' Marion rolled her eyes. 'Can we not do this today please.'

'Okay, okay. I was just paying you a compliment.'

'Save them for someone who is interested in what you think,' Marion said, smiling coldly.

'Are you still mad at me?'

'For following me to my home, stalking my social media and bombarding me with text messages?' Marion asked. 'You're a weirdo. Fucking right I am mad with you.'

'Oh dear. When you calm down, we can talk about things properly,' he said.

'Fuck off, David.'

'Charming.' David sulked.

'If you want me to leave, I can go now,' Marion said, gesturing to the door.

'Do you need the key for the chemical cupboard?' he asked, quietly. He knew when to back down from Marion.

'Yes please,' Marion said. She could smell him as she approached the bench; the smell was familiar in a stomach turning way. He opened a locker on the wall and gave her a single Chubb key. Marion took it and left the gym, heading further down the corridor. She reached an unmarked door, half the height of a normal door and stooped to unlock it. There were three shelves of untouched cleaning supplies. She took the scouring powder from her bag and put it on the shelf, taking an identical empty tub from the cupboard. She put the empty into her bag and locked the door.

David junior was leaving the gymnasium as she walked back. He was typing on his phone. He smiled but she didn't return it.

'I was coming to look for you. Your invoice is the same as last month, I trust?' David asked. 'Four grand.'

'Yes,' Marion said, nodding.

'The Kleeni-Queen account?' he checked. Marion nodded. He tapped the screen a few times. 'There we go. Paid in full.'

'Thank you. Your stuff is where it always is.'

'Always a pleasure. I'll see you soon, I hope.'

'You might see me around here, but not how you want to see me,' Marion said. David grabbed her arm and pulled her to him, trying to put his mouth on hers. His hands went down to her ass and squeezed her. She could feel him stiff through her clothes and pulled away. 'Get off me!'

'Oh, come on,' he complained.

'I have told you until I'm blue in the face that I'm not interested. This contract is with your father and if he thought there was anything unprofessional going on, I would be sacked,' Marion said, angrily, her voice almost a whisper. 'Don't touch me again. There are cameras here.'

'But no one is watching them at this time in the morning,' David moaned, trying to kiss her again.

'I said, no, you stupid idiot. Don't touch me again or you'll be sorry. I'm warning you,' Marion said, pulling away. 'My staff are everywhere and so are yours. We agreed. No risks, no mistakes.'

'You're so fucking boring sometimes,' David muttered, sulking like a teenage boy. 'You change like the weather. One minute you're hot for me and the next, frosty as fuck.'

'Whatever, David,' Marion said, walking away. 'I'll take boring over prison every day of the week.'

'I can buy stuff anywhere, you know?' he called after her. 'I know loads of people selling stuff.'

'Fine. Do that and see how good it is and how long it is before you get arrested,' Marion said, turning to face him. 'You will attract the attention of the wrong people, David. Spoilt little rich kids are easy pickings for the sharks out there and they will tear you to shreds and fuck you over in the process.'

'Okay, okay.' He sighed and rolled his eyes, taking a deep breath. 'Look, I'm sorry. I'm really sorry. I'm out of order.'

'Apology accepted but don't ever try to touch me again, understood?'

'Understood. I'm sorry.'

'Let's put it behind us,' Marion said.

'What about us?' David asked, frowning. He looked like he was about to cry.

'Oh, my God. Are you fucking deaf?'

'No. I'm not deaf.'

'Good, then listen carefully. There is no us, David. It was a bit of fun,' Marion said, shaking her head. 'We were both drunk and high. It meant nothing to me. Go and find yourself a woman your own age.'

'I don't want a woman my own age, I want you, Marion,' David sounded wounded.

'You have a lot of growing up to do before you can handle a woman of my age,' Marion turned and walked on. 'Grow up and accept that it was a mistake, drunken sex and nothing more.'

'Funny, I felt pretty grown up when we were fucking,' David snapped.

'Not from where I was lying, you didn't feel like a grown man at all. I'm just glad it was all over in minutes,' Marion said, with a shrug. 'Enjoy your weekend.'

'Fuck you, Marion!'

'Not again, you won't,' Marion said. 'Not in your wildest dreams, David!'

'Bitch!'

'You better believe it.'

Marion reached the kitchen and breathed in the odours. They were delicious. Her stomach was rumbling.

'Your sandwich and tea are here,' Bernie said, gesturing to the wooden table in the centre of the kitchen. 'Did you find David junior?'

'I did,' Marion said. 'He needs a girlfriend.' Marion bit into the sandwich and savoured the bacon. It was thick and smoked. Her favourite. she washed it down with a slug of tea. 'This is the only reason I come here, you know.'

'Well, it's always nice to see you,' Bernie said. 'How is your daughter doing?'

'She's dating a sixteen-year-old loser and she's pregnant,' Marion answered before she could think about her words. Bernie stopped what she was doing and walked over to her, holding her tightly.

'Oh no,' Bernie said. 'Last time you talked about her, you said he was a waste of time. How far gone is she?'

'We think she's about eight weeks,' Marion said. 'I'll take her to the doctor on Monday. We can talk about what to do next once we know for sure.'

'Persuade her to get rid of it,' Bernie said, lowering her voice. 'She's got all her life in front of her. Having a child at seventeen is so difficult, especially as a single mum. I know some people cope really well but they're barely adults themselves at that age.'

'I agree with you. If she has that child, Leo will be in her life forever,' Marion said. 'If I thought I could get away with murder, I would throw him in the river. He will never amount to anything. I hoped he was just a phase that she was going through and that she would get bored of him, but she moved in with him. They struggle to feed themselves week to week and I left her to it hoping she would get tired of being skint all the time but pregnancy changes everything.'

'It's terrible news for you. I'm sure you will sort her out. Let me know how you get on,' Bernie said. 'I must take this food to the dining room. Will you still be here when I get back?'

'No, Bernie,' Marion said. 'I need to get home before she wakes up alone. I don't want her having a change of heart and going back to him.'

'I'll see you next week,' Bernie said.

'You take care,' Marion said, finishing her sandwich, rinsing it down with her tea.

She put her cup and plate into the sink and rinsed them under the tap. Through the window, she could see leaves blowing across the empty tennis courts, the nets hung low weighed down by the water. Rain ran down the glass in rivulets, blurring her view. The clouds were as grey as her mood, and they scurried across the sky. She felt the need to be at home with her daughter.

Marion left her cleaning crew there and drove home to Penny Lane. She parked and went into the house, hoping beyond hope that Abi hadn't woken up and felt sorry for Leo. Abi loved him, no matter what he was. She wasn't sure how long she could convince her to stay at home with her. If Leo stayed on the ket or went on a bender, feeling sorry for himself, she might see how weak he was. She hoped that he would implode and fail. There is nothing more unattractive than spineless. Abi's father had been spineless; she wanted more than that for Abi.

Marion crept upstairs and peeked into her room. Abi was curled up, snoring gently in the same position she was in the last time she looked. Marion decided to leave her to sleep. She must need it. She felt her phone vibrating and pulled the door closed, tiptoeing down the stairs. The number was withheld, which was unusual. She thought about ignoring it but answered it anyway.

'Hello,' Marion said.

'Marion. It's Bernie from the Goodstone house.'

'Hello Bernie. The number was withheld, so I didn't realise it was you. Is everything okay with the cleaners?'

'No.' Bernie sounded like she was crying. 'One of your cleaners was working in the corridor and found David junior and his sister Rebecca unconscious in the gymnasium.'

'Fucking hell. When did this happen?' Marion asked, confused.

'About ten minutes after you left here,' Bernie said, sniffling. 'Their faces were all swollen, lips blue and they weren't breathing properly. We called an ambulance, and they said it looked like anaphylactic shock.'

'What, like an allergic reaction?' Marion said, shocked.

'Yes.'

'What happened?'

'We don't know exactly but they have been allergic to all sorts of stuff since they were babies. David senior was always panicking that we checked the ingredients when we bought in stock because they both have severe allergies to nuts.'

'Nuts,' Marion repeated shocked.

'Yes. They've had severe allergies to all sorts but, especially to nuts.'

'I didn't know that they suffered with allergies,' Marion said. 'Are they okay?'

'No.'

'They're not, okay?'

'No.' Bernie sniffled. Marion could hear her sobbing. 'David junior died while the paramedics were working on him,' Bernie said, her voice breaking. 'They couldn't bring him back.'

'Jesus Christ,' Marion muttered. 'What about Rebecca?'

'She was in a terrible state,' Bernie said. 'She couldn't breathe, so they did a tracheotomy.' Bernie was sobbing and blew her nose. 'She turned blue, Marion, I literally mean blue in the face. It was terrible, like she was suffocating right there on the gym floor. I don't think she'll make it.'

'I don't understand what happened to them,' Marion said. 'Did they eat anything?'

'No.'

'Then what have they reacted to?'

'We don't know for sure, but between me and you, the ambulance lady found some wraps containing white powder.' Marion froze, her heart quickened.

'White powder where?' Marion asked.

'She said there was powder in their nostrils.'

'So, they had snorted something?'

'Yes. That's what the lady said to her colleague, but surely you can't sniff nuts?'

'I doubt it, but the paramedics said they had both snorted something?' Marion asked.

'Yes. There were wraps near them and powder up their nostrils. They hadn't eaten anything from the kitchen, so I can't see what else it could be,' Marion said. 'David senior was in such a panic. I've never seen him panic about anything.'

'How many wraps did they find?' Marion asked. Her guts twisted and she felt nauseous.

In her mind she was thinking. Wraps.

White powder.

Dead client.

'How many, what do you mean?'

'I'm trying to make sense of this, Bernie,' Marion said. 'If they had taken drugs, it could have been an overdose, so how many wraps did they find?'

'David senior asked the paramedic the same question and she said it was an allergic reaction, not an overdose.' Bernie paused. 'They both have issues with drug misuse. David senior has sent them both to detox clinics in the past, but it's a family secret.'

'Don't worry,' Marion said. 'I won't repeat anything we say.'

'Okay. There were two wraps next to them on the table. They must have taken the powder in the gym and then collapsed right there, immediately.'

'Only two wraps?' Marion asked. Bernie sniffled again.

'Yes.'

'Are my people still there?'

'Yes,' Bernie said. 'David senior sent them away from the gym and told them to finish their work elsewhere.' She sniffled again. 'He's followed the ambulance to the hospital, but I thought you would want to know.'

'Of course, I do, thank you,' Marion said, quietly. 'I'd better come back and make sure the staff are okay.' Thoughts raced through her head. 'Have the police been called?'

'Yes. It's a suspicious death,' Bernie said. 'The paramedics called it in.'

'Okay. I'll see you soon,' Marion said.

'I'll be here,' Bernie said. 'David senior said to carry on with preparing lunch, but I can't think straight.'

'I'll be there in thirty-minutes,' Marion said, her mind whizzing at a million miles an hour. Her instincts told her their deaths were something to do with the cocaine she had delivered. She needed to speak to Kenny Fulshaw and scrolled through her phone for his number. She pressed connect and waited. The voicemail kicked in straightaway. Marion cursed beneath her breath and tried again. It rang three times before he answered.

'Marion. To what do I owe this pleasure?' Kenny said, chewing something.

'That gear you gave me is dodgy,' Marion said. 'Two of my clients had a serious reaction to it and one of them is dead.'

'Whoah, whoah, whoah, bald eagle,' Kenny stammered, nearly choking. 'What the fuck are you talking about?'

'I dropped the stuff with my client. His sister and him snorted a wrap each and had an allergic reaction. The brother is dead, and the sister was rushed to hospital.'

'Fucking hell, Marion,' Kenny snapped. 'What did you do to it?'

'I didn't do anything to it, Kenny,' Marion argued. 'I don't even look at that shit, never mind interfere with it.'

'You cut it with something you shouldn't have,' Kenny said, accusingly. 'What did you use?'

'Fuck off, Kenny,' Marion said, angrily. 'This is on you.'

'I sold you the gear. The responsibility is on you,' Kenny snarled.

'They had an allergic reaction to the shit, Kenny. They're both allergic to nuts,' Marion said, as calmly as she could. 'I bought cocaine from you, and I haven't touched it, so you have a massive problem because if you have sold a lot of that batch, you're going to have more dead people on your books.' Kenny was silent. 'I suggest you have a good think about what could have gone wrong or you're going down for a long time because no one is going to protect the fucking idiot who sold them contaminated cocaine.' There was an uncomfortable silence.

'How much of it did you sell to them?' Kenny asked, panicking now.

'All of it,' Marion said. 'I don't deal, Kenny. I just pass it on in one transaction for more money.'

'Fucking hell, if the police get hold of that, we're all fucked,' Kenny said.

'Calm down. I don't think anyone knows where the stash is,' Marion said. 'If they had found it, I think I would know by now.'

'What are you saying?' Kenny asked.

'I'm saying that if the powder is where I left it, no one will find it,' Marion said. 'I may be able to recover the cocaine before anyone else does when the police have gone, and the dust has settled but, in the meantime, you need to find out what the fuck went wrong.'

'Don't talk to me like I'm an idiot,' Kenny said, angrily.

'You need to get down off your high horse and worry about more dead people turning up,' Marion said. 'I'll be in touch when I know more. Do not contact me in any way, shape or form until this dies down.'

'Wait...'

Marion hung up the call and grabbed her car keys. She needed to know what had happened at the Goodstone residence.

Chapter 14. Cuckoo.

When I need you, I just close my eyes and I'm with you, and all that I so want to give you, It's only a heartbeat away...

LEO HAD SPENT THE NIGHT sniffing some of the ketamine that Marion had bought. He was floating in and out a deep sleep. The drug quietened the receptors in his brain and allowed him to sleep. He needed it to quell the pain of withdrawal and to numb the pain of Abi leaving him. She was pregnant with his child; their child and he didn't think he could live without her. He cried the tears of a tortured soul, trapped in a situation that he couldn't escape from or change. Being a father at sixteen wasn't the plan but neither was being a ketamine addict and now he was both. Father and addict, they were polar opposites; he couldn't look after himself, how could he bring up a child?

If he was going to win back the mother of his child, the love of his life, then he needed to be clean and he needed money. A lot more money than he was earning at the moment and to do that, he needed to ditch the ketamine, which was far easier said than done. He had to focus on staying sober, change his priorities and try to be a functioning human being. Maybe then Abi and her bitch mother might give him a chance.

The problem with addiction is the drug becomes essential. Ket covered all his raw nerves with a soothing blanket of numbness; it suppressed his emotional pain and anxiety. It was an anaesthetic, strong enough to be used on horses and other huge animals, so the effect on humans was far more powerful. It had aways been his escape from the emotional turmoil of life and he was mentally addicted the very first time George Madern had given it to him. The numbness and feeling of not being inside himself any more were euphoric. The disassociation was what he needed emotionally, and the physical addiction followed soon after. George had thought he was doing him a favour by helping him cope with his grief and separation issues, anxiousness and anger at losing his entire family but it just added addiction to his list of issues. The long-term effect was catastrophic.

George had a soft spot for Leo, and he protected him and carried him but when he retired and Barry stepped up, Leo's champion was no longer there. Leo was not in Barry's top tier of employees. He was deemed a junkie and unreliable, which made him expendable, with no real value to the organisation. Leo felt like he had been part of a family again, only to be an outcast once more.

Leo had to change the perception his superiors had of him, or nothing would change. If he could function properly, he could earn a lot of money. Enough money to look after Abi the way she deserved to be looked after. He could do it if he spoke to the Tickle brothers and asked them for more work. Work that paid a decent amount of money. If he could impress them, they would tell their bosses and maybe Barry Madern would give him a break like his father had.

A loud knock at the door startled him. Leo stood up quickly and blood ran to his head; he waited for the dizziness to pass. He staggered to the door, almost on tiptoes, hoping beyond all hope it was Abi. But Abi had a key, so why knock, and on the odd occasion she had forgotten to take one out, she never knocked that loudly. He couldn't understand why anybody would be knocking on his door at this time, whatever time it was. It still felt like the early hours of the morning, but time was dragging in his drug fuelled world. In his head the alarm bells began ringing and his instinct was not to open the door. He walked away from it.

Leo went to the window and peered through the curtains. The road and pavements were wet and puddles had formed in the potholes. Everything was bathed in the dull yellow light of the streetlights but there was a brighter patch of clouds on the horizon. Morning had broken. Crime scene tape flickered in the wind. The cordon was unmanned now, and Angela Deacon's house was in darkness. The crime scene tape was the only clue that a life had ended abruptly in that house yesterday. He looked up and down the street, concealing himself behind the curtain, trying to see if there were any vehicles which didn't belong there. Everything appeared to be as normal as it could be. Lights were burning here and there, and the estate was waking from its slumber but would remain quiet for the next few hours.

Another knock on the door startled him and dragged him from his ketamine haze for a moment. The knock was louder this time, more insistent, almost urgent. Leo knew that whoever it was at the door, they were bringing bad news with them.

He had no heart for any more trauma, and he stepped away from the window, making his way to the front door. He looked through the peephole and recognised Ged Tickle standing on the landing, looking agitated and nervous. Ged was a big man with dark hair and Turkey teeth. He was wearing one of his signature Hugo Boss tracksuits, which he owned in every colour of the rainbow. There was another man with him, but he couldn't see his face as his head was covered by his hoodie. Whoever it was, he didn't want to talk to them. His mind was in turmoil, and he couldn't cope with any drama.

Ged Tickle was the fairest of the brothers and Leo would rather deal with him than any of the others that worked for Barry Madern. Most of them were arrogant bullies at best and raging steroid-munching psychos at their worst. Ged was about to knock on the door again when Leo decided to open it. He unfastened the bolts and safety chain and turned the latch, and the door was pushed open before he could invite them in. Leo was knocked backwards against the wall, and he was shocked into silence for a moment. His reactions were slowed by the ketamine.

'Fucking hell, Leo, you took your time,' Ged said, walking to the living room window. Leo noticed his new Nike trainers. They were limited edition and cost hundreds. 'Didn't you hear me knocking?'

'Yes, I heard you but it's early and I'm a bit fucked,' Leo said, closing the door. The second man removed his hood and Leo recognised him as the burglar who lived in the flats across the road. He was an arsehole. 'What the fuck is going on?'

'This is Les,' Ged said, without turning towards him. His attention was on the house across the road.

'I know who he is,' Leo said. 'But why is he here, in my flat?'

'We need to do a recce on the place across the road,' Les said, trying to sound mysterious. 'I've got a bit of business to do there.'

'You've got a bit of business in an empty house?' Leo asked, frowning. Les was a scruffy chav, wearing dark sportswear and unbranded shoes. 'That sounds dodgy to me but then you are a thief.'

'Yes. It is well dangerous, mate. And it needs to be done sooner rather than later.' Les took out his cigarettes. 'Do you smoke?'

'Not in here and neither do you,' Leo said. 'Don't light that.'

'I have a job to do, and cigs calm my nerves,' Les argued. 'Have a fucking day off, mate.'

'I'm not your mate and what the fuck has that got to do with me?' Leo asked. 'Don't light that in here, I said.'

'Put the cigarette away,' Ged said. Les tutted and rolled his eyes.

'Can you please tell me why you are here?' Leo asked.

'You have a view of the side of the house and the lean-to on the back,' Ged said. 'I need to study it properly without being seen.'

'Why?' Leo asked, confused.

'That is the way out.'

'The way out?' Leo said, shaking his head. 'Are you breaking into Angela's house?'

'You don't need to know what we're going to do,' Les said. 'It's a need-to-know basis.'

'Is he for real?' Leo asked, Ged. 'If you're weighing up the way out of her house, you're clearly going to break in first.'

'There are no flies on you, Leo,' Ged said. He sat down on the settee. 'Sit down. I have a proposition for you.' Leo slumped in the armchair opposite him. Les stayed at the window, peering through the curtains from several angles. 'Is your missus still asleep?'

'No,' Leo said, shaking his head. He felt himself tearing up, but he fought the emotions. 'She's looking after her mum. She's not been well.'

'She looked fine when she left here last night,' Les said, turning towards them. 'Your missus had a suitcase with her.'

'I don't believe this twat is in my flat,' Leo said, glaring at Les. 'Why were you watching what was going on outside my home?'

'I was watching the Dibble at Angela's house, actually,' Les said. 'I just happened to see your missus and her mum arriving and leaving soon after with a suitcase.' Les pointed his finger. 'She's fit your missus. I'd give her one. You're punching well above your weight there, and don't call me a twat again.'

'Did he just say he would give my girlfriend one?' Leo asked, astounded. Ged nodded and grinned. 'Why is this twat in my flat, Ged?' Leo asked. The ket gave him the feeling of invincibility. 'I don't want him here.'

'Listen to me, Leo,' Ged said, leaning forward, lowering his voice. 'There are some parcels in the house that Angela was looking after for us.' He paused to let it sink in. 'We need to get them back before the Dibble find them.'

'I see,' Leo said. 'And you're using this twat to break in and recover them?'

'I'm going to break his nose,' Les said, angrily. 'I've warned you, you little rat.'

'Shut up, Les. You're not going to break anyone's nose because Leo is right, you are a twat, but I need you to focus on the job in hand.' Les thought about arguing but Ged's expression deterred him. 'I agree that he's a twat but he's very good at gaining entry into houses,' Ged said. 'I have a plan but I'm going to need another pair of hands and somewhere close to store the stuff until we can move it, safely.'

'This is really fucked up. Are you asking me to help him to break into a house surrounded by crime scene tape?' Leo asked, smiling. Ged laughed and nodded. 'I thought so.'

'It's got to be done, mate,' Ged said, shrugging.

'Do I have a choice in this?'

'Nope.'

'And is there going to be a decent pay out if I agree to help?' Leo asked.

'Yes,' Ged said, nodding. 'I'll look after you, lad.'

'I want some better jobs than I'm getting at the moment,' Leo said. 'I need some decent money.'

'Help me with this and I'll look after you,' Ged said.

'Okay, let's hear the plan,' Leo said.

'I'm not working with him,' Les said, walking towards the front door. Ged stood up and grabbed him by the throat, lifting him off his feet and slamming him against the wall. 'I can't breathe...'

'You need to be very clear in your head as to who is in charge here, Les,' Ged said, tightening his grip. 'You're only here because your cousin asked me to use you for the job as a favour to him. Barry specifically wanted you to do this for him, so I agreed because if it was my choice, you would be the last person I would work with.' Les was turning red. 'You will do as your told and if you cause me any problems at all, I will hurt you and have you buried in Delamere

Forest with your fingers and toes stuffed down your throat.' Les gagged and nodded, spittle running from the corners of his mouth. Ged let him go and he collapsed onto the floor gasping for breath. 'Do as I tell you and we'll get on fine but don't think for one minute that this is a democracy, understand?' Les coughed and nodded. 'I didn't hear you, Les. Do you understand me?'

'Yes.'

'Okay, let's get back to the job in question,' Ged said. He went to the window and gestured for Leo to join him. 'We have to assume the Dibble know there are packages stashed in the house, which means they're probably watching the gaff, waiting to see who turns up to recover it.'

'That's what I thought,' Leo said. 'Isn't it impossible to get in and out without being caught?'

'If someone was to break in and then walk out carrying the packages, they would be arrested and locked away for a long time, but I have a plan,' Ged said, tapping his nose. 'The genius burglar over there will break in through the patio doors to the rear, behind the lean-to. Then he will lock them, before moving on to the front and back doors, locking them and then he will drill screws into the frames, so no one can get in easily,' Ged explained. 'That will give him time to work. They won't move in to arrest him until he leaves the building. Once the ground floor is secure, he will locate the packages, remove them and toss them out of the side window, right there above the lean-to.'

'I see,' Leo said. 'And I'll be there to pick them up?'

'Exactly, clever boy,' Ged said. 'I want you to pick them up, put them into a haversack and then jump the back garden fences like a Grand National horse. You make your way along the street until you get to the back of your block, let yourself in, then stash them in here until I call you with instructions. By the time the police realise Les isn't coming out, you'll be snoring in your bed.'

'What about Les?' Leo asked. 'How does he get out of there?'

'He doesn't,' Ged said. Leo looked confused. 'He is going to take some weed with him, have a joint or two and wait until they break the door down and find him asleep in the bed.'

'I don't get it,' Leo said.

'What has he done wrong?' Ged asked. 'He has broken into an empty house and fallen asleep. There's nothing on him that they can link to the packages because they're not there anymore, no gear, no crime.' Ged shrugged. 'What do you think?'

'I think you're clever as fuck,' Leo said, smiling as the penny dropped. He stopped smiling for a minute. 'If I get caught with drugs on me, I'm going down for a long time. How much am I getting for this?'

'They won't get near you. They'll be watching from a distance, and you'll be gone in seconds. I'll give you two grand,' Ged said.

'No chance,' Leo said, shaking his head. 'The risks are huge. Five grand, minimum and you get me regular good jobs.'

'Don't push your luck,' Ged said. 'Three grand, last offer.'

'Four and I'll shake your hand right now,' Leo said.

'Deal.' Ged shook his hand. 'We will go tonight once we check the Dibble have retreated far enough. Get some sleep, Leo, you look like shit.'

Chapter 15. The world has gone nuts.

*T**he shadow on the wall tells me the sun is going down, oh Ruby, don't take your love to town...*

RUBY KISSED HER CHILDREN goodnight and turned out the light. The dull glow of a night-light bathed their bedroom in warm amber. They didn't wake up often in the night but if they did, they were not in total darkness. She pulled the door too, leaving it open a few inches. There was something too final about closing them in completely. She had been locked in her room for hours when she was a child, with no food, water or toilet. It was the punishment imposed by her father for pretty much anything she did. Being made to go without food and water was simple enough. She learned to hide a few biscuits and a bottle of water in her room, and it made the hours bearable but needing the toilet was the worst. If she did make a mess in her room, her father would beat her, force her to clean it up, make her bathe in freezing cold water and then lock her up again as punishment. Maybe that was why she didn't shut her own children in their room. Maybe.

There were lots of people who had challenging childhoods, some scarred for life, others appearing unscathed throughout their adulthood, and nobody would know the difference. Ruby came from an abusive background, but it did not define her. She chose not to carry it like a cross, never spoke about, rarely thought about it and appeared to be a balanced individual.

Her mother, whom she loved dearly, died of cancer when Ruby was twenty-one, which meant that after the funeral, she didn't have to go to her parents' home anymore. Her father played the victim at the wake and even tried to hug her. She whispered 'fuck off' as she pushed him away. The last time he had embraced her, he digitally penetrated her; she was nine. Ruby never told her mother, but she suspected something because her behaviour changed. Her father tried hard to make things appear normal, but Ruby never looked him in the eyes again. She would leave a room if he was in it, and they barely spoke again; if he asked a question, she blanked him and it became obvious, something was wrong between father and daughter.

On her deathbed, her mother apologised for whatever he had done, but Ruby still didn't disclose to her. She didn't want her to die knowing that her husband of a lifetime was a paedophile of the worst kind; the kind who prey on their own children. Her mother's funeral was like cutting the final thread of their relationship. She was finally free of the bastard. She didn't see or hear from her father again. He died a lingering death, suffering from dementia in a nursing home only ten miles away from where she lived but he might as well have been on the moon for all she cared. She was the only person at his funeral, and she only went to make sure he was dead. He was cremated and she never went for his ashes. She didn't give a toss where they ended up.

Life had its ups and downs, but she had made the most of it. She had two beautiful children and a decent job in the Liverpool Women's hospital as a phlebotomist. The father of her children was a prick and had left for a younger woman when she was pregnant with Dana, her youngest. Dana was five now. Her brother, Jack was seven. They were mini-Rubys with blue eyes, red hair and cheekbones that made them look Elvish. Their father had seen them sporadically for a while but one letdown too many, led to Ruby refusing to let him see them at all. He didn't appear to be bereft with grief and sent birthday cards with a twenty-pound note in them the first year but never afterwards. If they wanted to see him when they were old enough to decide, she wouldn't stop them but until then, he was dead to her.

Ruby was a good mum, didn't party, sleep around or feed them frozen crap. Her only release was a wrap of cocaine on a Friday night with a bottle of white rioja. She showered and climbed into her fleece PJs, poured a glass of wine and tapped out her powder onto her chopping board. She sniffed a line and walked to the settee. Before she could sit down, her throat had restricted so tightly, that she couldn't breathe. Her eyes were streaming, and snot ran from her nose. She grabbed for her mobile, but it was upstairs in the bathroom. Ruby thought about her beautiful children and what would happen to them as her heart stopped beating and the darkness descended.

KENNY FULSHAW CHECKED his messages on multiple phones and found only one which concerned him for now. It was from a small-time dealer called, Gaz, who lived in Bootle. He sold twenty-pound wraps along the Strand opposite McDonalds. Gaz was a professor at the university in a previous life, teaching art and drama to BA students; but that was before drugs took a hold of him. Most of the money he made was used to fund his own heroin addiction. He had left a message for Kenny to contact him urgently and because it was Gaz and he was an intelligent man, it would be foolish to ignore him. Kenny swapped SIM cards and called him.

'Alright Kenneth, lad,' Gaz mumbled, his voice thick with alcohol. His accent was nondescript but educated. 'Thanks for ringing me back. I've been very concerned about a couple of incidents last night.'

'What's the problem, Gaz?' Kenny asked, bypassing the niceties.

'Don't take this the wrong way, Kenneth but there's something wrong with the gear you gave me yesterday,' Gaz said, apologetically. 'You know that I don't like to make a fuss, but this is serious.'

'Why, what has happened?' Kenny asked, his nerves jangling. He felt sick to the stomach and knew what was coming.

'A young girl bought a wrap and sniffed it across the road in the carpark behind Maccies,' Gaz explained. 'She had a fit straightaway, Kenneth. Her eyes were bulging, tongue swollen, and she couldn't breathe. I called an ambulance, and the paramedic said it was anaphylactic shock. They tried to treat her there in the ambulance, but she couldn't breathe, and her lips turned blue. They rushed her into the Royal.'

'So, she had a bad reaction to a class-A drug,' Kenny deflected but he knew the truth. 'It happens.'

'I would agree with you, Kenneth but her brother was there, and he said she is allergic to nuts and nothing else,' Gaz said. 'I know it's unusual and I wouldn't bother you with it if it was a one off, but it happened again later on, only this time the young male who had the reaction was rushed into hospital and a friend of mine who is a porter there, told me he is dead.'

'Fucking hell,' Kenny muttered. 'Are you sure it was the coke?'

'I've never seen reactions like this to any powder. It happened twice, mate. Right in front of my eyes. As soon as they sniffed it, they were gasping for air.' Gaz was cautious but to the point. 'There is no other explanation. It must be the gear.'

'Fucking hell,' Kenny hissed. 'Have you sold it all?'

'No mate,' Gaz said. 'I've got seventy wraps left and I've stashed it. I figured the coke is contaminated and you might have other incidences of this allergic reaction. That's why I've called you and left an urgent message.'

'Okay, Gaz. Don't sell any more of it,' Kenny said. 'I'll replace what you have left, like for like.' He paused. 'Seventy wraps, right?'

'Yes, seventy.'

'I'll replace them with a few extras as way of compensation for your trouble,' Kenny said.

'No one in Bootle is going to buy from me again if this gets out, Kenneth,' Gaz said. 'My reputation will be ruined.'

'Then you'd better make sure it doesn't get out, hadn't you?' Kenny said, becoming annoyed. 'I've said I'll compensate you.'

'When?'

'Fuck off, Gaz,' Kenny snapped. 'I said I'll replace it, and I will but I need to find out what is going on first. I can't magic the fucking stuff out of thin air.'

'Okay, okay, don't bite my head off,' Gaz said. 'Can I give you some advice?'

'What?' Kenny asked, agitated.

'I would look at wherever it was bagged up,' Gaz said.

'Why?'

'Because once it's in the wrap, it can't be compromised unless it's opened again.'

'You might be right,' Kenny said, reluctantly. 'Thanks. I'll be in touch.' The call ended.

'I might be right?' Gaz muttered to himself. 'Where else could the powder have become contaminated, you retard?'

Gaz looked at the screen on his phone and thought for a moment. He scrolled through his contacts until he found the number he wanted. He dialled it and waited.

'Professor Garry Ledson,' the voice said, answering. 'It's been a long time.'

'Detective Howard,' Gaz said. 'I have some information you will want to hear.'

'To do with what, exactly?' the detective asked, sounding disinterested. 'Another dealer working on your patch again?'

'There's a batch of contaminated cocaine being sold, and a young lad died last night,' Gaz explained.

'Are you shitting me?'

'Nope. I can tell you who it came from and where he bags up, but I want paying for the information,' Gaz said.

Chapter 16. Teamwork doesn't always work.

A*ll day long they work so hard, till the sun is going down, that's the sound of them working on the chain gang...*

JO LILLY WALKED INTO the transfer meeting feeling like it was Groundhog Day, and she was the condemned about to face the firing squad again. The duty team managers would be there with their lists of cases which needed to be transferred into the assessment teams; each manager with their own agenda. In an ideal world, the duty teams worked cases for just a few weeks from initial contact until they were ready to be moved to an assessment team, which would work them to their conclusion.

Unfortunately, the world isn't ideal, and the assessment teams didn't always have the capacity to accept any more cases. Jo had the unenviable task of representing the assessment teams, every week. She took her seat at the table and the three females opposite stopped chatting. Their greetings were cordial but guarded and the atmosphere was tense. It didn't feel like a department meeting, it felt like battle was about to commence.

'Good morning, lovely people. Here we are again, bright and breezy.' No one spoke. 'I can feel the spirit of cooperation oozing from every pore,' Jo said, smiling. No one replied or smiled or commented. 'Okay. I can sense you're all frustrated, so I won't waste your time by beating around the houses.' Jo's superpower was using the wrong word at the wrong time. 'As you are all aware, because of the decision to cull the use of agency staff, the experimental impact team has been disbanded as of last Monday, leaving the assessment teams with fifty-six children to allocate and we're already at full capacity.'

'What exactly are you saying?' Tina asked. Tina had the ability to suck the fun out of a room in minutes. The atmosphere was darkening every time she took a breath. She wasn't a glass half full or half empty type of girl. Her glass had broken and left her with six stitches. 'Just spell it out for us loud and clear.'

'Bloody hell. I thought that was crystal clear,' Jo said. 'I'm saying that the assessment teams have no capacity to accept any transfers from duty at the moment.' She smiled thinly. 'Sorry, but we're swamped.'

'This is a joke,' Tina muttered, shaking her head. 'What is the point in having this meeting when you move the goalposts every week and throw roadblocks up all the time?'

'Firstly, if it is a joke, I'm not laughing, Tina. Far from it, lovely,' Jo said, trying to remain calm. 'I have seven social workers with over thirty cases each at the moment. They should be on twenty-one. Some of them are close to burn out and we're drowning,' Jo's expression hardened. 'There is absolutely nothing to joke about when another fifty-six children are being dropped on us like a sack of shit. The case files are some of the worst I've seen and the drift and delay is dangerous. We have a crisis situation that we're trying to deal with. Without losing any social workers.'

'I've heard some of the other assessment team managers saying how bad the cases are,' Barbara said. The other two duty managers glanced at her disapprovingly. 'What are you looking at me like that for?' she said. 'How can they take any cases from us?'

'You have heard right, Barbara,' Jo said. 'They're shite, visits not recorded, visits out of time, some children haven't been seen for weeks, at least twelve final evidence reports are late for court and haven't been completed and our social workers don't know the families or the children but are expected to complete them.'

'That's impossible,' Barbara said. 'You can't write a court report if you don't know the family.'

'It is impossible, but who else is going to do them?' Jo asked. 'They have to be done.'

'This is how mistakes are made,' Barbara said.

'Why don't you go and work in assessment?' Tina muttered.

'This is not a competition to see who can be the most awkward department.' Jo looked each one in the eyes. 'It's a crock of shite. A nightmare. We've got legal crawling up our backsides and complaint forms backing up.' Jo shrugged. The three managers looked deflated. 'I take no pleasure in coming here and pissing you off, but the facts are the facts and this week, the assessment teams have no capacity. We simply cannot take any cases from duty. You'll have to work them until we have capacity.'

'Duty teams are supposed to be a revolving door,' Tina said, shaking her head.

'I understand how the system is supposed to work, Tina,' Jo said, sighing. 'Unfortunately, we have a spanner in the water.'

'Works,' Tina said.

'What?' Jo said, confused.

'You said water,' Tina said, agitated. 'It's works.'

'Ah, I see.' Jo smiled but there was no warmth in it. 'Unfortunately, we have a spanner in the waterworks.' She winked.

'This is getting beyond annoying,' Paula said. 'While I'm here, we sent you the Massey case last week and it's been sent back. That is nothing to do with the impact team. What are we supposed to do when you won't take the cases we send over?'

'That's an ambush, Paula. You know better than that.' Jo tapped the table with her fingers.

'It's a transfer meeting, isn't it?' Paula argued. 'I transferred a case to you, and you've sent it back. Let's discuss the reasons why cases are not coming over, shall we?'

'You shouldn't be bringing up a specific case in this meeting but as you have, if you had checked the case file before you sent it, you would have seen that there are no visits logged for six weeks, core group meeting notes either haven't been done or haven't been recorded and the plan is a cut and pasted mess. There is no chronology and the family members have not been explored.' Paula shifted uncomfortably in her seat. 'I refused to take it because it's a crock of shit and I'm not accepting it in its current condition.' Jo watched Paula's face darken. 'It took me all of five minutes to identify the issues in the file. I suggest you do your job properly in the first instance, check the cases are up to date first and then we won't have to send cases back to you.'

'Well, that's me told.' Paula gathered her things and put them into her briefcase. 'I'd better go and do my job properly.' She huffed as she walked out of the room. 'I don't see the point in coming to these meetings.'

'It's so we can disappoint each other face to face,' Jo said, shrugging. Barbara smiled behind her hand. 'I do tell the AD when we have no capacity before we meet, but she insists we have the meetings, so here we are. I can't do anything to change the situation.'

'Let's be honest. You're not going to clear the backlog in a week, are you?' Tina asked.

'Not a chance,' Jo said, shaking her head. 'We've got to allocate the impact cases and get the social workers below thirty cases. We will be stepping down on some next week, but it will be one step forwards and ten back. Unfortunately, it will be the same story next week.'

'We're obviously going to have to speak to our head of service about this,' Tina said, standing up, her face like thunder. 'She will not be happy.'

'Of course, you are, and she already knows the situation because she is a head of service but feel free,' Jo said. 'But unless she can pull half a dozen social workers out of her floop, the game doesn't change.' Jo stood up and picked up her pen, pad and laptop. 'I'll see you ladies next week.'

'Good luck with the impact cases,' Barbara said. 'I don't know who had that bright idea, but they need sacking.'

'You and I both know it was a knee-jerk reaction to the OFSTED visit the year before.' Jo shrugged. 'It was an experiment which backfired.'

'What did they do exactly?'

'They set up a team made up entirely of agency staff, run by an agency team manager, answering to nobody. It was a slight of hand answer to poor recruiting and now we have to pick up the pieces,' Jo said, walking to the door. 'We'll get there eventually. But I appreciate your sentiment. At least one of you realises we're supposed to be on the same team.'

'It does feel like it's them and us sometimes,' Barbara said. 'See you next week.'

'Same time, same place,' Jo said, leaving the meeting room.

The office was as hectic as it always was although since covid, people only worked from the office once or twice a week. It suited Jo and she achieved more in her office at home because there were no interruptions, questions, chats or travelling time sitting in traffic. She spotted Phil sitting at his desk. He was chatting to their boss, Hayley. She saw Jo coming and waved hello.

'Good morning,' Jo said. 'It's nice to see a couple of friendly faces.'

'How did the transfer meeting go?' Hayley asked, frowning.

'It was a crock of shit,' Jo said. 'Talk about, don't shoot the messenger. I'm going to wear a stab vest next week.'

'That bad?' Hayley said, frowning. 'I'm sure it wasn't a surprise. Everyone knows about the impact team folding.'

'Tina Wells says she's going to her AD and Paula walked out of the meeting in a sulk and said she's not coming to another one for a year,' Jo said, shrugging.

'Did she really say that?' Hayley asked, looking concerned.

'No, but I heard her thinking it,' Jo said. 'I'm sure you'll be getting a call from Sandra to tell you I'm moving roadblocks and throwing up goalposts.' Phil smiled. 'Moving the goalposts, I mean.'

'Sandra is as aware of the situation as we are and the duty teams are struggling too, but we all have a job to do, so they will have to cope until we can free up some capacity,' Hayley said. 'Any news on the Deacon children?'

'We've spoken to legal to get PR and a DNA test done on them,' Phil said. 'That reminds me, Jane Bennet from the PVPU called while you were in your meeting. She asked if you would call her back.'

'There must be some news about Angela,' Jo said. She turned to Hayley. 'I'll give her a ring and let you know what she says.'

'Keep me posted,' Hayley said, walking away. 'I've got a bad feeling about that one.'

'Thanks Hayley,' Jo said, scrolling through her phone. 'I hate it when she says that.'

'Why?' Phil asked.

'She's a bringer of doom,' Jo said.

'Harbinger,' Phil said.

'What?'

'It's harbinger of doom,' Phil corrected her, while pulling up a report on his laptop.

'Not to me it isn't,' Jo said. 'When I said she's a bringer of doom, that's exactly what I meant. No one brings the doom as well as our Hayley. One minute the sun is shining, the next, boom! She brings the doom.' Phil shook his head and laughed. Jo dialled Jane's number and she answered immediately. 'Jane, it's Jo returning your call.'

'Thanks for calling me back,' Jane said. 'I have an update and a few important questions for you. Have you got time to talk now?'

'This sounds like I need to find a room,' Jo said. 'Give me a minute.'

Jo went back to the meeting room she had been in earlier. It was empty. She stepped in and closed the door, quieting the buzz.

'Okay,' Jo said. 'Fire away.'

'Firstly, they found some electrolytes in Angela's blood, which indicate she may have consumed flunitrazepam.'

'Rohypnol.'

'Exactly,' Jane said. 'CSI recovered skin and hair samples, prints and secretions from the bedroom and from her body.'

'They have semen samples?'

'Yes,' Jane said. 'Whoever was in her bed is going to be easy to identify, if he's in the system.'

'Good. Nail the bastard,' Jo said.

'We need your help with that,' Jane said. 'Whoever drugged her knocked on the door and talked to her first. They were invited into the house, and we think the children might be our only witnesses.'

'I see,' Jo said. 'We're in court for PR and to access their DNA but they won't be required to attend for either.'

'Where are they?'

'With emergency foster parents in Southport,' Jo said. 'I can ask them some questions, separately and see if they saw anyone at the house.' Jo paused. 'Do we have a timeline?'

'The rape was yesterday,' Jane said. 'We still don't know what killed her but she's being processed this afternoon. Until they open her up, we don't know if this is a murder or not.'

'When will you know?' Jo asked.

'Later on, today but we think the chief will give this to MIT to lead, with Matrix and us assisting, so they will get the report first. Once they decide what the case actually is, we'll be informed.'

'Okay,' Jo said. 'I'll arrange to see the children as soon as we can. Yesterday is a long way away for kids this age.'

'I know. Do what you can,' Jane said. 'I'll speak to you later.'

'You will,' Jo said. 'Bye for now.'

Jo ended the call and walked back through the office. The buzz of chatter and dozens of phone calls being made was almost overwhelming. She had worked as a social worker for eighteen years and never noticed the volume of noise in the office until covid came along and everyone had to work from home. The silence had been deafening at first, now the noise made her agitated. She reached her desk and Phil was talking on the telephone. He called her over, a serious look on his face. The call ended and Phil rolled his eyes.

'Have a guess whose solicitor has contacted legal this morning?' he asked.

'Oh, fuck off,' Jo said, shaking her head. 'Please don't tell me it's him. Barry Madern?'

'Yup,' Phil said. 'He wants to know where his children are and when we're going to court for Parental Responsibility. He wants to contest it.'

'I knew this was going to happen,' Jo said, sighing. 'I could feel it in my water. This is going to get messy.' She paused to think. 'Get on to the foster parents and tell them we will be there in an hour or so. We need to talk to the children and ask them if they can remember anyone being in the house yesterday.'

'Okay,' Phil said, nodding. 'Do you know something that I don't?'

'I'll explain on the way,' Jo said. 'We need a pool car to drive, so see if there's one available.'

'Really?' Phil looked surprised.

'Absolutely. He could have people watching the barrier waiting for us to leave so that they can follow us to the children. Under no circumstances do you go to where the Deacon children are in your own car, understand?'

'How would he know who we are?' Phil asked.

'There were dozens of people filming outside the house yesterday,' Jo said. 'Some of them will be on his payroll, one hundred percent. He will already have pictures of us, our vehicles and anyone else who was at the scene.'

'Do you think so?' Phil looked unsure.

'Do not underestimate this man,' Jo said. 'Surveillance is an absolute must in his business. It's how they survive and stay out of prison, understand?'

'Yes. I understand.' Phil looked worried. 'I know a fair amount about him from what Leo Tomkins tells me but is this Madern guy that dangerous?'

'He's the most dangerous man that you've come across so far in your career,' Jo said. 'He's a well-known OCG leader with an army of violent nutcases on his payroll and he thinks we're going to take his children away from him again. He lost his first son and if Calvin and Coco are his, we're not going to just hand them over to him and he knows this. He'll try every dirty trick in the book to put pressure on us.'

'We don't know they are his children yet,' Phil muttered.

'He clearly thinks they are,' Jo said.

'Surely, he wouldn't dare to intimidate us, personally?'

'My partner is in the motor trade and Madern had a beef with the owner of one of the car dealerships Lenny is friendly with,' Jo said. 'His car was set alight on his driveway in the middle of the night. His house nearly burnt down.'

'You're worrying me,' Phil said.

'Good. You don't use your own car, except to come to the office and although it's a pain in the arse, don't use your own mobile until further notice.'

'My work mobile is knackered,' Phil said.

'Get another one issued today,' Jo said. 'We need to be on our toes with this case because it will get personal.'

Chapter 17. A Tough Nut to Crack.

The cycle repeated, as explosions flashed in the sky, all that I needed was the one thing I couldn't find...

KENNY FULSHAW DROVE into the city centre and then took the Scotland Road turning onto County Road. There was nothing suspicious behind him. He turned right, heading for Anfield and drove past the stadium. Once he was sure he wasn't being tailed, he turned right again towards Kensington. It's a rundown area and he did a lot of business there, but it was also a dangerous place if you weren't careful.

Kenny parked up his car opposite a small mini market. It would be safer where there were people coming and going. He locked it and headed across the road to a row of terraced houses. They were in a state of poor repair and some of them were boarded up and derelict. He spotted a group of teenagers, eyeing him. One of them waved a hand and he nodded almost imperceptibly and pointed to his car. The youth gave him a thumbs up.

Fifty yards on, he knocked on the door of a house, which had been converted to bedsits. It was in decent condition in comparison to its neighbours. The door buzzed open, and he stepped into the dimly lit hallway. The smell of cannabis and curry was strong and unpleasant. Junk mail was piled behind the door and stacked on a console beneath a broken mirror. The laminate floor was sticky to walk on and had warped at the edges. A black face appeared from a door to his left. The man was rubbing his eyes as if he had just woken up. He was heavyset and filled the doorway.

'Can I help you?' the man said. His eyes focused on Kenny. 'Oh, it's you, Kenny. What are you doing here? I wasn't expecting you today.'

'What the fuck has been going on, Biggy?' Kenny asked. He was deliberately vague. Biggy looked at his feet, nervously.

'What's the problem?' Biggy asked. 'I bagged everything just as you taught me, like always. Madern will never know we've been cutting the gear.'

'That's the problem,' Kenny said. 'Something is wrong with the gear, Biggy, so what have you done differently?'

'Nothing, man,' Biggy said, shrugging.

'You bagged up exactly the same way?'

'Yes. Straight up.'

'In the same place?'

'No.' Biggy shook his head. 'You said to change it each time.'

'I've got customers choking to death on my gear. That's not good for business, so do you want to tell me what the fuck is going on?'

'I don't know nothing about people choking to death, Kenny,' Biggy said, shaking his head. His jowls wobbled. 'What are you talking about?'

'Where did you bag up last time, Biggy?' Kenny asked. Biggy looked confused. 'It's a simple question. Where have you been bagging up?'

'Upstairs, in the top flat. I cuckooed him. The lad in there does as he's told and keeps his mouth shut,' Biggy said.

'Take me up there,' Kenny said. 'I want to see what the fuck went wrong.'

'You want to see his flat?'

'Are you fucking deaf?'

'No. Of course not,' Biggy said. 'Come on. I'll show you. The guy is cool, man. I told you. He does as I tell him and says nothing.'

'Have you been letting him bag up alone?' Kenny asked.

'No way, man. Do you think I'm stupid?' Biggy asked, panting. The climb was hard work at twenty-stones. 'I don't trust no one to bag up alone.'

Kenny couldn't see his face, but he sensed Biggy was lying. They reached the top landing and Biggy knocked on the door. It was opened by a slight man with darker skin than Biggy. Central Africa, Kenny guessed. He peered between the door and the frame.

'What do you want, Biggy?' he asked, abruptly. The smell of something cooking drifted from the flat. 'I'm very busy at the moment.'

'Tell him to open the door before I take it off its hinges,' Kenny said.

'We need to have quick look around,' Biggy said. 'Open the door.'

'I told you that I'm busy,' the man said. 'I'm working.'

Kenny stepped forward and pushed the door open. The man was knocked backwards.

'Hey!' the man protested. 'You can't just barge in like this.'

'I can do what I like,' Kenny said, looking around. He walked through the living room, which had a three-piece suite and a smart television. The floor was covered with cheap laminate. 'What's the smell?' Kenny asked.

'I'm baking,' the man said. 'I told you I'm busy. I bake. It's my job.'

'What are you baking?' Kenny asked, curious. 'It smells good.'

'These are my brownies,' the man said. 'Look, I'm Sulliman. People call me Sulli.'

'Hello, Sulli,' Kenny said, walking into the kitchen. Every surface was occupied with bowls and trays. There were bags opened here and there and the surfaces were covered in powder. 'This looks like you are cooking for hundreds. How many are you making?' Kenny laughed.

'I'm making a dozen chocolate and a dozen walnut today,' Sulli said. I sell them to some of the coffee shops near the hospital. 'They're organic.'

Kenny looked around and alarm bells started ringing. He saw the label on a bag of powder. 'Organic ground walnuts?'

'Yes. I use it instead of flour in the walnut brownies,' Sulli said. Kenny looked at Biggy and Biggy looked away. 'Can I ask why you are here in my kitchen?'

'I'm looking for answers, Sulli,' Kenny said. 'People have been having a nasty reaction to my product. Product that you two bagged up.'

'He sat in the living room watching football, lazy twat. It took me all day,' Sulli said, moaning. 'I cut all the powder with benzocaine, exactly the right weights. I use my cooking scales.'

'Let me get this straight. The last time you bagged up, you did it in this kitchen using this equipment?' Kenny asked. The men looked at each other and nodded, neither aware of the problem. 'So, you put the cocaine on these worktops, which are covered in ground walnuts?'

'It's just a bit of flour,' Biggy said, confused. 'We don't sterilise the place.'

'It's not a bit of flour, it's fucking nuts!' Kenny said. 'Walnuts to be exact. Even people who aren't allergic to nuts can react to walnuts. Did you know that?'

'I never thought,' Biggy mumbled.

'I put these stickers on the wrappers,' Sulli said, proudly. 'To warn people with allergies.'

'Do you, indeed?' Kenny sighed.

'Yes.'

'But we don't put a warning on our product to warn people that the cocaine is contaminated with nuts, do we?' Kenny asked, calmly.

'Maybe you should,' Sulli quipped. He grinned.

Kenny punched Sulli in the face, breaking his nose. Sulli grunted like a piglet. Kenny hit him again, connecting with his chin. Sulli's knees folded, and he sat down on the floor with a bump, his eyes wide with shock. Kenny took a step backwards and then kicked him in the throat. Sulli fell back, struggling to breathe, blood spraying from his mouth. He gurgled as if he was drowning.

'What are you doing, Kenny?' Biggy asked, panicking. 'He's a good lad.'

Kenny picked up an iron frying pan and smashed it into Biggy's face. There was a metallic ping as the bridge of his nose cracked. Biggy doubled over, grasping his nose. He raised it again and brought it down onto the top of Biggy's skull. There was a clunk as the base connected with the bone and Biggy fell forwards like a felled tree. Kenny brought the heavy pan down on his skull again and again until his head was no longer spherical. His brains had spilled onto the laminate like a puddle of gooey pink porridge.

Kenny wiped his hands on a tea towel and turned on all the gas rings before opening the oven and walking out of the flat. He pulled the door closed and jogged down the stairs, banging on all the doors as he passed them.

'Get out of the building!' he shouted. 'There's a fire. Get outside as quickly as you can!'

Kenny reached the bottom of the stairs and others followed, asking questions of each other.

'Where is the fire?'

'Who is he?'

'It's on the top floor,' Kenny shouted. 'Get out. I can smell gas.'

The men reluctantly headed for the front door. Kenny ran into Biggy's flat. It smelled of BO and pizza. He went into the kitchen and turned on all the gas rings and the oven. He opened the cupboard and took out a cardboard packet of some type of cuppa soup. Jamming it into the toaster, he switched it on and ran.

There were a handful of dark-skinned people on the front path, some African, some Middle Eastern and Afghan.

'I can't see any smoke. Why are we outside?'

'Where is the fire?' another one of them asked.

'Get away from the building,' Kenny warned and jogged down the road towards his car.

'I can't see any smoke. Can you?' one of the men said.

Kenny ducked as Biggy's flat exploded, and the windows shattered, spraying the men with shards of glass. The noise was deafening. A second later, the windows on the top floor blew out into a million pieces.

Chapter 18. Marion.

*L*ike a million miles away from me you couldn't see how I adored you, so close, so close, and yet so far...

MARION DROVE TO WOOLTON in record time, trying not to crash or attract attention to herself. The traffic was heavy but moving. She arrived at the security gates and entered the code, but nothing happened. The communication box crackled.

'Hello, can you state your business please,' a voice said.

'Is that Duncan?' Marion asked, recognising the voice of the Goodstone's security guard.

'Yes,' he said, 'Is that you, Marion?'

'Yes.'

'All your cleaners have gone, now Marion,' Duncan said. 'I'm not supposed to allow anyone else into the property.'

'I am worried that David senior might think we've rushed the job and I want to double check the pool area and leisure areas.'

'The gym is out of bounds at the moment,' Duncan said. 'The police and CSI are in there.'

'I realise that, but Bernie mentioned the corridors between the kitchen and pool areas might not have been cleaned. You know how musty it gets down there. Can I just check them?' 'Not a chance, Marion,' Duncan said. 'I'm not risking my job for the sake of a bit of dusting.'

'I'm worried about the health and safety aspect in the areas where the children might stray from the pool,' Marion said. 'You know the cleaning cupboards in the corridors have dangerous chemicals in them and must be locked at all times, but I haven't had chance to do a final check. You're not the only one with their job on the line here.'

'I have keys to all the cupboards,' Duncan said. 'I'll check they're locked for you to put your mind at rest.'

'That would be great,' Marion said, disappointed but resigned to the fact she wasn't getting back in. 'Much appreciated, thank you.'

'No problem,' Duncan said. 'I'll see you when you're next here. Bye for now.'

The call ended and Marion turned the car around and pulled into the traffic. The cocaine was paid for, and it was hidden and unlikely to be found, even if it was looked for. She thought about David senior and his children. One was dead, the other hanging on by a thread. She felt sick to the stomach. It wasn't her fault, but it felt like it was. She had a huge part in the death of David junior and there was a money trail. It could be explained away at first glance but if it came under forensic scrutiny, she would be arrested. There was no way to change it now. All she could do was go home and hope no one would touch it until she could get back into the house.

Chapter 19. PVPU.

S trange places we never see, but you're always there, like a ghost in my dreams...

JANE BENNET WAS SCROLLING through a report which had just arrived from social services. Her DS brought two cups of coffee and put them on her desk.

'We have another cuckoo report,' Jane said. 'This is becoming unmanageable.'

'It's out of control,' Gill said, sipping her brew. 'Where is this one?'

'Dovecot. A vulnerable man William Hughes, sixty-nine is being preyed upon by some local thugs. The social worker has one name, Elliot Cann, who he thinks is the ringleader. They're knocking on his door and hounding him day and night for money. William has been giving them five pounds a time just to get rid of them.'

'They have no fear or morals anymore,' Gill said, shaking her head. 'Respect for the elderly is a thing of the past. It's disappeared.'

'Yesterday, they asked to use his toilet and get a drink of water, but they were actually stealing his belongings, including a laptop and his phone.'

'The poor old man must be terrified.'

'William broke down to his social worker and disclosed that a few days before they had barged their way into his house, raided his kitchen of food and used his dining table for six hours to bag up some powder, which he couldn't identify.' Jane picked up her coffee and grimaced. 'It's going to be difficult arresting these little scrotes unless William is prepared to make a full statement.'

'Shall I get uniform to have a word in the meantime?' Gill asked. 'We can put a marker on the address.'

'Yes, let's do that and find out where Elliot Cann lives,' Jane said. 'I want to knock on his door myself.'

'I want to be with you. Consider it done,' Gill said, enthusiastically.

Jane scanned the rest of the report. An email popped up on her notifications. It was from Laura Lunt at the Matrix team. She opened it and read the message.

Call me at the office when you get a sec.

Jane found Laura's direct dial number and called her. It rang twice.

'DI Lunt,' Laura answered.

'Laura, it's Jane. I've got your message,' she said. 'Have you got any news?'

'I have and it's not good news, unfortunately,' Laura said. 'Not for us anyway.'

'That doesn't sound good,' Jane said. 'What is it?'

'Angela Deacon died from a pulmonary embolism,' Laura said.

'A pulmonary embolism is a blood clot on the lungs, right?' Jane asked, confused.

'Yes. She had a deep vein thrombosis in her left calf and the clots broke away and went to her lungs and that was lights out for Angela,' Laura said. 'Technically, we have no crime to investigate.'

'Fucking hell,' Jane muttered. 'We can't get a conviction for an assault or sexual assault without a victim. She obviously can't make a complaint or tell us who did it. The CPS will toss it before the ink is dry.'

'Exactly,' Laura said. 'We have nothing, but the drugs found upstairs, and we can't lay them with anyone unless they go back to the house for them.'

'Do you think they will?' Jane asked.

'The house is under surveillance for now, but we don't have the budget to drag it on longer than a few days. The housing association want the property handing back within seven days.'

'And it's no longer a crime scene?'

'Nope. If it was a murder, we would be able to keep them at bay and have an investigation running at full steam ahead, but this is an explainable death.'

'I can't believe it. It beggars belief at her age.'

'Apparently, she smoked and was taking the contraceptive pill, which makes you more prone to DVT but it's a lottery.'

'It's very sad. Thanks for letting me know,' Jane said. She felt bitterly disappointed. 'Is that it as far as Madern is concerned?'

'We're going to pull him in before the postmortem is released and rattle his cage for a few hours, but I don't think he'll be phased by it,' Laura said. 'It's all part of a day's work for that prick. He might give us something else to focus on that we don't know already but it's more likely to be a 'no comment' interview if we pick at something uncomfortable.'

'Good luck with that,' Jane said. 'I hope you uncover something to nail the bastard on.'

'We can only hope but don't hold your breath.'

Chapter 20. Jo Lilly.

I *miss you, like the deserts miss the rain...*

THE DRIVE TO SOUTHPORT was not an easy one. It was mundane and Jo felt like she was wasting time sitting in the car when she had so much to do. There were a million things more important than driving for hours but the children needed to be seen face to face. They were too young and too vulnerable to delegate to another social worker for now. Phil was driving, which allowed her to clear some emails and make some calls on the way. She received a text message from Jane Bennet, asking her to call. Jo knew it wasn't going to be good news. She called her mobile.

'Hello Jane, I got your message,' Jo said. 'Is there any news?'

'It sounds like you're driving,' Jane said.

'I'm out and about but Phil is doing the driving,' Jo said. 'We're about five minutes away from where the Deacon children are staying.'

'Great timing. I've just spoken to DI Lunt from the Matrix team,' Jane said. 'The postmortem discovered that Angela had a pulmonary embolism.'

'Oh no, that's not good. The poor woman,' Jo said. 'It's a blood clot on the lungs, right?'

'Right.'

'So, it's not a crime anymore?'

'No. It's a sudden death but not a criminal one.'

'Fucking hell. That's the worst news. It doesn't help us finding out who attacked her.'

'Officially, without a complaint, there is no crime to investigate.'

'Someone is going to be very relieved about this,' Jo said, shaking her head. 'What about the rape?'

'Without a victim who can testify, it's almost impossible to pursue it. It's hard enough when we have a victim.'

'What if you got a confession?' Jo asked, 'Surely you could prosecute that without her statement. She was drugged anyway, so her testimony would be useless. It's the DNA and injuries which could convict, isn't it?'

'We'd be clutching at straws. You know the figures on convictions when we have evidence from the victim but with the victim deceased from natural causes, we're struggling.'

'This is such a crock of shit,' Jo said. 'We can't get justice for this poor woman.'

'If we knew who it was, we could put the pressure on. With a confession we might have a shot,' Jane agreed. 'But it's a very long shot.'

'We'll ask the children what they can remember and go from there, shall we?' Jo said. 'If we know who was at the house, we have a starting point.'

'Okay. Let me know how you get on.'

'I will.'

'But don't get your hopes up.'

'I won't. Before you go, we've had contact from Barry Madern this morning,' Jo said. 'His brief has been on to legal to determine when we are going to be in court to seek PR. He wants to contest it.'

'He's an arsehole,' Jane snapped. 'What is he going to do with two young children, get them delivering ket on their skateboards?'

'I think it's about his ego,' Jo said. 'He strikes me as a narcissist, and unfortunately, we can't just tell him to fuck off. It would be so simple if we could. Not that he would listen anyway.'

'People like Madern don't listen to anyone,' Jane said.

'The problem is that he has a lot of money,' Jo said. 'Money will get him represented in court by some heavy hitters.'

'Does he have any chance of getting PR?' Jane asked.

'Not a chance in hell but we can never say never. We must follow the process,' Jo said. 'He's influential and we have no idea how far his influence reaches.' There was a knowing silence between them. Justice wasn't always blind and balanced. 'I'll see what the children say and call you later?'

'No problem, talk later,' Jane said.

The call went dead, and Jo had the urge to smoke a cigarette, despite it being three years since she packed them in. A spell of high blood pressure was the trigger to quit. Her father had suffered multiple heart attacks before one finally killed him. She didn't want to go the same way, so she packed them in, but the cravings lurked in the darker reaches of her brain.

The grey clouds parted for a second and shafts of sunlight beamed down over Southport. She could smell the salt in the air. They were close to the sea now. The Royal Liverpool golf course was to their left, the acres of manicured fairways were pleasing on the eye. She watched a golfer drive off from a tee. The ball hit a small tree and bounced back, stopping near his feet. She smiled.

'Angela Deacon died from a pulmonary embolism,' Jo said.

'I got most of the conversation,' he said, nodding. 'I'm not sure if I'm happy she wasn't murdered or not, if that sounds right?'

'It sounds okay to me because I want someone to blame, someone to pay for it but this leaves us and the police with nowhere to go,' Jo said. 'There is no crime to investigate.'

'What about the rape?'

'Alleged rape,' Jo corrected him. 'We're assuming there was a rape. Angela didn't report a rape therefore the police don't have a victim who can testify. The only way they could have a chance of a conviction is if they got a confession.'

'And if they withdrew the confession, there's no victim to contradict them?' Phil said.

'Exactly. The whole thing is a crock of shit.'

'No one is going to come forward to confess to raping a dead person,' Phil said. 'Surely not.'

'Let's ask the children who was at their house yesterday and maybe we can salvage something from this mess,' Jo said. 'These children are without their mum, so it's up to us to make sure the truth comes out. They will want to know what happened to her, one day.' She sighed and looked out of the window. 'If we can find out who attacked her, great, if not, so be it.'

Chapter 21. Mad Madern.

Tell me lies, sweet little lies...

DETECTIVE SERGEANT Howard and DC Johnson were the officers selected to speak to Barry Madern. He had been arrested on suspicion of breaching an injunction by uniformed officers outside of his office in Lark Lane. They put him into a marked patrol vehicle, in front of diners and drinkers in the many wine bars and tapas joints. It was highly embarrassing, and he was beyond angry when he arrived at the custody suite. He was processed and stripped of his gold chains, Tag watch, belt and shoes and left in a cell to sweat for three hours. His brief was Alister Clement from Clement, Darling and Moss, a firm who specialised in criminal law and defended the city's richest rogues. Their client list was a who's who of Merseyside's gangsters. Clement was wearing a dark blue Hugo Boss suit, his dyed-too-dark hair was gelled back. In contrast, Madern was wearing a grey tracksuit from the same designer. He had piercing blue eyes, cropped greying hair and wore a diamond stud in his left ear. His arms and torso were covered in ink from his hands to his neck.

Eventually, Madern and his brief were shown into an interview room, which was cold and smelled of vomit, and made to wait for another forty minutes. Clement complained several times and was told to wait for the detectives to arrive as they were busy working another case. The detectives walked in and nodded greetings, the male introduced himself as DS Howard and the female was DC

Johnson. Madern was drawn to the female detective; her black leggings hugged her slim hips.

Howard was middle aged, skinny with a mop of grey hair, wearing faded Wranglers and a check shirt. Johnson was in her twenties, attractive and from a Pakistani background. Her black hair was pulled into a ponytail which reached her waist. She had eyelashes that a drag queen would die for.

'I'm switching this on. For the camera, Detective Sergeant Howard and...'

'Detective Constable Johnson have entered the room.'

'Also present are Alister Clement and...'

'Barry Madern and for the record, I'm already fucked off with playing your games,' Madern said. 'Delay tactics might work with the dumb fucks you bring in here and bully into confessions, but I've been around the block. You lot must think I was born yesterday, fucking muppets.'

'There's no need for the language, Barry,' Howard said, smiling.

'Fuck you, it's all about having respect,' Madern said, smiling back.

'Respect?' Howard said. 'Do you know how to spell it?'

'Fuck you, Dibble,' Madern said. 'If you treat me like a cunt, I'll behave like one.'

'So, we all know where we stand,' Howard said. 'Barry is going behave like a cunt.'

'Can we get on with this?' Clement said. 'Enough postering and game playing.'

'We're not playing games, Barry.' DS Johnson said, opening a file.

'Mr Madern to you, love.'

'Sorry. Mr Madern,' she repeated. 'I'm DC Johnson, not love.'

'We haven't met but let me tell you that you're not good enough to play games against me, darling,' Madern said, glaring at her. 'Are you the token Muslim detective?'

'No, I'm not a Muslim,' Johnson said, shaking her head. 'Actually, I'm an atheist.'

'You must be a lesbian then?' Madern asked, shrugging. 'Why else would you be here?'

'I'm married to a man,' Johnson said. 'I'm a detective because I applied for the post and passed the exams, not because of my religious beliefs or because I have a vagina.' Madern smiled, sourly. 'This is Angela Deacon. Do you know her?'

'Yes,' Madern said, nodding. He yawned. 'She's the mother of my children.' He paused. 'We have three children.'

'So, you're in a relationship?'

'It's complicated.'

'Relationships can be,' Johnson said. 'When did you last see her?'

'The day before yesterday,' Madern said.

'Wednesday?'

'I can see how you made detective,' Madern said. 'Yes. I was with her Wednesday in the early hours of the morning, and I left before the kids woke up, about six-thirty.' He paused. 'We had sex twice, both times were consensual. We have been having sex for over eight years and I have never raped her.'

The detectives glanced at each other. 'Who mentioned rape?' Johnson asked. Madern looked shocked for a moment. 'No one has mentioned rape.'

'I have friends in the area,' Madern said, shrugging. 'Some of them spoke to the plastics and were told they suspected Angela had been raped.'

'Plastics for the camera, are PCSO and volunteer officers,' Howard said. 'It seems a bit odd you would feel the need to say you didn't rape her.'

'You lot are slippery bastards and you're going to ask me if we had sex and if we did, was it consensual,' Madern said. 'I just got it in there first.'

'Okay,' Howard said, nodding. 'Thanks for clearing that up.'

'Did you use a condom?' Johnson asked.

'Nope.' Madern stared into her eyes. 'I'm not a pulling out at the last second type of guy.' Johnson nodded. 'Do you use a condom, DC Johnson?'

'Let's not be childish,' Johnson said, shaking her head. 'My contraception is not relevant and if you're trying to embarrass me, you are wasting your time.'

'My client is here because he was in breach of an injunction,' Clement said. 'Why is his sex life being interrogated?'

'There is evidence of a sexual assault, so we have to investigate.'

'And you have DNA evidence?' Clement asked. 'Secretions?'

'We can't tell you that, I'm afraid,' Johnson said.

'Okay. Are you charging my client with rape?' Clement asked.

'We're investigating a serious sexual assault,' Johnson said. 'At this point, we're just gathering the facts.'

'Angela is dead, so did she make a complaint against me before she died?' Madern asked.

'We're investigating at the moment, that's all we can say,' Howard said, deflecting the question.

'My client has admitted to having sex with the deceased and he has asked a very valid question, detective,' Clement said, removing his glasses. 'Did Angela Deacon make a complaint of rape before she died?'

'There is solid evidence that a sexual assault took place,' Howard said. 'And there is evidence she was drugged.'

'Drugged with what?' Madern suddenly looked interested.

'Flunitrazepam,' Johnson said.

'Rohypnol?' Madern asked.

'Yes,' Johnson said.

'Angela was drugged and raped?' Madern asked. He looked angry. Johnson nodded. 'Do you have any other suspects?'

'We're investigating at the moment,' Howard said. 'Hence you are here.'

'Do you have DNA?' Madern asked.

'We can't say.'

'You asked me if we used a condom,' Madern said. 'So, you have semen.' He studied the detectives. 'Then, when you get your results, you will know who attacked her, won't you?' Madern said. 'And you will know it wasn't me, fucking idiots. Why would I drug Angela?'

'We have to explore all avenues,' Howard said.

'So, if she was drugged and raped, she was murdered?' Clement asked.

'We can't disclose her cause of death yet,' Howard said. 'We found two sets of digital scales and a number of wraps of powder in a spare bedroom.'

'So what?' Madern said, shrugging. 'They're nothing to do with me.'

'Angela Deacon wasn't dealing class-A drugs,' Johnson said. 'She had no money in the electric meter and no food in the cupboards.'

'Looks like you have a mystery to solve, detective Johnson,' Madern said. 'Best get your magnifying glass out and look for clues.'

'The room was being used by a dealer, definitely,' Howard said. 'The door was locked, and we haven't found the key in her house.'

'I always wondered what was in that room,' Madern said, shrugging.

'Do you know who the dog in the back garden belonged to?' Johnson asked.

'My client doesn't know anything about a dog,' Clement said, shaking his head. 'Do you have any relevant questions or are we done?'

'The dog belonged to John Trent,' Howard said. 'He's a friend of yours, isn't he?'

'I know of him,' Madern said.

'He was paying Angela to keep the dog in the back garden,' Johnson said. 'Maybe he was paying her to use the spare bedroom too?'

'Fuck me, this is amateur hour,' Madern said, shaking his head. 'Have you got anything that links me to a crime, because this is boring the shit out of me?'

'I have to agree with my client,' Clement said. 'Is there anything to incriminate Mr Madern in any way, shape or form?'

The detectives looked at each other and shrugged. 'We have to ask these questions.'

'Then we're ending this interview with immediate effect unless you're going to charge my client with a crime?' Clement said, putting away his pen and pad.

'Not at this time,' Johnson said. 'But for the record, you admit to being in breach of an injunction, preventing you from approaching Angela Deacon or the property she lived in?'

'Lock me up and throw away the key,' Madern said. The detectives smiled. 'I guess not. Then I'll be seeing you.' Madern made to stand up.

'Before you go,' Howard said, holding up his hand. 'Are you aware of any recent drug related deaths in the city?' Madern looked at his brief and his brief shook his head.

'We won't be answering any more questions about this or anything else,' Clement said, standing up. 'You have wasted enough of my client's time with your fishing trip.'

'You will have to answer our questions at some point, because there are four people dead already and another five in a serious condition in hospital,' Howard said. Clement looked shocked. 'It's touch and go on some of them.'

'Four people dead?' Clement repeated. 'What on Earth are you talking about?'

'They're having a laugh,' Madern scoffed.

'This really is serious,' Johnson said.

'They're taking the piss,' Madern said, shaking his head. 'Four people dead?'

'Yes.'

'Connected to my client, how exactly?'

'We are absolutely sure that there is a connection,' Howard said. 'Sit down and we'll explain.' Madern leaned forward in his seat.

'Come on then. What has this got to do with me?' Madern asked, outraged.

'You're not aware of any recent drug related deaths?' Howard asked.

'No. Because they're nothing to do with me.' Madern folded his arms. 'Why are you asking me about them?'

'I'm advising you not to say anything,' Clement said. 'We should leave. This entire interview is a fishing trip.'

'Before you walk out, let me explain it all to you.'

'I'm advising you to leave now,' Clement said.

'You must be curious?' Johnson asked. 'I know I would be.'

'I'm listening,' Madern said. 'You have five minutes.'

'It appears that someone has been distributing a batch of cocaine, which is contaminated,' Howard said.

'My client is not involved in the distribution of cocaine,' Clement stated. 'Nor is he involved in the distribution of any illegal substances.'

'Duly noted,' Johnson said. 'Someone has a batch of contaminated cocaine which is killing people.'

'Contaminated with what?' Madern asked. 'People don't die sniffing a bit of cocaine.'

'All the victims who died had one thing in common, severe nut allergies,' Johnson said.

'Nut allergies?' Madern said, smiling. 'Tell me how that works.'

'They had severe allergies, inhaled the contaminated cocaine, reacted immediately and died within minutes.'

'They sniffed cocaine and died because they had nut allergies?' Madern said, shrugging.

'Severe nut allergies,' Johnson said.

'Nuts?' Madern repeated. 'You're fucking nuts if you think I'm listening to this old bollocks.'

'It's a very serious situation,' Johnson said.

'Serious?' Madern scoffed. 'You've been on the space biscuits, love.'

'This is very real, Mr Madern,' Johnson said. 'People are dying.'

'So, you've said but I'm not having any of it,' Madern laughed. 'You're so far out there with this one, that I can't take you seriously.'

'You know David Goodstone, don't you?'

'The dentist?'

'Yes.'

'We're both members at Blundell's Hill. I play golf with him, every now and again.' Madern said. 'What's he got to do with anything?'

'I can't advise you enough, not to say anymore,' Clement said. 'This is a fishing expedition and they're reeling you in.'

'I need to hear this,' Madern argued. 'This is comedy gold.'

'There is nothing funny about it. His son and daughter both died yesterday,' Johnson said.

'What?' Madern asked, frowning. He suddenly looked concerned. 'David junior and Rebecca are dead?'

'Yes,' Howard said. 'David died in their home gym and Rebecca died forty minutes later in the Royal. They had both inhaled cocaine.'

'They had sniffed a wrap of cocaine each. They both suffered from severe nut allergies, and they died of anaphylactic shock,' Johnson said. 'There's no doubt about what killed them.'

'I have never heard anything so fucking ridiculous in all my days,' Madern said, shaking his head. 'You're telling me the Goodstones had a bit of sniff and it killed them?'

'Exactly that,' Howard said. 'Along with several others and the number is climbing.'

'And why are you telling me this?' Madern asked. 'Where do I come into this shit?'

'Barry...' Clement cautioned his client. 'You shouldn't be engaging...'

'Will you shut the fuck up for a minute, please!' Madern snapped. 'I can't think straight here with you whittering in my ear. I want to know why you are telling me this?'

'All the incidents are in your post codes,' Howard said. 'The cocaine was sold on your patch.'

'I have post codes now,' Madern said sarcastically but he looked worried. 'Is that what you do, allocate post codes to people you're trying to fit up?'

'We have to track the areas where known criminals operate,' Howard said. 'These incidents occurred in your post codes. The areas where Kenny Fulshaw deals for you, to be more specific.'

'That's outrageous!' Clement said, standing up. 'My client does not distribute drugs in any capacity. I insist that this interview is suspended. It's clearly an ambush and must be terminated right now.'

'Oh, come on!' Johnson said, shaking her head. 'Let's not do the innocent charade when people are dying. You can play the legal chess game all you like but eventually you will lose it. We all know Kenny Fulshaw works for you.'

'Kenny who?' Madern asked, coyly.

'Fulshaw. He works for you, mostly around Allerton, Smithdown Road and all the way across the city to Kensington.' Johnson showed him a colour coded map of the city. 'The Tickle brothers operate in the other post codes here, here and here.'

'We need to end this right now,' Clement insisted.

'I don't know what you're talking about,' Madern said. He looked concerned. 'Fucking nuts in the sniff. You two are fucking nuts.'

'We're presenting you with the facts as we know them,' Johnson said.

'Do you remember the advert on the telly, nuts whole hazel nuts,' Madern asked. 'Cadburys take them, and they cover them in chocolate...' No one replied. 'That's you two. Fucking nuts, the pair of you.'

'The truth is that Kenny Fulshaw is key to the contaminated drugs, and he works for you.'

'Never heard of him,' Madern said, folding his arms.

'There's plenty of evidence linking him to you, video and audio but now is not the time to delve into all that,' Howard said. 'He was seen today by witnesses who put him parking his car here, and then entering this HMO in Kensington.' Howard pointed to a map on his laptop screen. 'He was seen jogging away from it minutes before it exploded,' Howard said. 'Do you know anything about an explosion?' Madern blushed red.

'That is nothing to do with me,' Madern said, shaking his head. He looked furious.

'It was a gas explosion on the face of it, but the remains of bodies have been found on the top floor. Two of the residents are missing. It's very suspicious and we suspect arson, possibly murder,' Johnson explained. 'Perhaps he was destroying evidence linked to the contaminated batch?'

'This is like listening to Jackanory,' Madern said, sighing heavily. 'Tell me another story, Jackanory, boom, boom.'

'We have intelligence that he may have been cuckooing the property, using it to store and process drugs,' Howard said. 'So, he probably torched the place to conceal evidence.'

'Really?' Madern smiled but he looked shaken. 'What happens in the end, does everyone live happily ever after?'

'You won't. We think he was trying to conceal evidence of a contaminated batch of cocaine, which he distributes for you,' Johnson said. 'So, you can see where the link to you comes from.'

'We're leaving right now,' Clement said opening the door. Madern didn't move. 'Barry, we're leaving!'

'You genuinely didn't know, did you?' Johnson said, smiling. 'Kenny Fulshaw hasn't told you what has happened. I can see it in your eyes. You didn't know about the deaths.'

'That's fucking priceless. No one has told you yet, have they?' Howard asked, chuckling. 'I wonder why they didn't tell you?'

'Because it's nothing to do with me,' Madern said. His demeanour had changed. His expression was stoney.

'Four people dead and five seriously ill. This will filter all the way back to the top,' Howard said. 'I would get my story straight if I were you. All the worms will turn when we start bringing people in for manslaughter. They always do.'

'Don't say anything, Barry,' Clement said. 'My client is making no comment to any further questions.'

'Someone cut your shit with something they shouldn't have,' Johnson said. 'Of course, they will say they got it from you and didn't touch it.' Madern stared into her eyes, but his focus was elsewhere. 'No one will admit to cutting your gear because that would be a capital crime in your world, eh Barry?'

'Mr Madern to you, bitch,' Madern growled. He stood up and walked out of the door in a hurry. 'That is so much bullshit. Fucking nuts.'

'I told you not to engage with them,' Clement said.

'Oh, shut the fuck up!' Madern moaned. 'You're doing my head in. It's all Billy bullshit.'

The detectives listened to them bickering as they went.

'Are you sure it is bullshit?' Clement asked, 'It all sounded very real to me. You need to do a fact-finding mission and see how much of what they said is factual.'

'What are you saying?' Madern asked, offended. 'That I don't have control of my business?'

'Is it possible you don't know about the incidents they are asking about?' Clement muttered. 'If they're a surprise to you, someone is hiding the facts from you.'

His brief was lecturing him as they walked down the corridor. They could hear them arguing all the way to the door.

'I think that will do the trick,' Johnson said, smiling. 'We wanted to rattle his cage, and we have.' Johnson stood up. 'Did you see the expression on his face?'

'He was genuinely stunned. Their mobile phones will be red hot tonight.' Howard turned off the cameras. 'We're monitoring their chatter and we have eyes on their top people wherever we can, but we haven't got enough bodies to watch them all.'

'What do you think about the stash at the Deacon home?' Johnson asked, frowning.

'I think it might have slipped down the priority list for sure,' Howard said.

'Fulshaw will be number one on the list, of course,' Johnson said. 'But we don't know where he is. He's fallen off the radar since the gas explosion.'

'We'll find him. He'll be more worried about Madern than the fire,' Howard said. 'Whoever has fucked up the supply is in big trouble.'

'We're going to find casualties along the way through this,' Johnson said. 'Madern will be on the warpath once he realises what's happened.'

'Good. Fuck them all,' Howard said. 'I hope they kill each other; it saves us the job.'

Chapter 22. Leo.

I *go to sleep, sleep, and imagine that you're there with me...*

LEO COULDN'T SLEEP but he tried to. He checked his phone to see if Abi had messaged him, but it was blank. Her mother would have something to do with her not replying to him, the bitch. Marion hated him and he hated her right back. He typed another text.

Hey starling how are you? I'm missing you like the deserts miss the rain. Please don't give up on us. I will do whatever it takes to keep us as a family, me and you and the baby. We will be forever parents, not like ours. Our dads fucked off and left us when we needed them the most. I won't leave our baby, not ever. I've got a good job coming up and it's paying a lot of money. I can't say too much but I'm being trusted on an important gig. Ged has promised he'll look after me if I do this job tonight, so we'll have money. I love you Abi, please don't leave me. Everyone I've ever loved has left me and I can't live without you. I can't stand to lose you too. Love you starling. x

KENNY FULSHAW WAS SITTING outside of a café in the Albert Dock, called the One O'clock Gun. Across the dock, he could see the Liver Birds standing proud against the dark clouds, sentinels to protect the city from danger approaching from the sea. Tourists were milling around the docks, enjoying the museums, galleries and shops. Some of the tall ships were moored near the Tate gallery, majestic in their stature. His phones had been ringing non-stop all morning, but he hadn't answered any of them. He listened to his voicemails. Some of the calls were from his sellers, who wanted more product but most of them were urgent calls about people reacting badly to his cocaine. The contaminated drugs problem was out of control. It had started as something he thought he could supress and manipulate to a decent conclusion, but it had spiralled into something huge and deadly.

He had taken the risk of cutting Barry Madern's gear to make more money, which was not tolerated. Madern had a reputation for selling decent cocaine. His father had always sold quality gear. Most of the powder in the city was bash. Bash is so cut with shite, it barely has any cocaine left in it. Bottom feeders buy small amounts of the powder and cut it again and again and sell it on. By the time it reaches the pubs and clubs, it's crap.

Madern had strict quality rules. Don't cut my cocaine or ketamine, or you will get hurt, simple. Those who did, usually ended up in a hospital bed, if they were lucky enough to survive the punishment beating. Kenny rolled the dice. It had been an educated gamble which had made him thousands with no problems until now. This fuck up would have repercussions of epic proportions.

The one call he knew he had to answer came through. The phone it was coming from was encrypted, meaning it was Madern.

'Hello Barry,' Kenny said, nervously. 'I've been expecting a call from you.'

'I bet you were expecting a call from me,' Madern said. He could hear the menace in his tone. 'I bet you've been sitting there staring at your phone, waiting for me to call.'

'I was just going to call you, actually.'

'Were you, indeed?'

'Yes.'

'Why don't I believe you?'

'I know it sounds like crap, but I was.'

'It does sound like crap. You should have called me sooner than this, Kenny,' Madern said. 'You should have called me yesterday when you found out what a monumental fuck up you've made.'

'I was waiting until I had answers for you,' Kenny said.

'Waiting is never the answer. I have had a very embarrassing conversation with two Matrix officers, who couldn't catch a fucking cold, but they knew all about what you've been doing.' Kenny stayed quiet. 'Why don't I know that you've fucked up and killed four of your customers, so far?'

'I have been trying to sort it out, Barry,' Kenny said. 'I couldn't believe it at first. It was just too weird, but the Bootle professor called me, and he had seen two people react to the gear with his own eyes.' Kenny took a slurp of his pint. 'I had to take it seriously then. There was no denying it after that. He's a clever man, so I had to listen to what he had to say.'

'He's not that fucking clever,' Madern said. 'He's selling twenty-quid wraps on the Strand for you.'

'He's fallen on hard times,' Kenny said. 'But he's still switched on.'

'And what did the professor have to say?'

'He said the gear was contaminated and to check where it had been bagged up,' Kenny said.

'Because?' Madern prompted.

'Because it's the only place the gear can be contaminated, once it's wrapped,' Kenny said, sighing.

'But it was wrapped when you got it,' Madern said. 'So, what you're saying is that you were cutting my product?'

'Yes.'

'You're a cunt, Kenny,' Madern said. 'You're a stupid greedy cunt.'

'I know.'

'What did you cut it with?'

'Benzocaine,' Kenny said. 'I wasn't taking the piss, Barry. I cut it by ten percent. It was still a decent product.'

'Benzocaine doesn't kill people, so what went wrong?' Madern asked.

'I gave the gear to Biggy to cut,' Kenny said.

'Biggy from Kensington?'

'Yes.'

'He's as thick as pig shit,' Madern snapped. 'What happened?'

'Biggy was bagging it up in a flat on the top floor of his gaff. He had the guy in his pocket, storing gear and money for him.' Kenny sighed again. 'The bloke bakes brownies to sell to some cafes near town. He does it for a living on the side. No hygiene certificates or EHO involved,' Kenny explained.

'This is all very interesting but get to the point,' Madern snapped, impatiently.

'He was using ground walnuts instead of flour and it contaminated the cocaine.'

'He was cooking brownies to sell to cafes and ground walnuts got into my cocaine and that's destroyed your business?' Madern asked. His voice sounded strained. 'How much do you think he made from selling his brownies?'

'I don't know,' Kenny said.

'As much as you were making?'

'No, Barry.'

'No Barry. You're a fucking idiot!' Madern shouted. 'You are a massive fucking idiot. The biggest fucking idiot I've ever encountered in my life!'

'I'm very sorry,' Kenny said.

'Not as sorry as I am, Kenny,' Madern said. 'Do you know how difficult it is to keep the Dibble looking in the opposite direction?'

'I'm trying to fix it,' Kenny said. 'Honestly, I'm trying to straighten things out.'

'You can't straighten out killing four people, you twat!' Madern shouted.

'I can try and make it right.'

'How are you doing that, exactly?' Madern asked, a touch of sarcasm in his voice. 'You tell me how the fuck you're going to make this right?'

'I'm trying to trace every last wrap of that batch, and take it off the streets,' Kenny said.

'And how is that going for you?'

'I've traced most of it,' Kenny said.

'How did David Goodstone's children get hold of it?'

'Who?'

'David Goodstone.'

'I don't know him.'

'He's a retired dentist, lives in Woolton,' Madern said. 'His son and daughter, both in their twenties, died yesterday after sniffing a wrap of cocaine. Your cocaine.'

'In Woolton?'

'Yes.'

'I sold two-grand to a woman who has a cleaning company over that way,' Kenny said. 'She did ring me to tell me they'd had a reaction, but I don't know the family. That must be them.'

'What did she tell you?' Madern asked.

'She said the son and daughter had a bad reaction to something, but I didn't believe it could be the cocaine,' Kenny said. 'I thought it must have been something else.'

'Now you know differently.' Madern went quiet. 'She bought two grand's worth in one buy?' Madern asked.

'Yes.'

'Where is she dealing?'

'Nowhere,' Kenny said. 'She moves it off the grid in one sale. It doesn't' go onto the streets.'

'How often does she buy from you?'

'About monthly, give or take.'

'Sounds like she just sells it on in one hit,' Madern said.

'That's the impression I have.'

'So, if the Goodstones had a wrap each, where is the rest of it?' Madern asked.

'I'm trying to find out.'

'What's her name?' Madern asked.

'Marion,' Kenny said.

'Marion who?'

'I don't know her surname,' Kenny sighed. 'She runs a commercial cleaning company called Kleeni-Queen or something like that.'

'She buys two grand from you, and you don't know her surname?' Madern asked.

'I've known her for years. Her daughter lives with Leo Tomkins,' Kenny said, trying to calm the conversation.

'Little Leo, the ket-head?' Madern asked.

'Yes.'

'He's a fucking waste of fresh air,' Madern said. 'Please don't tell me he has anything to do with this?'

'No.' Kenny backtracked. 'He doesn't know Marion buys from me.'

'Get that fucking cocaine back from her today, Kenny!' Madern said.

'I will,' Kenny said. 'I promise you I'll get it all back.'

'The second thing that I know fuck all about, is what happened at Biggy's house?' Madern asked. Kenny remained quiet, thinking of his answer. 'Because the police know you were there before it exploded, and they have found bodies in the top flat.'

'I went to tie up all the loose ends,' Kenny said. 'I couldn't get my head around what they had done.'

'So, you think there are no loose ends anymore?' Madern scoffed.

'There were loose ends at the house,' Kenny explained. 'There was too much forensic evidence there, so I torched the place.'

'Who are the bodies?' Madern asked.

'Biggy and the baker twat, called Sulli. It was his flat, and they bagged up the gear. They knew what had happened,' Kenny said. 'They both live there.'

'Not any more they don't. They're dead.'

'They fucked this up. Idiots. They had no idea what they had done. I just lost the plot.' Kenny sighed. 'I had to shut them up. There'll be no evidence there.'

'You're missing the point, Kenny,' Madern said. 'People are dead. That doesn't go unnoticed or unpunished.'

'I can't change the way things happened,' Kenny said. 'I was careful.'

'Careful?' Madern repeated. 'Did you go in your car?'

'Yes.'

'Did anyone see you?'

'One kid who does some running for me sometimes,' Kenny said. 'But he won't say anything.'

'He already has.'

'What?'

'The police know where you parked.'

'He won't make a statement.'

'Did you have your mobile on you?' Madern asked.

'Yes.'

'So, to sum it up, you drove in your car with GPS in your pocket, let witnesses see you entering a house where you then murdered two men,' Madern asked. Kenny didn't answer. 'Then you torched the place and added arson to the list.'

'I was trying to fix it,' Kenny said.

'That's six dead and five seriously ill,' Madern said. 'I don't think this can be fixed, Kenny. You're fucked up beyond all recognition, mate.'

'What do you want me to do?' Kenny asked. There was a long silence.

'It's a fucking mess, Kenny,' Madern said. 'I can't see any way out for you.'

'What do you mean?'

'You need to vanish, one way or another,' Madern said. There was an uncomfortable silence. 'I will say one thing though, it doesn't add up,' Madern said. 'The police know way too much, too soon.'

'What doesn't add up?'

'The timelines. You're a total wanker and you've left a trail that an idiot could follow but the police connected all these random bad reactions to the drugs, and put them all at your door, overnight.' Kenny dwelled on the facts but didn't speak. 'That is amazing police work,' Madern said. 'They're not that good.'

'What do you mean, they placed it all at my door?' Kenny asked.

'They named you,' Madern said. 'They know you supplied the contaminated drugs, and I didn't believe them until I spoke to you myself.'

'They know I sold the gear?'

'Yes. That can only have happened if someone gave them your name,' Madern said. 'Why did they connect you to the fire in Kensington?'

'I don't know,' Kenny said, baffled. 'Do you think someone grassed me up?'

'I don't think they did, I know they did,' Madern said.

'I'm fucked, aren't I?' Kenny mumbled.

'Stop feeling sorry for yourself. Do the honourable thing, fall on your sword,' Madern said. 'But first, recover the contaminated gear, then find the grass and waste them, Kenny.'

'I'll find them,' Kenny said. 'What about me, Barry?' Silence was the reply. 'Barry, are you there?'

The line was already dead.

Chapter 23. Jo.

When I need you, I just close my eyes and I'm with you...

Jo was sitting at a dining table next to Calvin, who was holding a glass of blackcurrant juice in two hands. His lips were stained purple. The foster parents were nice people, and they said that once the children were settled, they had fallen asleep almost immediately. They said Coco had woken up just once in the night to go to the toilet and Calvin had taken her and waited outside the door to make her feel safe. They had slept until nine-thirty and eaten boiled eggs with toast soldiers for breakfast. Calvin had asked if their mum was dead, but Coco hadn't spoken about her at all. Phil was looking after Coco while Jo talked to Calvin.

'I want to talk to you about what you can remember about yesterday,' Jo said. 'Can you remember waking up in the morning?'

'Yes,' Calvin said, nodding. 'It was cold and dark; the electric had run out again.'

'That happened a lot, didn't it?' Jo said, nodding.

'Mum said the meter was a thief.'

'Your mum was right, it is,' Jo said, smiling.

'Is my mum dead?'

'Yes, Calvin, she's gone over to be with the angels,' Jo said, softly. 'She became really poorly, and her lungs stopped working.'

'Why did that happen,' Calvin asked, 'Was it because she smoked cigarettes?'

'Smoking cigarettes does kill people but that's not why your mum went to heaven,' Jo said. 'It was something that just happens. No one knows why. It just happens to some people.'

'Where has she gone?' Calvin asked. He appeared remarkably calm.

'She's right here with you,' Jo said. 'She'll always be here with you, and she'll never leave you.'

'I can't see her,' Calvin said.

'No, but I bet you can feel her,' Jo said. 'Inside there.' Jo pointed to his chest. 'Does it feel funny, like an ache?' Calvin nodded. He started to cry, and Jo held him while he sobbed. 'What you can feel in your chest are your heart strings.'

'Heart strings?' Calvin said, his bottom lip quivering. 'What are they?'

'They are what connect you to your mum,' Jo explained. 'They're invisible but you can feel them, can't you?'

'Yes,' Calvin said.

'When you feel that ache, your mum is pulling at your heart strings, letting you know she's next to you.'

'Is she next to me now?'

'She'll always be next to you.'

'I can feel the ache in here,' Calvin said. Tears ran down his cheeks.

'Whenever you think of her, she'll let you know she's here and you'll feel that feeling in your chest. You'll never be alone, Calvin. She'll always be with you.'

'Always?' Calvin sobbed.

'Always and forever,' Jo said. 'She'll never leave you and Coco, and you'll feel her, whenever you think about her.'

'Will I see her again?' Calvin asked.

'Yes. If you close your eyes, can you see her?' Calvin nodded. 'Whenever you think of her, close your eyes and you'll see her and feel her inside, pulling at your heart strings.'

'What about Coco?' Calvin asked. 'Does she have heart strings too?'

'We all have them,' Jo said. 'Coco has them too and yours are connected because you're brother and sister. When you think of Coco being sad, what do you feel?'

'Like the ache inside,' Calvin said. 'Is that my heart strings too?'

'Yes,' Jo said. 'You can feel them when you think of someone you love, even if they're in heaven.'

'How do you know my mum has gone to heaven?' Calvin asked.

'Because she was a good person. So, of course she has gone with the angels,' Jo said.

'But you said she's here,' Calvin said.

'She is able to be both,' Jo said. 'That's how it works when you're an angel. Can you feel her?' Calvin nodded. 'She can feel you too and she can hear you.'

'She can hear what I'm saying?' Calvin asked, smiling through his tears.

'Always, Calvin. Speak to her whenever you want to,' Jo said. 'I told you that you'll never be alone. She'll always be with you and when you want to talk to her, you can speak aloud, or you can talk to her in your head. Either way, she'll hear you and you will feel her in there.'

'I can feel my heart strings,' Calvin said, touching his chest. 'Inside here.'

'Good, that's your mum letting you know she's going nowhere,' Jo said. 'She'll never go away from you.'

Calvin wiped his nose on his sleeve. He rubbed his eyes and appeared to be less distressed. Jo wiped his face with a tissue.

'It's okay to be sad, Calvin,' Jo said. 'Don't ever be afraid to cry if you feel sad. We all feel sad sometimes and when we're sad, we can cry. Your tears are the sadness coming out of your body. That's how we get rid of it.'

'My friend says big boys don't cry and if you cry, you're a girl,' Calvin said.

'Your friend has been taught that but he's wrong,' Jo said. 'Crying doesn't make you weak. Girls are just as strong as boys and we all cry.'

'Do you cry?' Calvin asked, sniffling.

'Of course,' Jo said. 'My dad is with the angels too and when he died, I was very sad, like you are now. I cried and cried, and I still cry when I think of him. But that's because I loved him very much. He still pulls at my heart strings when I think of him, and I talk to him all the time.'

'Does he talk back?' Calvin asked.

'In more ways than one,' Jo said. 'I hear his voice in my memories. I know he'll always be next to me because of that feeling in my chest.'

'I can feel it,' Calvin said, nodding.

'You will always be able to feel it,' Jo said. 'Your mum will always be your mum. That never stops.' Calvin nodded. 'I'm trying to piece together what happened yesterday,' Jo said. 'Are you okay to talk about it?' Calvin nodded. 'I'm wondering what you can remember. Did you have any breakfast?'

'We had a yogurt,' Calvin said. 'There were three left, so we had one each.'

'What flavour did you have?'

'Strawberry,' Calvin said.

'What did you do after breakfast?' Jo asked.

'We got dressed and went to nursery,' Leo said.

'Who takes you to nursery?' Jo asked.

'Rosemary,' Calvin said.

'Does Rosemary have children?' Jo asked.

'Tina,' Calvin said. 'We walk together, and she brings ice pops when we walk home.'

'Did anyone come to your house before you left for nursery?' Jo asked.

'Tony Knobhead,' Calvin said. He looked down at his hands. 'That's what mum says his name is, but my friends don't think it is his real name.'

'Tony Knobhead?' Jo chuckled. 'I think you might be right. Is he the man who lives next door?'

'Yes,' Calvin said. 'He was walking through the side gate when we were walking down the path.' Calvin wiped his nose again. 'He had a bottle in his hand.'

'What type of bottle?' Jo asked.

'A green one,' Calvin said. 'Like a wine bottle.'

'Was he there when you got home?' Jo asked.

'No. Mum was asleep on the settee and then you came a bit later,' Calvin said.

'That's been very useful,' Jo said. 'You've been a great help.' Jo smiled. Calvin sniffled and nodded. 'I need you to look after your sister, Calvin. Wherever you go, she'll need you to look after her, even when you grow up to be adults.' Calvin nodded. 'You'll always be her big brother and it's your job to take care of your sister, okay?' Calvin nodded again. 'As you get older, it will always be you two. Other people will come and go in your lives but Coco will be there always. You need to look out for each other, and your mum will watch over both of you.'

PHIL AND JO WERE EMOTIONALLY drained when they began the journey back to Liverpool. The children were safe and being looked after. The process of finding a forever family for them would be complex and thorough, but the siblings would remain together. The complexity would be in dealing with Barry Madern and his millions, but Jo was confident that his criminal record and profile would present a significant danger to the children. Building a case to demonstrate the danger would take time and effort. Jo scrolled through her phone to the last call she had made. She pressed redial. DI Jane Bennet answered almost immediately.

'Hello, Jo,' Jane said. 'How are the children?'

'Confused and distressed,' Jo said. 'They're safe and that's the main thing.'

'Poor little things,' Jane said.

'I had a talk with Calvin,' Jo said. 'He remembers seeing the next-door neighbour approaching the house when they were leaving for nursery.'

'That's interesting,' Jane said. 'Do you know his name?'

'Tony Knobhead,' Jo said. Jane laughed. 'I can hear Angela saying it. Apparently, he was carrying a bottle of wine.'

'CSI took some bottles from the kitchen bin but it's unlikely the entire bottle was doped. It's far more likely that her glass was spiked.'

'Does it help?' Jo asked.

'I'm not going to lie to you, we have very little to get a warrant but that doesn't stop me having a conversation with Tony Knobhead. I can ask him to give us a sample and we'll see what he has to say. We have DNA, so fingers crossed, we might get a match.'

'Fingers crossed,' Jo said.

Chapter 24. The Burglary.

So much for the golden future, I can't even start, I've had every promise broken, there's anger in my heart...

LES CHECKED THE TIME and took a drag of his cigarette. This was it; crunch time. Time to go to work and do what he was best at. Breaking and entering; it was his profession, after all. This was not a job like any other. It was a job he was undertaking purely because his cousin, mad Madern, had told him that he needed a favour doing. When Barry Madern said he needed a favour, that meant do it, no questions asked, no matter what the consequences. There were no discussions and no debate and the option to decline the requests didn't exist. He had been assured he would be looked after when he went to prison, which was a certainty for a serial burglar caught red-handed in a property that didn't belong to him. His cousin shotgun Degsy had said they would pay money into his account while he was in prison, so he could buy extra food, drinks, chocolate and the like from the prison shop. He would also be able to buy contraband, like hooch and drugs.

The plan was clear, and he was told not to deviate from it under any circumstances. That was rich coming from his cousins, who couldn't organise a piss up in a brewery. He had gone over the plan a couple of times, and it was simple enough, but he could have come up with it himself. It was hardly rocket science. Les stubbed out the cigarette and went to his fridge. He opened the door and looked inside. There was half a bottle of apple juice and a lump of cheddar.

He took a bite and put the rest of the cheese into the bin and took out the juice and swigged it down in three gulps, tossing the bottle. There was nothing in the fridge that would rot and stink when he finally came home.

He had done a twelve month stretch last time and come back to a fridge full of putrefied milk, cheese and bacon. The stench was horrendous, and he couldn't shift it, no matter how many times he bleached it. That time, he had been arrested coming out of a garage workshop that he had burgled to steal the money from the vending machines and as many tools as he could carry. He had triggered a silent alarm and the police were waiting for him when he came out. The police locked him up and he was denied bail, hence he didn't get to tidy up at home before going to prison. At least this time, he had the chance to put his affairs in order but that was the only positive that he could think of.

He looked around his flat and felt anxious. It wasn't much but it was his home, and he would be away from it for months. Being in prison wasn't a problem, there were three meals a day, hot water and clean sheets but being unable to access his drug of choice was an issue. That gave him the jitters. Just thinking about clucking made him feel sick. Withdrawal was horrendous and the prison doctors were unsympathetic to repeat offenders. Prisons were full of drugs but not always the ones he needed. Spice was most accessible as it cost just pennies on the street, but it was also shite and more addictive than opiates. Les did not like spice one bit and he had struggled to get off it the last time he came out. Beggars can't be choosers inside and he knew that he would have to take whatever was available.

He felt angry that Barry Madern had asked him to do this 'favour' when anyone with a bit of bottle could do it. He didn't need Les to do it. It wasn't like the owner was going to wake up, she had snuffed it. Barry Madern was all about control and turning people into puppets that he could make dance when it suited him. Using Les was a demonstration of the assets he had control over. Les often flouted his name as it offered him protection, but the truth was, he actually didn't like the man. He was a bully.

Barry had always been a bully, even when they were kids and their parents visited each other. The children were all roughly the same age and played together. Les knew he was different at a very young age although he didn't know what gay was then. He was attracted to boys and not girls and he thought that Barry had a sneaking suspicion that he was different and bullied him. He always called him a little queer, a puff, a fairy, twinkle toes, bumboy and faggot were his favourites. His experiences with his older cousin, who was hard as nails, shaped his adult life; it made him embarrassed to be himself. He felt worthless and dirty because of his sexuality, and he spent his life denying who he was. Les had never so much as kissed another man or woman, and he supressed his feelings with drugs. One thing led to another until he tried heroin and it had been his constant crutch ever since. Drug addiction is expensive and incapable of gaining decent employment, Les began to steal to fund his habit. He became a burglar and the title stayed with him like his shadow, always there, it defined who he was. Les the scummy burglar. Imagine what they would call him if they knew he was gay.

Les grabbed his bag of tools and put on his burgling gear; dark tracksuit, black trainers and baseball cap. He pulled on leather gloves even though leaving prints wasn't an issue on this one. It was a one-way ticket to the cells regardless of what he did. Les went to the front door and opened it, taking a last look around before stepping out. He locked up and walked across the hallway to the main door. The cold night air touched his skin and sent a shiver down his spine. His nerves were jangling for some reason. Was it because the final result was already etched into stone or was it something more? He checked his phone. There was a message.

The Dibble are parked on Bluebell Lane.

That meant the police were to his right about two-hundred meters up the road. He jogged to his left until he reached the pavement, then he slowed down to a quick walk. There were no people around. A bus drove by and he crossed the road and headed for the T-junction at the end of the street. The parked cars that he could see were empty, but he checked them all again, to be sure. One last look up and down the road.

He climbed a low wall and jogged across the lawn, then vaulted over a wooden fence into the back garden of Angela's neighbours. The police were watching from the opposite side of the street. He ducked low and made quick work of the adjoining fence and approached Angela's house from the rear. There were sliding patio doors between him and the inside of the house. He took a crowbar and slotted it into the rail beneath the doors, pressing his bodyweight down, he lifted the doors out of their track.

Les was inside in seconds, and he lifted the doors back into their track, making it secure again. He took out his drill and screwed three metal fixings to each side of the doors. The only way for the police to get in through them was to smash the glass. He moved through the dining room to the front door and drilled three long screws through the wood into the frame, top, middle and bottom. It wouldn't stop a forced entry with a battering ram, but it would slow them down. He walked into the kitchen and repeated the process on the backdoor.

With the doors screwed into the frames, the ground floor could not be breeched without making a lot of noise, which would give him warning that they were coming to arrest him. He didn't want to make it too easy for them. The police wanted him to steal something and leave the property, that way they had a cast iron case for the CPS to prosecute. Barry had a different idea and Les had to follow the plan. If he didn't leave the house, technically, he hadn't stolen anything.

Les gathered his tools and headed upstairs. The small bedroom was on his right and he stepped inside. He took a torch and twisted the head to its minimum, making the light as dim as possible. He searched the floorboards for the tailored pieces and spotted them almost immediately. Taking a blade, his lifted the boards and exposed two kilo bricks of powder. There were no signs of any firearms. He looked at the edges of the floorboards and ran his fingers over some recent markings. He took out his phone and sent a simple text.

The Dibble are onto this.

He didn't expect a reply. The police had found the stash and had to remove the weapons, so the bricks were left as bait. Degsy had said that we had to assume that's what they were doing. They had laid a trap and Les was to trigger it but not how they thought he would. Les wasn't sure why Barry would be so concerned about a couple of kilos of gear. It was a drop in the ocean for him, but he couldn't ask questions; he just had to do as he was told.

Les took the bricks and put them onto the desk. He took his hammer and dragged the desk away from the wall. There was a patch of new plaster and he aimed for the centre and hit it, cracking it with the first blow. Two more and he could pull big chunks of plaster away. He exposed a small plastic bag, smaller than his thumb. No guns, no bag stuffed full of fifty-pound notes, just a memory stick. He wondered what was stored on it that was so valuable, it had to be retrieved.

Les took the plastic bag and made it as tight as he could. He took his knife and made a small slit in the wrapping of one of the bricks. He slid the memory stick into the parcel and then taped over the hole. His instructions were clear, and he followed them to the letter. He taped the bricks together with duct tape and then went to the window. He checked his watch and opened it. He waited for the second hand to tick around to twelve and dropped the powder to the left of the downpipe next to the lean-to kitchen roof. Very specific, don't fuck it up, Les. It made no noise and he assumed someone had caught it. It was supposed to be Leo Tomkins; the little tosser. Les didn't like the cocky little prick.

A few seconds later, he could see a shadow climbing over the fence. He moved quickly and silently, to be fair to him. He disappeared into next door's garden before reappearing at the next fence, then the next one and the next. He lost sight of Leo at the fifth garden and closed the window. There was no sign of the police chasing him. The unlikely duo had followed the plan and pulled it off. His job was done. All he had to do now was wait for the police to arrive. He had nothing on him that didn't belong to him, so there could be nothing too serious to charge him with. The drugs were gone but there was no evidence to corroborate any possible charges.

Les rummaged in his bag of tools for his works. Syringe, sponge, spoon, lighter, elastic strap and special wrap of gear from his cousin Shotgun Degsy. Degsy said it was from Barry as a thank you for the gig. It was quality brown, cut with a little ket. Degsy said it would be the first of many when he came back out. Barry was grateful and he knew Les loved his smack. Les melted the powder, all of it. He was going away for a while, so a decent hit was just the ticket. He loaded the syringe and wrapped his arm, then injected into his forearm and released the strap.

Seconds ticked by. The blood flowed and reached his brain and turned every nerve ending in his body into something indescribably beautiful. His entire being was earth-shatteringly orgasmic, yet his mind was beyond peaceful. The pleasure he felt was cosmic. The warmth flowed through his very being and took him far away from his body. So far, that he didn't want to go back. He was flying through colours so bright that he could hardly keep his eyes open. The sense of weightlessness and flight was incredible. He soared higher and higher. There was nothing but joy around him.

At the back of his mind, he knew this was not just opium and ketamine, but he was past caring. It was too intense to be a safe dose. As he drifted from this world into the next, he heard the front door being smashed to pieces. His last thoughts were that his cousins had murdered him, and he didn't care.

Chapter 25. Marion.

I guess you'd call it cowardice...

ABI HAD STAYED IN HER room all day, moping around and sulking. Marion had left her to it and decided to wait until she came around of her own accord. Taking her away from the flat she shared with Leo wasn't as hard as she thought it would be because Abi knew in her own mind that she couldn't stay. Being pregnant changed everything and she realised that herself, but she did tend to sulk.

Marion had done the right thing and she didn't have the time or the inclination to pander to her when it was obviously the right thing to do. Abi would have to come to terms with it in her own time. She had talked to her until she was blue in the face, but it was like talking to a brick wall at times. The sulky teenager would resurface, and the walls would go up. Taking her away from Leo was the best thing that any mother could have done in that situation, but did she get any thanks for helping her? Nope.

Marion would challenge any mother to be in the same situation and not take their daughter home if they could. Protecting her child was not optional; it was instinctive. Having a child was her greatest achievement and her greatest challenge. Trying to steer her daughter in the right direction, encourage her and protect her had been the number one focus in her life. Abi was her life, but Abi didn't always appreciate that fact. She could be downright ungrateful.

Abi didn't realise how low she had sunk and how much lower she would go, if she stayed in that toxic relationship with a baby to feed and look after. Rock bottom was a long way down and she wasn't going to stand by and let her sink any lower than she already had. Abi was bright and intelligent and had so much potential and it was heartbreaking to see her future with a baby and a man like Leo Tomkins as her partner.

Leo was immature in so many ways, still a boy in his head. Abi was in love with him but the boy she loved was trapped by addiction and circumstance. He could escape neither of those things and if she stayed, she would be dragged down with him. Becoming pregnant was the game changer. It was no longer her choice to make alone. There was a baby to think of now. Marion had to protect her daughter and her grandchild and Leo Tompkins could go and whistle. He was not high on her priority list. Abi was her only concern and would remain that way, even if she didn't appreciate it just yet. In time, she would.

Marion flicked on the news and searched for any coverage related to the Goodstone family but there was nothing to see. It would trickle out eventually. The press would be all over it once the news broke because of their standing within the community. They were a rich family, supported charities and local schools but David and Rebecca had also made the news for the wrong reasons. Their visits to rehab were well documented and a major embarrassment to their relatives. Marion sent a text message to Bernie.

Hello lovely. Any news?

She waited impatiently for a reply, when it came, she was stunned.

David senior has warned everyone to keep it quiet, but Rebecca died in hospital. That didn't come from me.

Of course. That's terrible news.

I can't talk to you. The police have told us not to talk to each other until they've spoken to everyone.

Okay, lovely. Take care or yourself.

You too.

Marion felt like a deflated balloon. She had hoped the doctors would be able to save Rebecca. The news was a hammer blow. Guilt began to eat away at her confidence. David junior had been a spoilt brat and she should never have gone near him, but she had. It was a drunken fuck that meant nothing to her but had meant much more to him. He had become obsessed. That couldn't be changed now, and she felt guilty for treating him the way she had earlier even if he had crossed the line. Trying to kiss her while she was working was immature at best and an arrogant assault at worst.

She sighed and shook her head. There was no way to wind the clock back. He was dead and she had sold him the powder which killed him. The guilt was simmering below the surface, but she couldn't allow it to boil over. She had no idea what was in the cocaine that would cause a fatal reaction, but that was academic. It had killed him and his sister, and she had sold it to him. If the police found out that she had supplied them, she would be sent to jail for a long time. She wouldn't be around while Abi had her child alone and struggled to bring it up and she couldn't allow that to happen. Her guts clenched and made her grimace. This was unbelievable. The anxiety was going to put her into an early grave. Just like David and Rebecca Goodstone. The drugs had been supplied by Kenny Fulshaw and she hadn't touched them before she sold them on.

Marion had told Kenny not to try to contact her and then blocked him but now she wished she could call him. It would be foolish to do so, but her curiosity was monumental. Had anyone else been affected by the drug or was it a one off? She wondered if it could be something in the container, she transferred the wraps into but dismissed the idea quickly. The wraps were sealed; therefore, it was the powder inside that had caused the reaction. That wasn't her fault. But selling it to David was her fault and she couldn't avoid that guilt. Her mind went back and forth. She would have to wait until

David senior allowed people back onto his property to recover the cocaine but for now, she knew it couldn't hurt anyone else. When she was allowed on the property with her cleaning team, and had the opportunity to access the cupboard, she would make sure the entire batch was thrown down the drains. There was nothing that she could do until then and she needed to focus on the things she could influence.

Marion made two cups of hot chocolate and broke open a packet of biscuits. She bit into one of them and munched on it. She liked the dark chocolate flavour; it was her favourite. Marion took a deep breath and walked to the bottom of the stairs.

'Abi, I've made hot chocolate,' she shouted. There was no reply and no footsteps to be heard. 'Abi, stop sulking and get your arse down here. I've got biscuits!'

Nothing.

Marion put the cups down and stomped up the stairs. She was expecting to see Abi sitting in the corner of the room, hugging her knees like she did when she was a little girl who couldn't get her way. She was going to tell her to get a grip and stop being so childish. If she was going to have this baby, she needed to grow up sharpish.

'Why are you pretending that you can't hear me?' Marion said as she opened the door. 'Oh, my God!' she screamed. 'No, no, no!'

Abi was hanging from a noose that she had fashioned from her sheets. Her face was deep purple, her ears blue, eyes rolled back into her head. Marion instinctively ran to her and lifted her up, to take her weight from the noose. Her body felt warm but limp. Marion tried to lift her from the hook she had made from coat hangers. Abi had twisted several together and then tied them to the light fitting in the centre of the ceiling. It didn't look very strong, but it was holding her. Marion pushed her up again and shouted.

'Abi, what have you done!' Marion screamed. 'Abi, Abi, Abi, don't you leave me like this!' Marion became hysterical. 'Not like this, Abi. Please stay here darling! Abi....please, please, please, please, don't leave me...'

She couldn't unhook the fastening. Marion pulled her from the waist and used her weight to yank at the coat hangers, but they held fast. A rasping noise came from Abi's throat, like air rushing from a balloon.

'Abi, don't die, darling, don't die, don't die, please, don't die,' Marion became hysterical. 'Abi, come back, come back, come back, Abi, please, please, please!'

Marion heaved Abi as high as she could to relieve the pressure on her throat. Her body was limp as if her bones had liquidised. She couldn't maintain her grip.

'Abi! Abi!,' Marion screamed. 'Please don't die, baby girl. Don't you die on me now. Stay here with me, Abi. Please, please, please, don't die...'

The hangers snapped and Abi fell to the floor with a thump. Marion loosened the noose and felt for her pulse but there was nothing. She dialled 999 and began CPR.

Chapter 26. Leo.

Little donkey, on the dusty road, keep on plodding onwards with the precious load...

LEO WAS BREATHLESS when he reached his building, but he didn't stop to see if he was being followed before he entered. He felt like a child, afraid of the dark, running from an invisible monster that was closing in on him with every step; the fear was suffocating him, driving him to run faster despite his heart threatening to burst. His lungs were burning, and it felt like he had been running for hours but it was more like minutes. There were cuts and bruises all over him and blood was running from his left elbow and right knee. He could feel a nasty graze on his stomach. Climbing fences in the dark was a hazardous business. He ran up the stairs and put his key in the door, opening it too quickly and it hit the wall with a loud bang. The noise echoed down the stairwell, and he cursed beneath his breath. He didn't want his neighbours to hear him. None of them could mind their own business. Most of them shunned him when they saw him in the shared areas and pretended, they hadn't seen him. He couldn't trust any of them not to say something to the police if they were questioned.

Once inside, he closed the door quietly and sat behind it, sliding off the rucksack; his chest was heaving as he tried to catch his breath. Sweat trickled from his forehead, running down his cheeks and his back was soaking wet, his tee-shirt sticking to his skin. He lifted the bag. It felt heavier when it was on his back, hurdling fences. He tossed it aside and kicked it away from him as if it was something dangerous, threatening to bite him. There were two kilos of class-A powder in there, which added up to a long jail sentence. What the fuck was he doing?

Ged Tickle said he would give him four grand to collect the package and stash it in his flat. It had sounded so simple at the time, and he needed the money. If he was going to get Abi back, he needed a regular income. But when it had come to creeping over garden fences to get to the house across the road, where a young woman had died, he had questioned if this was something he should be doing. His knees had felt weak, and his hands were shaking as he'd waited for the package to drop. The urge to run away was overpowering.

He was thinking that if he had been caught, Marion would never let him see Abi and their baby. The urge to go back to the safety of his home had been overwhelming but he had resisted. He would have been sent to jail if the police had intercepted him on the way back to his flat with two kilos on him. That was intent to supply and that was a heavy sentence. What if they had been watching him all the time and they knew he was in his flat right now with two kilos of powder in a bag? What if they kicked the door in? He had no defence, caught in the act, red-handed with the goods in his possession.

He was more afraid now that he was at home than he had been outside. Leo looked at the rucksack and his mind began working, but not in a good way.

Two kilos of powder.

Two kilos of powder.

Two kilos of powder.

It was uncut and it was twelve inches away from his feet. Ged wouldn't know if he had a little bit, would he? He could take a few grams out of each parcel and tape them back up. Who would know? They were unlikely to weigh the fucking things when they came to collect them. It could be a little reward for all his effort and the danger he had put himself in. The drugs were calling to him.

"Just a little bit, go on, you know you want to..."

The temptation was enormous, but he couldn't risk it. Ged would send someone to collect, surely, he would. That was another of the questions he needed to ask. How long was he expected to store the drugs in his home? The longer they were there, the greater the risk. Who would take them away or would mad Madern expect him to act as the mule and carry them to wherever they were going? Fucking donkey more like. Stupid dumb little donkey carrying the risk.

They were making other people take all the risks, people who meant nothing to them. All the risks were spinning around his mind like a tornado of the worst possibilities. A maelstrom of negative endings raged in his mind, and he felt sick and confused. He had asked Ged to give him more work, work that paid well but that meant dangerous work. It meant if he got caught, he was going to jail and that would be him and Abi finished forever. He was trapped between the devil and the deep blue sea and there was no easy way out. There was no way he could survive in the normal world of nine to five, where rules and regulations would be against him at every turn, but could he become a trusted soldier for Barry Madern? Probably not.

He tried to silence the thoughts from his brain and took out his phone. There was still no reply from Abi. He thought her mother was probably telling her that she was not to message him because he was a useless junkie. It was true but she needed to have a day off from being a bitch-on-his-case all the time. Abi would still be in the flat and they could have worked things out if Marion hadn't come poking her big nose in their business. It had to be Marion because Abi loved him, and she wouldn't ignore his messages. There was no other explanation. He typed a text.

Hey starling, how's it going? I Hope you're feeling okay. Are you fat yet, ha ha? I can't believe we're going to be parents. Me and you, being mum and dad. Do you want a girl or a boy? I don't mind either way. What about names? Can we look online for boy's names and girl's names and pick two each? Then we can narrow it down and have a row about it, ha ha. I've been busy tonight, doing a job for Ged. It was an important job and I'm getting a lot of money from him for doing it. I'm going to get some good jobs from now on. I know you're sick of hearing me say it but I'm going to get clean and then we can be together with our baby. Love you, starling. X

Your Leo. Love you to Pluto and back.

Chapter 27. Jo Lilly. The SHIELD Teams.

O*h no, love you're not alone...*

JO WAS SITTING ON A grey leather-hide settee with her feet up, watching Hacksaw Ridge for the umpteenth time on a screen that filled the media wall. Every explosion reverberated, threatening to blow her out of her seat. The media wall was a recent addition to the house and part of an extensive renovation and extension, which they had undertaken through lockdown. Covid-19 had closed the restaurants and pubs that they frequented. Lenny and Jo decided that socialising at home would be their most likely future, so taking down all the walls from the ground floor and extending made sense at that time.

The project had dragged on for months because of the shortage of both materials and tradesmen. Everyman and his dog had the same idea through lockdown, and it made building work virtually double in price. They had been without a kitchen and hot water for three months. Lenny had rigged up a garden fence sprayer, filled from a catering urn so that they could shower with hot water standing in the bath, although it meant that one hand was constantly employed on the pump handle, leaving the other to soap, shave and scrub. It had been a very stressful time, but Lenny was a very calm person, who kept Jo's feet on the ground while the build dragged on and on. By the end of the second week, they were sick of the sight of takeaway food. The project went overtime and way over budget, but the result was stunning, and they loved their new living space. Staying in was their going out and they loved entertaining family and friends. Lenny was a keen pool player and had bought a dilapidated table and refurbished it. It lived on the patio beneath no less than four waterproof covers unless the weather was dry, then he would spend hours practicing. It was a popular addition when they had barbeques and people played on it all day. Although Lenny was sometimes a bit precious about the cloth and his cue.

Lenny emptied his rioja and picked up Jo's empty glass. He stood up and made his way to the kitchen, to top up the wine. She watched him walk away. He was broad and muscular, both arms covered with ink from shoulder to his hands. People thought he looked scary, but he was a pussycat, a gentle giant with a heart of gold and she idolised him.

The white sauvignon was an experimental brand as her favourite wine had climbed to fourteen pounds a bottle which Lenny said was daylight thuggery. He had suggested buying homebrew equipment and making their own wine, which Jo had deemed as one of the shittest ideas he had ever had, almost as shit as the garden sprayer shower, so he didn't mention it again.

'What's this new wine like?' Lenny asked as he walked away.

'Shite,' Jo said, checking her phone. A message had appeared from Cara, who worked in safeguarding and managed the SHIELD team. SHIELD worked with exploited children involved in county lines operations. 'It's possibly the crappest wine ever put into a bottle.'

'The reviews were good,' Lenny said.

'I think the reviewers were paid by the vineyard owners or they gave them enough samples to make sure they were pissed enough to say anything,' Jo said. 'Or they have never tasted another wine to compare it to. It is definitely in my top three worst wines of all time.'

'Oh dear,' Lenny chuckled. 'I guess you don't want another then?'

'I'll try another just to make sure,' Jo said, smiling. 'Never give up, my old dad used to say, bless his soul.'

'Are you sure?' Lenny said. 'I can pour it down the sink, if you don't like it.'

'Fuck off, Lenny. I'm not a quitter,' Jo said, reading the message on her phone. 'I'll try another. The truth is in the pudding.'

'No, it isn't,' Lenny said, chuckling to himself. He struggled with the cork in a new bottle of rioja.

'What are you laughing at?' Jo asked, distracted.

'The truth isn't in the pudding,' he said. 'I think, the proof of the pudding is in the eating, is the phrase you were thinking of. It doesn't mention the truth.'

'Bog off, Lenny,' Jo muttered. 'It's the same thing. Stop being a smart arse.'

'Pardon?' Lenny said, laughing. 'Did you swear at me?'

'No.'

'What did you say, then?'

'Nothing,' Jo said. 'I need to make a call to work.'

'At this time of night?' Lenny said, returning with the wine. 'I thought EDT or whoever sorted out nighttime emergencies.'

'They do, smarty-pants,' Jo said. 'This is a friend giving me the heads up about something. Put my cheap wine on there and I'll grab it in a minute.' Jo scrolled through her contacts and found Cara. She rang the number and Cara answered on the second ring.

'Don't rip my head off for messaging at this time of night,' Cara said, sounding stressed. 'I had to speak to you in person.'

'Don't be daft,' Jo said. 'What's up?'

'Our little friend, Leo Tompkins has excelled himself,' Cara said. 'I know he's been on the books forever and always been a handful but he's really in the shit this time. This is trouble with a capital T.'

'Leo couldn't stay out of trouble in an empty room,' Jo said. Her heart sank. Leo was a favourite, because he had been through so much tragedy. His heart was in the right place, but his decision making wasn't good at all. 'What has he done this time?'

'I know you're working on the Angela Deacon case, and this is connected to her house,' Cara said. 'I've had a heads-up, so, this must go no further than us until it comes out?'

'Of course, that goes without saying,' Jo said. 'Let me grab my wine. This sounds like I'm going to need it.'

'Join the club. I've just poured myself a large pinot. What are you drinking?' Cara asked.

'It's supposed to be Sauvignon Blanc, but Lenny is exploring the cheaper brands on the market because the gas and electric have gone up,' Jo explained. Cara laughed. 'I think this is the wine equivalent to, Utterly Butterly.'

'We call it, 'fuck all like butter',' Cara said.

'This is, utterly shite, in a bottle,' Jo said.

'Or it could be, 'I can't believe it's not Sauvignon'?'

'That's the one. I appreciate the gas has doubled in price, but to be honest, I would rather be cold and smelly than drink this shite at night. The central heating and hot water shouldn't be his priority.'

'Oh dear,' Cara said. 'Perhaps you should give him a list of wines not to buy.'

'Anyway, enough of Lenny's economic disasters. Tell me what Leo has got himself into,' Jo said.

'Angela Deacon's house is under surveillance because the police found a quantity of powder and some firearms beneath the floorboards in a locked bedroom, so they left the drugs in place as bait,' Cara explained.

'Oh, no!' Jo sighed. 'Please don't tell me Leo has gone for the bait, has he?'

'Yes, he's involved. There were several people involved from what I can gather. Someone broke in through the patio doors at the rear of the house and recovered the packages from upstairs. The drugs were then dropped into the back garden from an upstairs window and Leo collected them.'

'You're kidding me?' Jo said, shaking her head. 'What on Earth was he thinking?'

'The police had a drone up and he's been identified catching the packages as they dropped.'

'Has he been arrested?'

'Not yet,' Cara said. 'He's taken the drugs back to his flat and the police are waiting to see who turns up to collect them or where Leo takes them.'

'He's taken them to his flat?' Jo asked, shocked. 'He's never been the brightest bulb in the box but that's absolutely ridiculous.'

'On the tree,' Lenny said, sipping his wine.

'What?' Jo asked.

'Brightest bulb on the tree,' Lenny said, whispering behind his hand. 'Not in the box.'

'Bog off, Lenny,' Jo whispered, smiling. 'Sorry, Cara.'

'No problem. I feel sorry for him,' Cara said. 'He's probably been bullied into it or promised money to retrieve them. However, they have coerced him, it's CE.'

'Leo is the poster boy for CE. The Maderns have had their hooks into him for years,' Jo said. 'I know his file like the back of my hand. It started when he was in care, given a bike and a delivery round at twelve. The kid has never been able to break their hold on him.'

'They're not as smart as they think they are. The police have been building a case against Madern for nearly two years and Leo was just on the periphery of it but now he has put himself in the middle of it. He doesn't know the police have been watching the entire area, not just the Deacon property. They're on to him now.'

'The Maderns won't care if Leo burns with them. They're using him to take the risk as usual,' Jo said. 'He's had a terrible time, but he keeps going back. I know he's been forced to carry drugs up his backside on trains to North Wales, earlier this year. His social worker was really concerned about bruises on his face, but he said he had fallen. On one trip, he was threatened with a knife. Apparently, it was a very close call. Leo was traumatised by it and promised to stay away but he went back a few weeks later. He's anchored to them by the ketamine.'

'We're fighting a losing battle against that shit,' Cara said.

'It's a vicious circus but someone has to try, lovely,' Jo said.

'Circle,' Lenny said.

'Bugger off, I'm having a conversation,' Jo whispered. 'Poor Leo. He has no idea they're watching?'

'None. He'll be sitting there thinking he's got away with it but he's in for a nasty shock and I'm really worried that we won't be able to help him this time,' Cara said. 'Exploitation is our trump card but he's not a twelve-year-old.'

'I know. This is so messed up. So, the police let the SHIELD team know what's going on because Leo is involved?' Jo asked. 'Was it official?'

'No. It's a live operation but one of the detectives is on the MACE team. She's familiar with Leo and knows he's vulnerable and he's being exploited, she gave me the nod.'

'That kid drives me insane,' Jo said. 'We all know that he's being exploited, but two kilos puts him in the big league.'

'The big problem is that he's seventeen next month. They'll treat him as an adult,' Cara said.

'Next month. Oh, no,' Jo said. 'I didn't realise his birthday is so close. That's not good.'

'Exactly. I want to give you the chance to get your social workers primed. The police have lost patience with Leo and because he's nearly seventeen, they may see an opportunity to flip him. If they pile the pressure on him, they can make him give evidence against Barry Madern and his cronies.'

'He would be in grave danger if he testified against them,' Jo said. 'Leo is a cheeky little bugger when he wants to be but he's nowhere near as tough as he makes out. He'll say whatever they want him to.'

'If they go down that road, I'll make sure they consider his vulnerability. They would have to offer him the safest option available to them,' Cara said.

'That would mean witness protection?' Jo said. 'Leo wouldn't last five minutes in prison, but I don't see him in WP either. He's too reliant on others to cope alone.'

'I agree,' Cara said. 'If they took him into the program, there's no getting off. They'll find him accommodation in the middle of anywhere which is nowhere near here and get him a crappy job, which he won't be able to hold down. I can't see it being a real option for him.'

'He can't even function here with our support,' Jo said. 'This is so sad. I thought he had turned a corner. He seems really settled with his girlfriend; she's been a positive influence on him. I can't believe he's got involved in something as big as this. We're going to struggle to help him.'

'Once he's arrested, things will move very quickly, and he won't realise that his girlfriend won't be included in any deal they offer him. Not a chance. He would be whisked away. You know the score,' Cara said. 'He will never see her again if he stays in WP and if he can't cope and comes back here...'

'He's a dead seventeen-year-old.'

'Exactly.'

'How long has he got?' Jo asked.

'How long is a piece of string?' Cara asked. 'Leo is a little fish in a big pond. They want the big ones to turn up for those drugs but they're not going to wait long. If no one shows, Leo will cop for it.'

'I feel so sorry for that kid. It makes me very upset,' Jo said. Her eyes filled up with tears. 'The poor little bugger has never been given a break. Everything he touches turns to crap. I wish there was something we could do!'

'I'll do whatever I can at this end,' Cara said. 'If he is lifted tonight, I'll call you after nine tomorrow.'

'Thanks for the heads up, Cara,' Jo said.

'Enjoy your wine.'

'Like rat's piss, but apparently, a bargain, none the less,' Jo said, sniffling. Lenny chuckled to himself and sipped his wine. 'What are you laughing at?' she asked, ending the call.

'Nothing,' Lenny said. 'Are you okay?'

'Not really,' Jo said. 'I can't go into detail, but this kid has had everyone he loved taken from him since he was a little boy and he's traumatised. He has been passed from pillar to post. It's no wonder he's struggling with addiction. He's made a lot of poor decisions, but this one is spectacularly bad.' She wiped a tear from her cheek. 'He's mixed up with something he might not get out of, and I don't think we can help him this time. It's made me really upset.'

'I know it's upset you,' Lenny said. 'It's not hard to upset you though. You're a sensitive soul, you cry at adverts.'

'Fuck off, Lenny,' Jo said, cracking a smile.

'Drink your rat's piss,' Lenny said. 'There's another two bottles of that left.'

Chapter 28.

Suicide is painless, it brings on many changes, and I can take or leave them, if I please...

MARION WAS SITTING in the relatives' room, holding a barely warm cup of something beige. She was numb. Abi was in resus and there was nothing that she could do to help her but wait. It was cold and she was wearing a cotton tee-shirt; she hadn't thought about grabbing a jacket when the ambulance was leaving. She hadn't thought about anything but Abi hanging from the ceiling. She wondered if David Goodstone had been sitting in the same place waiting for news about Rebecca, knowing that his son was already dead. She couldn't help but think this was karma, and the bitch was biting back. Marion had sold the drugs that killed two people and here she was waiting to find out if her daughter and grandchild were alive or dead. What goes around, comes around. Two lives in payment for the two she had a hand in ending.

The door opened and she looked up at an older version of herself. Her sister, Liz rushed to her and held her tightly. She always smelled of Armani Si and looked like she had come from a riding stable without changing. Wax jackets and boots were here forte.

'I came as soon as I could. Is there any news?' Liz whispered.

'No. Not yet,' Marion said. 'Did you come on your own?'

'No. Mitch is trying to park the Defender,' Liz said. 'The car park was designed for much smaller vehicles than we own.'

'I came in with the ambulance,' Marion said. 'It felt like it took forever to get here.'

'Are you okay?' Liz asked. 'Stupid question, I know.'

'I can't get the image of her hanging out of my head, Liz.' Marion sobbed. 'She was purple. Her ears were blue. I can't get it out of my mind. Why didn't she just talk to me?'

'How awful for you,' Liz said. 'I can't believe she has done this. Was she struggling with something?'

'Yes. Her waste of space boyfriend.' Marion clenched her fists. 'I would strangle him if I could get my hands on him.'

'Don't get angry. Try not to think about him if he makes you angry. You stress out when you're angry,' Liz said, squeezing her. 'It's not going to be helpful for you. Take a deep breath and tell me what happened?'

'It's all that useless junkie bastard's fault,' Marion said, angrily. Her mascara had run. 'If I could get my hands on him right now.'

'I don't understand why it is Leo's fault?' Liz asked. 'Tell me what he did.'

'She's pregnant,' Marion said.

'Oh, no! Don't tell me that,' Liz said, shaking her head. 'They're not adults themselves. What were they thinking?'

'Exactly,' Marion said, sniffling. 'I've told her a thousand times to use condoms every time she has sex with him. She's on the pill but you know how unreliable they can be. I warned her but she said Leo didn't like wearing them and obviously he didn't. The stupid little shit, he is.'

'I bet that was a nasty shock. What did you say when she told you she was pregnant?'

'I probably overreacted but you should have seen the state of her. She looked like she's wasting away and hadn't had a decent meal in weeks,' Marion said, lowering her voice. 'Leo had sent her to get him some more ketamine because he was clucking but had no money to buy it. He can't even feed his own habit.' Marion sighed. 'He sent my daughter to beg for credit from a drug dealer.'

'Okay,' Liz said. 'I can see why you're angry.'

'I can't believe she ever got involved with the little shit.' Marion cried and Liz let her settle. 'They had no food in the flat and no money in the meter and she told me she was pregnant. So, I took her home with me and before we left, I told that fucking junkie not to contact us until he was off the ketamine.' Marion shook her head, tears streaming down her cheeks. 'I should have talked to them like adults, but I was angry and took control when it wasn't my place to. If I hadn't interfered, she wouldn't have tried to take her own life.'

'Oh, no, you can't know that for sure,' Liz said, shaking her head. 'These things can't always be predicted. We do things because we think they're right at the time.' She paused and let Marion calm down. 'How far gone is she?'

'Eight weeks, she thinks,' Marion said, sniffling. 'Oh, that poor baby inside her. What if she dies, that baby will die too before it was born.' Marion began to shake. 'I can't even think straight.'

'Try to remain calm, Marion,' Liz said. 'You're tormenting yourself and it will solve nothing.'

'I feel like my head is going to explode!' Marion said. 'I made hot chocolate while she was hanging from the ceiling, choking to death.' She shook her head. 'I was eating a chocolate biscuit while she was trying to commit suicide. How fucking deluded can a parent be?'

'You didn't know what she was doing,' Liz said. 'How could you possibly of known that she was suicidal?'

'I could have asked her how she felt instead of telling her what she had to do,' Marion snapped. 'But I was too busy messing about with my own problems to worry about my daughter.' Marion clenched her hands into fists and hammered on her knees. 'I should have known. How could I not know that my own flesh and blood didn't want to be in this world anymore?'

'You're not a mind reader and Abi must have seemed okay to you,' Liz said. 'You can't blame yourself.'

'Who else can I blame, apart from that twat, Leo?' Marion said. 'I can put some of the blame on him but not all of it. I made her come home and took her away from him. This is on me.'

'You could not have known that she would react this way. People who commit suicide seldom appear to be disturbed. They hide it well. Who knows what was going on in her mind?' Liz said. 'It's impossible to see these things coming sometimes.'

'I should have known, Liz,' Marion said, sobbing. 'She was pregnant, and I took her away from her boyfriend and forced her to come home. I should have asked her what she wanted. She loved the useless bastard, and I took her away from him. I should have known it would disturb her. She's so sensitive and fragile.'

'I understand what you're saying, and I would have expected her to be angry with you or upset about Leo but not hang herself,' Liz said. She held her sister tightly and let her cry. 'You mustn't blame yourself. Everything you have done is with best intentions. You can't take the blame for other people and the choices they make.' Marion was hysterical and didn't reply. Liz squeezed her. 'I'm glad you called me. You can't do this alone.' She paused. 'Does Leo know?'

She felt her sister stiffen at the mention of his name. Marion was distraught and maybe seeing Leo wasn't the best idea, but he was her partner and the father of her unborn child. Liz felt it was terribly wrong to keep it from him, but she didn't want to rile Marion. Her head was in a spin. Introducing Leo into the mix, might send her over the edge. She sensed vitriol in her voice when she spoke about him as if everything wrong with her daughter was his fault. Liz knew that Abi hadn't recovered from her father leaving them, no matter how long ago it had been. She was emotionally damaged and vulnerable. Leo had shown her love and loyalty, despite his addiction. Marion would never see that in a million years, especially not right now.

'He's to blame for all of this,' Marion sobbed. 'Why couldn't she fall in love with a nice young lad, who wanted to go to college and university and have a good life?'

'Because they would leave her,' Liz said. Marion looked up, a confused expression on her face.

'What do you mean?'

'They would leave her to go to college, surrounded by pretty young things and if they survived that, they would leave her for three years to go to university,' Liz explained. 'Leo was with her morning, noon and night and he would never go away and leave her. She knows that Leo will always be by her side and that's the attraction. She feels secure with him.'

'Is she that damaged that Leo Tompkins is the best option that she thinks she has?' Marion said, shaking her head. 'Does she really think that he is the best she can do?'

'I don't know but I'm guessing she's still suffering from her father leaving her. She's vulnerable and feels that people she loves might desert her again,' Liz said. 'Who knows what went through her mind. We can't put ourselves inside her head. Not even for a minute.'

'Oh, my god,' Marion said, her voice a whisper. 'Is she that broken that I couldn't fix her, what have I done to my baby?'

'You looked after your little girl,' Liz said. 'No one is a better mother than you. Don't ever think anything else.'

The door opened and two doctors stepped in, one male and one female. They both looked too young to be qualified. Their expressions were dour. It was obvious that the news wasn't good.

Chapter 29. Leo.

When you walked out that door, I swore that I didn't care, But I lost everything, darlin', then and there...

LEO CHECKED HIS PHONE again, but Abi hadn't replied. His stomach cramped and he felt something was wrong. Marion must have taken her phone from her. It was typical of how she treated him as if he didn't have feelings too and if he did, they didn't matter. Marion had no idea about how much Leo and Abi loved each other. She couldn't know or she wouldn't interfere. The thoughts of her not being in his life we're completely incomprehensible. There was no alternative future without her in it. He wondered what she was thinking right now. Did she really think that they couldn't be together as a family or was she being railroaded into this decision by her mother? It was impossible to gauge where her mind might be. If this was just a temporary situation to give him the chance to get off the ketamine, then he could live with that. He intended to give it the best shot he could so that they could be mum and dad to their baby. It was everything he had dreamed of and more.

Leo went to the kitchen and got a pint glass from the cupboard. He turned on the tap and filled it full of cold water, drinking thirstily. It had been a long night and it wasn't over yet. Everything felt as if time was standing still, a state of limbo between events. Something was changing. He was waiting for a paradigm shift in his world, but he wasn't sure what it was going to be. Maybe it was a kind of premonition that something huge was about to happen. Or maybe it was just his imagination running wild. It wasn't every day he was involved in the recovery of two kilos of ketamine from a dead woman's house. Combined with watching Abi walk away from their house with her things in a suitcase, his head was completely mashed, and it was no wonder that he couldn't think straight.

He heard his phone vibrate and his heart skipped a beat, hoping Abi had found a way to reply to his messages. He looked at the phone and saw that he had a text message, but the number was encrypted somehow. He knew that Barry Madern and his cronies used encrypted phones, but he didn't really understand how they worked. He opened the message and read it. It said simply;

press your call button.

Leo pressed the call button, and a message began to download.

Read these instructions very carefully and do not deviate from them in any way. Follow them exactly and you will be well paid for your efforts tonight however if you fuck this up it will be the last fuck up that you will ever make. If you understand this message so far, then press the Y button.

Leo pressed the Y button and waited for their response.

Take the packages of ketamine out of the rucksack and check them for a small incision which has been made in the outer covering and has been covered over with black masking tape. Do it now and press the Y button on your phone when you have found it.

Leo went to the rucksack and picked it up, placing it on his dining table. Nervously he opened it and checked the parcels, looking for a strip of black tape. Sure, enough on the second package he saw a three-inch strip of black tape on the centre of the wrapping. He pressed the Y button on his phone.

Remove the tape from the incision and place your fingers inside the powder. You will find a small memory stick. Remove the memory stick and replace the tape over the incision. The memory stick is of great value and is now your responsibility. I need you to hide the memory stick somewhere in your flat and you are to tell nobody of its whereabouts. Some people will come to your flat shortly, to remove the drugs. They may ask you if there was anything else in the bag. It doesn't matter who asks you.

You will reply, no.

Once the bag has been removed, you are to forget the events of tonight and never speak of them to anyone again. If you are arrested by the police, you will make a full no comment statement and speak only to confirm your name and address. I will contact you directly when I need to. Until then, forget about it. This is your responsibility and yours alone. Do not deviate from the instructions. If you understand these instructions, then press Y on your phone.

Leo pressed Y.

He removed the tape and inserted his forefinger into the powder searching for the memory stick. It was buried an inch or so inside the parcel. He removed it as he had been instructed and then replaced the tape over the incision. Then he walked into the kitchen and opened one of the cupboards. He closed the door and opened the next, looking for an unobvious hiding place. On the middle shelf, there was a tub of strawberry milkshake powder, which Abi had bought and hardly ever used. Leo picked it up and removed the lid and then slipped the memory stick into the pink granules, shaking the tub until it was no longer visible. He wondered if strawberry milk shake granules could damage the memory stick and decided that he didn't care. He put it back onto the shelf and placed some open packets of pasta and flour in front of the tub. Sweat trickled down his back as he went back into the living room. He put the packages back into the rucksack and checked his phone again. There was no option to reply to the messages and as he looked at the screen, the instructions that he had received were deleted as if by some invisible hand.

Leo was confused and frightened, but the messages had said that he would be contacted at some point in the future about the memory stick and that the drugs would be removed from his flat soon. That gave him some degree of comfort as he wanted them gone and he didn't want to see them again. He wished he had never been involved in the first instance, but he couldn't change that now. He had to stay calm and manage the situation no matter how shit it was.

Tiredness caught up with him and the urge to sleep spread through his bones. He was exhausted. Leo yawned and thought about having a nap on the settee when suddenly, there was a knock on his front door. It was the type of knock that couldn't be ignored. Like an Amazon delivery driver on steroids.

Leo felt his heart racing as he went to the front door. He looked through the lens and saw three men standing there dressed in dark clothing. Their heads were covered by hoodies and baseball caps, but he could see from their features that both Tickle brothers were there. He didn't recognise the third man, but he was huge. The Tickle brothers were well-built, but this guy was juiced. Leo felt intimidated but it was almost a relief to see them there. They had come to collect Barry Madern's drugs and that was a good thing.

Leo opened the door and the three men rushed in without any greetings. Leo checked the landing to see if any of the neighbours were around. He walked to the top of the stairwell and looked down at the entrance area. It was quiet. He went back inside his flat before closing the door behind him. Ged was peering through the curtains at the street and the big guy went into his bedroom.

'Where is he going?' Leo asked.

'He's checking the place is safe,' Ged said. 'Where is the bag?'

'What does he think is in my bedroom?' Leo asked. 'A BBC camera team?'

'You've got a smart mouth, kidda,' Si Tickle snapped. 'I would keep it closed, if I was you.'

'Well, you're not me, and this is my home,' Leo said, blushing. He was scared but annoyed. 'There's no need to search my home.'

'Shut up. Where is the fucking bag?' Si asked.

'Hello Leo. How did everything go tonight?' Leo said, sarcastically. 'Thank you very much for your help in retrieving our valuable packages. You have done an amazing job.'

'Is this little prick really taking the piss out of us?' Si asked his brother. 'Does he realise who he's talking to?'

'Give him a break,' Ged said. 'He's a good lad or I wouldn't have asked him to do it in the first place but sometimes, he doesn't know when to keep his big mouth shut. Do you, Leo?'

'It has been mentioned before,' Leo said, shrugging. 'I can't help myself. The rucksack is on the dining table there.'

'Have you looked inside the bag?' Si asked, walking to the table.

'No. I haven't looked inside the bag because I don't want anything to do with what is inside it. I just carried it here.'

'Weren't you curious?'

'I did as you asked, and I was where you asked me to be at the time you told me to be there, and I caught the bag and then nearly killed myself vaulting over every garden fence between there and here. I'm scratched to buggery and knackered, so when I got back here, the last thing on my mind was what is in the bag.'

'So, you haven't even taken a peek?' Si asked, eying him suspiciously.

'No, I haven't looked in the bag,' Leo repeated. 'Do you want to ask me again, because the answer will be the same.'

'I don't like this prick,' Si said, shaking his head. 'He's way too cocky for my liking.'

'I'm not trying to be cocky,' Leo said. 'I tend to say what I'm thinking, which gets me into trouble a lot. I don't mean any offence.'

'Check the bag,' Ged said to the big man, who had returned from his search of the bedroom. 'Did you speak to Les at the house?'

'No, Ged,' Leo said, shaking his head. 'I didn't even see him. It was black as the ace of spades in that garden, and I was shitting my pants. I stood beneath the window and waited for the bag to drop then I was off on my toes, like a greyhound out of the traps.'

The big man emptied the bag and placed the two bricks of powder onto the table. He searched the other pockets and squeezed the material to make sure the rucksack was empty.

'That's it,' he said, gruffly. 'There's nothing else in there.'

'Then we have a problem,' Si said, staring at Leo. 'Have you taken something out of the rucksack, Leo?'

'I've told you,' Leo said. 'I didn't look in the rucksack, never mind take anything out of it.'

'I don't believe you.' Si turned to Ged. 'This doesn't add up and I can tell by the look in his eyes that he knows something.'

'Are you sure there wasn't anything else in the bag?' Ged asked. 'Be honest with me.'

'Listen to me, Ged. I have no idea what you are talking about,' Leo said, feeling the menace in the air. It was becoming clear that there was an issue at the top of the tree. 'I have done everything that you asked me to do, so please pay me my four grand, take your rucksack and whatever is in it and leave me alone.'

'Four grand?' the big man growled. 'How come he's getting four grand for this?'

'He's not getting four grand,' Si laughed. He patted the big man on the back, but he didn't look happy. 'Who told you that you're getting any money at all?'

'Ged.'

'Did you promise him four grand to run a few kilos across a couple of gardens?' the big man asked, angrily. 'I'm getting paid peanuts in comparison to this little baghead.'

'Don't call me a baghead,' Leo said, offended. 'Look at the state of you. Your big because you shove needles up your arse and what's in the needles, fucking scotch mist?'

'What did he just say?' the big man asked, angrily.

'I said that you inject drugs too, mate,' Leo said, shrugging. 'Tell me you don't, and I'll apologise.' The big man flushed red with anger. 'You're a habitual drug user, just like me, so you call it what you like but don't kid yourself it's different.'

'I'm going to smash his face in when we're done here,' the big man said.

'That won't be difficult because you're fucking massive and I'm a skinny kid,' Leo said, shrugging. 'I don't want to get my head smashed in, but Ged promised me, four grand,' Leo said, looking from one brother to the other. 'You did promise me four grand, Ged. I wouldn't have done it otherwise. Please don't tell me this is a fucking wind up.'

'You're missing some of your marbles, sunshine, if you think that you're getting paid that amount of money for picking up a bag and taking it home.' The big man stabbed a stubby finger in the air. 'No way.'

'And you're missing some of your marbles, mate, if you think that I was going to do this for nothing.' Leo shrugged. 'I didn't see anyone else queueing up to do this. We made a deal, Ged.'

'Forget your deal. Tell me exactly what was in the bag,' Si said. 'What did you take out?'

'I'm done with this shit,' Leo said. He shrugged. 'I did what you asked me to do, so pay me and fuck off out of my flat.'

'I'm going to have to break your head if you tell me to fuck off ever again,' Si said. his eyes darkened and he glared at Leo.

'You'll have to get in the queue behind the big man,' Leo said. 'He's already going to kill me.'

'This kid is doing my nut in,' Si said, angrily. 'Why don't you keep your gob shut?'

'Because you keep asking me stupid questions,' Leo said.

'That's it!' Si snapped and lunged at Leo. Leo dodged the attack and sidestepped him.

'Let's do the little gobshite!' the big man growled and grabbed at Leo, but he ducked out of the way.

'Okay, okay, calm down, all of you!' Ged said, stepping between his brother and Leo. 'We're all bit on edge here, so let's keep cool heads and sort this out.' He waited a few seconds for the men to calm down. 'Listen to me and listen well. We've got an issue, Leo.'

'No shit, Sherlock,' Leo said.

'I'm going to snap his neck,' the big man growled.

'Will you shut up for a minute!' Ged turned on him. 'I'm trying to get to the bottom of this.' The big man stepped back. 'Has anybody contacted you since you made the pickup?'

'Of course, they have,' Leo said, trying not to look as if he was lying.

'I knew it!' Si snapped. 'Who was it?'

'I don't know,' Leo said. 'The messages appeared on my phone with no number listed.'

'That's an encrypted phone,' Si said to Ged. 'What did they say?' Si asked. He became agitated, pacing up and down. 'It has to be Madern.'

'I had two messages, the first asked me if I had picked up the bag, and the second one told me that you would be coming to pick it up soon,' Leo explained. 'Both messages have gone. They deleted themselves a few minutes after I replied to them, which is clever as fuck because I've never seen anything like that before.'

'That's it?'

'Yes.'

'Did they tell you to take anything out of the rucksack?'

'No.'

'Are you sure?'

'Yes. I'm positive,' Leo said. 'Why would I lie to you?'

'Show me your phone,' Si said.

'Why do you need to see my phone when I've just told you that the messages disappeared as soon as I replied to them?' Leo asked.

'I'm not asking you if you will show me your phone, dickhead, I'm telling you to show me your phone right now. It is not a request,' Si demanded.

'I don't know why you need it?'

'Show me your phone before I tip you upside down and bang your head on the floor.'

'Is there any need for that?' Leo asked Ged.

'Don't look to him for help,' Si said. Ged looked uncomfortable but didn't speak. The big man was lurking, a permanent scowl on his face. 'There's an easy way and there's a hard way to do this. I would advise you to do this the easy way.'

'Don't break my phone.'

'I'm not going to break it.'

'My girlfriend is pregnant, and she is staying at her mums tonight and I'm waiting for a message from her to tell me that she is all right,' Leo said, backing away. 'I need my phone to be able to keep in touch with her. I'll show you my phone and you can see that the messages have gone but please do not take it from me or smash it up.'

'No one is going to smash up your phone, Leo,' Ged said. 'Si is a bit nervous at the moment because he thinks there's something shady going down with this pick up and we're a little on edge.'

'I understand,' Leo said. 'I'm not trying to be awkward, but I need my phone.'

'I'll be straight with you, we can't understand why anybody would risk recovering those drugs, which makes us think that there was something else and that bag,' Ged said.

'Like what?' Leo asked.

'A gun,' Si said, staring hard into his eyes.

'A gun. Fucking hell!' Leo said, genuinely surprised. 'I think I would have noticed the weight of a gun in the bag.'

'Show us your phone,' Ged said.

'Okay, Ged,' Leo said. 'You have always been alright with me, but I need to know if I am going to get paid for what I have done tonight, like we agreed. We shook hands on that deal, and I took you at your word. I need that money to get Abi and me on our feet. We're having a baby and I wanted to do right by her.'

'I said I would pay you for the job and I will stick by my word, but you need to show us your phone first,' Ged said.

'Are you paying this little baghead four grand for this?' the big man asked, angrily.

'Shut up, Dom,' Ged said, turning to face him. 'I told you the price that you're being paid for tonight and you agreed, so what he gets paid is none of your business.'

'Yes, but...'

'Shut up!' Ged shouted. Dom looked shocked. 'I'm sick of hearing you moaning. If you want to walk away now, then do it.'

'I'm just saying,' Dom said. 'He's getting more than me. A lot more. It's not fair.'

'Life isn't fair,' Leo said, shaking his head. 'They pay you to be big and stupid, which puts you at the bottom of the pay scale.'

'I'm going to kill that little fucker,' Dom growled.

'Enough!' Ged said, pointing at Dom. 'Back off and watch from over there. Move now.' Dom walked to the other side of the room. 'Show me the phone.'

'Okay,' Leo said, taking out his phone. His fingers were shaking as he took his phone from his pocket. He trusted Ged to a degree but did not like Si or Dom at all. There was a nasty aura around them, which made Leo very uneasy. He had a feeling that there was more to this visit than met the eye. Ged's disclosure that they were concerned about the integrity of the job had said it all. Leo had been questioning the motive to retrieve the drugs from the first moment it was mentioned to him. It did not add up. The maths we're not correct and the risks outweighed the rewards. It was obvious to Leo that the reason this risky operation had been organised was to retrieve the memory stick. Whoever had sent him the messages, had warned him that he would be asked about the contents of the bag. It had to be Barry Madern himself. The Tickle brothers answered to Barry Madern and no one else. There was something going on in the upper echelons of the organisation, which was beyond his comprehension and his caring. It was out of his league, and he didn't want to be involved in any infighting between a bunch of violent psychopaths. What he wanted was irrelevant, because this was like being on a roller coaster that was already running. He was strapped in and couldn't get off until it's conclusion.

'Here you go,' Leo said handing over his phone. Ged took the phone and scrolled through his messages.

'He's telling the truth,' Ged said. There was nothing to see and he handed the phone back.

'Now that we've established that I'm telling the truth, what about my money?' Leo asked. 'When am I going to get paid?'

'You just don't know when to keep your mouth shut,' Si said. He looked like he was about to explode, anger in his dark eyes.

'If you don't ask, you don't get.' Leo thought that maybe he should have kept his mouth shut but the bitter disappointment of not being paid was too strong to ignore. He had done the job in good faith, and he had done it to the best of his ability. He had gone above and beyond what he had expected to do. Not that the Tickle brothers would know or understand. Leo was carrying a responsibility that he hadn't asked for and didn't want and he deserved to be paid, one way or the other. Leo was genuinely scared for his life. The atmosphere in his flat was tense. He could sense the anxiety between the three men. They were as nervous as he was but for different reasons. Reasons that Leo neither understood nor cared about.

'If the gun wasn't in the bag, where is it?' Si asked his brother.

'I don't know,' Ged said. 'I told you to throw it in the river, but you gave it back to Barry and he's kept it.' He shrugged. 'He said it would never be found or put back into circulation, but we know he's a liar. He has a thing about weapons. For some reason, he keeps them. We only have his word for it that it was even in that house.'

'He keeps them because they give him a hold over us,' Si said. 'We should have put a bullet in his head a long time ago.'

'You shouldn't be talking like that in front of the troops,' Dom said, shaking his head. 'I'm going to have to pretend I didn't hear that. I don't want Barry Madern on my back.'

'We know you won't say anything, Dom,' Si said. 'Because if you did, I'd have to cut your tongue out.' Dom changed colour and looked uneasy. Simon Tickle took a blade from the pocket of his jeans and flicked a switch. The spring assisted blade opened with a metallic click and Si held it up at eye level, studying the edge. 'I'm going to leave you with something to remind you that you need to keep your mouth shut about what's been said tonight.'

'Stop him, Ged,' Leo said, frightened. 'I've never grassed on anyone, you know that.'

'Leave him alone,' Ged said. 'There's no need for that.'

'I'm going to cut your tongue in half, like a snake,' Si said. 'You can take it as a lesson for the future. It might teach you to be a bit more respectful, but I doubt it.' He took a step towards Leo.

Leo backed up as far as he could and then tripped. Si loomed over him with the knife.

'Go on, do the little baghead,' Dom shouted.

A deafening bang echoed across the room as the front door exploded in a shower of splintered wood. Armed police officers swarmed through the door screaming and shouting orders that Leo didn't have time to comprehend. He was thrown to the floor face down and his arms were pulled painfully behind his back, handcuffs clasp tightly on his wrists. He looked around and his eyes made contact with Ged's for a second. Leo was reassured to see pain and fear in his eyes. He was glad that he wasn't the only one who was scared. One of the policemen picked up the rucksack and looked inside. He held it up to another officer who had stripes on his sleeve.

'The bag is empty and there're two kilo packets of powder on the table.'

'Okay,' the sergeant said. 'Get him out of here.'

Leo was picked up by two officers and pushed unceremoniously towards the door. The Tickle brothers and Dom were held face down on the floor. Dom was crying like a baby, which Leo thought was amusing.

'Why are you taking that little baghead and not us?' Dom shouted.

'Because they can't pick you up, you fat cunt,' Leo said, laughing.

'He's got a point,' one of the policemen said.

'I'm going to kill him,' Dom shouted.

'You're going nowhere,' an officer said. 'He's being moved first because he's a sixteen-year-old kid and technically still a child and you have been exploiting him, so if I was you, I would be getting my story straight because the exploitation of children carries some serious time.'

'That's the biggest load of bullshit,' Si shouted. 'He's expecting four grand for tonight. How exploited is that?'

'Where is the four grand?' the officer asked Leo.

'He's a knobhead,' Leo said, shaking his head. 'Search me. I haven't got four pounds, never mind four grand.'

'Where is the four grand?' the officer asked Si. 'Or are you chatting shit?'

'Fuck you,' Si said. 'You're dead, you little fuck.'

'That's the fourth time he's threatened my life tonight,' Leo said. 'And he's tried to touch my arse. He's a massive paedophile.'

'I'm going to skin him alive,' Si shouted, wrestling against the policemen. One of them put his knee into his back and pinned him down.'

'It's the truth. He's a paedo and so is the big fat one,' Leo said, matter-of-factly. 'He tried to bum me. I want that on the record.'

'He's a dead liar,' Si said.

'Take no notice of him, he's a baghead' Dom said, angrily. 'You're dead, kid.'

The officers exchanged glances and ignored their protests.

'Are you taking him because he's a grass?' Dom asked. 'Snitches get stitches.'

'So do paedos,' Leo replied, grinning. 'You, big nonce.'

'I'm going to kill him,' Dom said, purple with anger.

'You're in enough trouble, so keep your mouth shut,' an officer said.

'He's not a grass,' another officer said. 'He's a kid. And I'll tell you now that he is not the one you need to worry about.'

'What are you talking about?' Si sneered.

'There are more important people being pulled in tonight, who will have a story or two to tell about you, Tickle and you don't have many friends out there.'

'Oh, fuck off,' Si snapped.

'The knives are out for you and your brother and we're going to take great pleasure in banging you away for a long time. That kid will be a grown man by the time you see daylight again.'

'I told you this was bent but you wouldn't listen,' Si shouted at his brother. 'Madern has had us over here, good and proper.'

'I told you we should have walked away months ago,' Ged said. 'When we had the chance, but you had to be the big man.'

'I'm telling you there was something not in that bag. Madern has stashed something. I told you that before you started recruiting retards to go and break into a house which was obviously being watched by the police,' Si shouted.

'Shut up, Si,' Ged said.

'You're a wanker, you always have been, and you always will be. I don't know why I listened to you in the first place.'

'You're always so smart after the event, Si, and I'm sick of hearing you whining like a bitch. You've been running around town for years like you own the place so it's no wonder we've got no friends left.'

Leo could hear the brothers arguing as they held him on the landing. The police were busy and organised, and they had the operation running like clockwork. Fully suited CSI officers we're climbing the stairs before they had even removed the suspects from his flat. That told Leo that the police had been waiting to spring a trap and he had walked straight into it with his eyes open. He had burned his bridges with the Tickle brothers, that was certain. Calling Simon, a paedophile wouldn't be forgotten. Leo felt the old familiar sinking feeling in his guts. It was the feeling he had when anything that could go wrong does go wrong and it was always accompanied by a deep, painful sense of helplessness.

Chapter 30. PVPU. The next day.

*T**ell me no secrets, tell me some lies...*

AFTER AN UNCOMFORTABLE night, Leo was led into a suite of interview rooms, which were identical to some he'd been in before. Being arrested was an occupational hazard, and he had been there several times. He thought one police station was just like another. None of them were a pleasant experience but they were memorable for all the wrong reasons. There were four adults already seated around a table, which was fixed to the floor.

'Sit down, Leo,' Phil Molt said, standing. He was over six-foot-five and towered above everyone. A social worker with presence. Leo liked Phil. He was one of the good ones, who genuinely cared. 'There's a cup of tea with three sugars there.'

'I take five sugars,' Leo said, sarcastically.

'I know, that's why you got three,' Phil said. 'I'm doing your teeth a favour.'

'Thanks Phil,' Leo said, nervously. He sipped the tea and looked at the other adults in the room. 'Am I in the shit?'

'Oh, you're in it up to your neck this time,' Phil said, nodding. He ruffled his hair. 'Has the doctor been to see you?'

'Yes, he's given me something to take the edge off it,' Leo said. 'It helps.'

'Are you clear enough to answer some questions?' Phil asked.

'Yes.' Leo sipped the tea and looked around. 'I know you two are bussies,' he said to the detectives. 'But I don't know her.'

'We have met but for the camera, I'm DI Jane Bennet from the PVPU.'

'And I'm DS Gill Alan, also PVPU.'

'I'm Linda Jones, working for Knowsley social services legal department. May I explain to Leo what is going on?' Linda asked. She had spectacles which covered most of her face and wore red lipstick a few shades too deep. Leo could smell her from across the table. Her perfume was eye wateringly strong.

'Please do,' Jane said, smiling at Leo. 'Is that okay with you, Leo.'

'Knock yourself out,' Leo said, nodding.

'This is an exploratory interview to establish where you're at with regards to capacity to be interviewed by the Matrix team at a later date,' Linda said. 'Do you understand?'

'Yes, I think so,' Leo said, nodding. 'Matrix are the big boys, aren't they?' Phil nodded. 'They chase all the OCGs and get nowhere.'

'I wouldn't underestimate Matrix, Leo,' Phil said. 'You haven't come across them before because of your age but that doesn't mean they're not aware of your role in Barry Madern's operation.'

'Your social worker is right. We're PVPU, Leo and we're talking to you about child exploitation by the Madern OCG,' Jane said. 'Matrix are running several investigations into the OCG, including conspiracy to supply class-A drugs, which is what they want to talk to you about.'

'Conspiracy to supply?' Leo repeated. 'I'm just a muppet.'

'Yes, conspiracy,' Jane said, nodding. 'Two kilos of class-A drugs are a significant haul, and they were in your possession, in your flat.'

'Yes, but they're not mine, obviously,' Leo said, frustrated. 'I'm just the mug they sent to pick them up.'

'The definition of a conspiracy is the planning with other people, to do something bad or illegal,' Jane said, shrugging. 'Breaking into

Angela Deacon's house to recover drugs took planning by a number of people, including you.'

'That's heavy. I'm just a muppet to them. If I get done for this, Abi will go mental.' Leo saw a flash in Phil's eyes. It was a reaction of some kind, but he couldn't say what it was or what it meant. 'Seriously, I'm trying to get out of this game. I love Abi and she loves me, but her mum hates my guts as it is. If I get charged, she'll hate me even more. This isn't going to help one little bit. What are they going to say when they find out?'

'Let's focus on you, Leo. Abi and her mum are not why we're here. You don't need to worry about them at the moment. Let's worry about you for now,' Phil said.

'I get that but do Matrix think I'm actually part of Barry's crew?' Leo asked. 'That couldn't be further from the truth.'

'Listen to what the detectives have to say and answer their questions honestly,' Phil said.

'Yes, but if they think I'm part of the conspiracy, what are they going to charge me with?' Leo asked. 'That's way over the top!'

'Calm down and listen to them,' Phil said.

'Do you think I'm part of their crew?' Leo asked, panicking. 'Because I'm not anything to them but a joke. They pick on me and make me do stupid shit for a few quid and a bit of ket.'

'That's what we're here to establish,' Jane said. 'I don't want you to panic. We need to establish the facts as you see them, okay?'

'Okay,' Leo said. 'But I'm not part of their crew. I'm just a kid they take the piss out of.'

'Okay, Leo,' Jane said. 'Have a drink of your tea and we'll get going, shall we?'

'Okay.'

'Why don't we start at the beginning and see where we end up, shall we?'

'Sounds like a plan,' Leo said. He looked at Phil and he nodded, sagely. Phil had a way of talking to him on his level. He never talked down to him or treated him as if he was retarded. 'What do you want to know?'

'Who came to you and asked you to be involved in recovering the drugs from Angela Deacons house?'

'One of Barry's crew told me about it.'

'Who was it and what did he say, exactly?'

'You're asking me to name names?' Leo asked, shaking his head.

'We need specifics, Leo,' Jane said. 'This isn't the time to be heroic. If you don't help us, we can't help you.'

'If they think I'm a grass, I'm dead.' Leo folded his arms. 'You know how this works. No one names them or they get burnt.'

'If you don't tell us what you know, Matrix will take it you're protecting them because you're a key part of the organisation,' Jane explained.

'I'm protecting me not them,' Leo said. 'They will know who said what and when they said it. They always do.'

'Nothing you say here will be used by Matrix,' Jane said. 'I told you; this is an exploratory interview. This is your chance to be honest with us.'

'You need to tell them what you know,' Phil said. 'If you don't, you'll be thrown into the adult investigation, and they will chew you up and spit you out.'

'Okay. It was Ged Tickle,' Leo said. He felt his stomach cramping and needed the toilet. 'If I tell you what happened, will you tell them that I told you because if they think I'm a grass, they'll hurt me again.'

'What you say to us will stay with us but what you say to the Matrix team could be used in any case against them. It's best to get it off your chest today,' Jane said. 'The more honest you are here, the better it looks for you.'

'Can you guarantee anonymity for Leo?' Linda asked.

'In a conspiracy to supply investigation?' Jane said. 'Not a chance. What I'm saying is, if we can establish the facts and the facts are that Leo is a pawn in the game, it's better for him'

'But if he names the people who forced him to do this?'

'At this stage, yes, we can keep his name out of the more serious investigation,' Jane said. 'We need to establish the facts as Leo sees them, then we can liaise with Matrix.'

'I need the toilet,' Leo said, standing up. His hands were shaking. 'I need to go, right now.'

'Oh really?' Gill asked, sighing.

'When I have to go, I have to go,' Leo said, shaking his head. 'Right now.'

'I'll walk him out,' Phil said, standing. 'Come on, mate. Have you got cramps?'

'Really bad,' Leo said.

Phil opened the door, and a uniformed officer greeted them.

'He needs the loo,' Phil said. 'Urgently.'

The officer took Leo down the corridor and ten minutes later, he returned, and he looked better. There was more colour in his cheeks. Phil waited for the uniformed officer to walk away before speaking.

'Are you feeling better?'

'Yes, mate,' Leo said.

'Do you need to see the doctor?'

'No. I'm okay for now.'

'Be careful what you say in there,' Phil said. 'Either tell the truth or say nothing at all but don't lie or exaggerate. Matrix will pull you up on it, and if they think they can nail you to Madern, they will, okay?'

'Okay, Phil,' Leo said. 'I'm sick of being their Joey. They just use me; they're not my friends and I'm here trying to keep my head above water and for what?'

'You're one hundred percent right. Just remember that when you're answering their questions.' Leo nodded. 'Remember that you're the most important thing in all this,' Phil said. 'You're the victim here but you need to put that on the record with names to back it up or it's not going to cut it with Matrix.'

'Okay,' Leo said. Phil guided him back into the room and they sat down. 'Thank you for the break. I feel better now.'

'That's good,' Jane said, smiling, although she looked agitated. 'We'll crack on, shall we?'

'Yes. Let's get on with it. I'm much better. The ket gives me the wild shites sometimes.'

'I realise that. No problem, back to the questions,' Jane said, changing the subject. 'You said Ged Tickle approached you.'

'Yes,' Leo said.

'And he works for Barry Madern?' Jane said.

'Is that a serious question?' Leo asked, shaking his head. 'You know he does.'

'What we know isn't the point,' Jane said, shrugging. Her expression was stern. 'We need to establish what you know.'

'Okay, okay,' Leo said. 'Ged Tickle told me, and he works for Barry Madern.'

'Great,' Jane said. 'Tell me how he approached you?'

'He came to my flat,' Leo said. 'Knocked on the door when I was sleeping off some ket.'

'Was it arranged?'

'What do you mean?'

'Did you know he was coming?'

'No. He just turned up. I was half asleep,' Leo said.

'Was he alone?'

'No.'

'Where you alone?'

'Yes, Abi was at her mums,' Leo said, nodding. The memory of her leaving squeezed his insides.

'Abi is your girlfriend?' Jane asked.

'We live together,' Leo said. 'We're going to have a baby. Imagine me being a dad!'

'Who was with Ged Tickle?' Jane said, ignoring the point. 'Did you know him?'

'A guy called Les,' Leo said. Leo thought it was odd that no one acknowledged that he was going to be a father. 'He lives across the road.'

'Les Smith?' Jane asked.

'I don't know,' Leo said, shaking his head. 'He's a smackhead and burgles people but I don't know his surname.'

'We'll assume it's Les Smith,' Jane said.

'Surely you know his surname. Didn't you arrest him?' Leo asked.

'He wasn't arrested,' Jane said, avoiding eye contact.

'Did he get away?' Leo said, sitting forward. 'Ha, ha! How did that dopey fucker get away?'

'A man was found dead at the scene,' Jane said, looking up. 'We're assuming he overdosed until the autopsy results are back. We think it is Les Smith.'

'Get fucked,' Leo said, shocked. 'Les died in that house?'

'Yes.'

'He's been a smackhead for centuries,' Leo said, astounded. 'He knows what he's doing with drugs.'

'What are you saying?' Jane asked.

'I'm saying, there's no way a smackhead like Les has overdosed,' Leo said, shaking his head. 'Not a chance.' No one replied but all eyes were on Leo. 'If he's dead after a fix, he's been spiked.'

'What do you mean?'

'Someone has given him a hotshot.'

'Can you clarify what you mean by hotshot, please?' Jane said.

'You know what it means,' Leo said, backtracking. He folded his arms again.

'I do but people reviewing this interview might not,' Jane said. 'Clarify it for us.'

'A hotshot is what they give to an addict who they want rid of,' Leo said, blushing. 'It has a little something extra in there to fuck them up.'

'Fuck them up?' Jane said, coyly.

'Send them across the line,' Leo said. No one replied again. He looked at Phil and he nodded. 'They put gear in there to kill them, make them overdose, fuck them up, whatever you want to call it.'

'Are you saying that you think Les Smith was murdered?' Jane asked.

'I definitely didn't hear Leo saying anything of the kind,' Phil said. 'Don't comment on anything outside of what happened in your flat. Les Smith is nothing to do with Leo and what he thinks is pure speculation anyway.'

'And I think it's best if we let Leo answer the questions, rather than you,' Jane said, eyeing Phil, angrily.

'As long as the questions are fair and relevant,' Phil said, nodding. 'I don't have a problem but if you're fishing, I do.'

'I have to agree with Phillip,' Linda said, taking of her glasses. 'The question about Les Smith and how he died is out of bounds.'

'Fine,' Jane said, grimacing. 'Okay, Leo. We've established Ged Tickle and a man we think is Les Smith, came to your flat and what happened?'

'Ged told me that they were planning to break into Angela's place and that they needed me to collect a package from the back garden,' Leo said. 'Les is a burglar, so he was going to break in and then drop the bag from the window.'

'Did he ask you to do it, or did he tell you?' Jane asked.

'They never ask. There's no, please or thank you,' Leo said. 'They tell me what to do. I don't have a choice.'

'What would happen if you said no?' Jane asked. Leo looked at Phil and Phil nodded.

'I would get a good hiding. I've been burned with lighters and cigarettes, shot with an air rifle, stabbed with a compass, battered black and blue and hung upside down from a block of flats,' Leo said. 'The list goes on forever. They always slap me around if things don't go to plan, even if it's not my fault.'

'So, you're saying you have been beaten up by these men many times before?' Jane asked.

'Often. All of us runners are abused,' Leo said. 'They're bullies and they give us money and drugs sometimes but never enough to walk away. They beat the shit out of everyone who works for them. It's how they operate.'

'Okay, to be clear. They told you that you had to recover a package from Angela's back garden?' Jane asked. 'What were their instructions?'

'Yes. I had to be under the window next to the downpipe at exactly midnight, catch the rucksack and bring it home to my flat.' Leo shrugged. 'There was to be no conversation and no deviation from the route home and no stopping.'

'And you did that exactly as they told you to?'

'Yes. Exactly as Ged had said.'

'Did you know what was in the rucksack?' Jane asked, looking into his eyes for a lie.

'No.' Leo lied. 'I didn't ask. I asked once and got a broken nose as the answer.'

'Did you have any idea what was in it?' Gill asked, frowning.

'I know you think I'm stupid but I'm not an idiot,' Leo said. 'I worked for Barry's father, George Madern when I was twelve. He had a shop on the Bluebell, and he gave me a bike and a paper round. He would give me deliveries to make, and I knew they weren't all mint imperials. They're drug dealers. I didn't ask what was in the bag, but I didn't think it was cheese.'

'Okay,' Jane said, smiling thinly. 'You were coerced into recovering a rucksack, contents unknown and then you took it back to your flat and then what happened?'

'I wasn't home long, and I got a text message,' Leo said. 'It asked me if I had the bag. I said yes and they said someone would come to pick up the bag.'

'Do you have the messages on your phone?' Jane asked.

'Nope,' Leo said, shaking his head. He sat forward and lowered his voice as if someone may be listening. 'They just deleted themselves a few minutes later.'

'That were sent from an encrypted phone,' Jane said, nodding. 'We know Barry Madern and his crew use them. What happened then?'

'The Tickle brothers knocked on my door with a big guy called Dom,' Leo said. 'They were there a few minutes, asking me questions and bullying me. They were really shady with me, but then the police broke my door in, and here I am.'

'The police report indicates that Simon Tickle was threatening you with a knife?' Gill asked, checking the notes.

'Yes. He's a knobhead,' Leo said. 'He was trying to touch my arse. He's a massive paedophile and so is the fat one, Dom.'

'They sexually assaulted you?' Jane asked, shocked.

Phil looked surprised and folded his arms. He stared at Leo. Leo glanced at him and looked away.

'They tried but I pushed them off,' Leo lied. 'I told him to fuck off out of my flat, so he said he was going to cut my tongue out to teach me a lesson.'

'Did he actually say that?' Gill asked, shaking her head. She looked shocked.

'Yes.'

'I think it's clear that Leo has no part in the wider conspiracy,' Linda interrupted. 'He's a child being exploited in more ways than one.'

'I agree, Linda. For the record, why did you tell him to fuck off?' Jane asked.

'He was bullying me and trying it on, paedo. He always bullies me. He threatened to kill me four times,' Leo said. He flushed red, uncomfortable with this part of the story. 'He kept on asking me if I had taken any of the drugs for myself and I repeatedly said no but he wouldn't give up accusing me.'

'To be clear, he was accusing you of skimming some of the drugs that you had recovered, so you told him to fuck off and he took out a knife and threatened to cut out your tongue?' Jane summarised.

'No.'

'No?'

'He said he was going to split my tongue like a snake,' Leo said.

'Okay, Simon Tickle tried to assault you and said that he was going to slice your tongue like a snake?'

Leo nodded. 'Say it for the recording, please.'

'In a nutshell, yes, that's what happened,' Leo said. 'Then the police arrived, and I was saved by the bell, so to speak.'

'Okay,' Jane said. 'It was noted by the officers in the room that when child exploitation was mentioned, Simon Tickle told them that he wasn't exploiting you, and that you were being paid a sum of four-thousand pounds for your part in the recovery plan.'

'Is that what he said?' Leo chuckled. 'I wish they had paid me something,' Leo said, snorting. He blushed again, not comfortable with the lie. 'I haven't got any money on me or in my flat. I never have any money.' He nudged Phil. 'Phil will tell you.'

'He never has any money,' Phil agreed.

'You've given me money for the chippy before now, haven't you, Phil,' Leo added. 'When I was starving and coming down. I get a craving for chippy food, really bad. It sorts me out but it's so expensive nowadays. The last time me and Abi had a chippy, it was seventeen quid. Phil had given me a twenty, so we got some pop as well.'

'That's very kind of Phil,' Jane said, nodding at the social worker. 'Above and beyond the call of duty.'

'He's a good egg,' Leo said. 'Helps me out a lot. He always texts back, not like some social workers I could name who don't really give a fuck. Phil is like a big brother, looking after me when I fuck up.'

'That's great to hear. So, back to the point,' Jane said, glancing at Phil. 'Was there ever a discussion about being paid any money to recover the rucksack from Angela Deacon's house?'

'Never,' Leo lied. 'Ged never said anything about any money. They never mention money.'

'Could anyone else have mentioned giving you money?' Gill asked.

'I didn't speak to anyone else about it,' Leo said. 'It was Ged and Les in my flat beforehand. That's it.'

'What about afterwards?' Gill pressed.

'I told you,' Leo said, tiring. He yawned. 'No one mentioned money.'

'Leo is getting tired now,' Phil said. 'I think we need to be wrapping this up.'

'I think I'll decide when we're done asking questions,' Jane said, frowning. She glared at Phil.

'I'll decide if he's fit to answer them or not. He has a short attention span,' Phil said. 'And physically, he tires quickly, which affects his capacity to think straight.'

'Does it?' Jane said, shaking her head.

'It's a side effect of his addiction.' Phil locked eyes with her, not backing down. 'Leo's health and wellbeing is my responsibility.'

'Point taken. This is very important, so I want to clarify the point,' Jane said. 'As far as you were concerned, there was no financial reward for doing the job?'

'No. Absolutely not.'

'Okay,' Jane said. 'I think we get the gist of what happened. There's nothing new or sinister in what we've heard from you, but the Tickle brothers may have a completely different take on events. It will be everyman for himself once people get locked up. Deals will be made and some of them will give evidence against others to have the chance of a lighter sentence from a judge. Some of them will tell lies to make sure their enemies get longer inside, like the accusation that you were being paid for your role in the operation.' Jane stood up. 'Tell the truth, Leo and everything will be okay. Don't try to be clever and don't deviate from what you've said today.'

'Okay,' Leo said, nodding. 'Are you letting me out?'

'Yes.'

'Can I go home?'

'I can't see why not. We'll leave it to your social workers to work out where you will be going,' Jane said. 'Once we know where, we'll release you on a tag but if you break your curfew, you'll be locked up, understand?'

'Yes,' Leo said. 'I'm not going anywhere.'

'Good. Thank you everyone, we'll get him processed and you can take him out of here.'

Chapter 31. Marion.

B*ut I was wrong, I will cry, I will love you 'til the day I die...*

MARION AND HER SISTER were standing, holding each other. Their tears were flowing and the terrible sound of a mother howling her grief, echoed through the hospital.

'No, no, no, no... please god no!' Marion cried, over and over again.

Abi was gone. The doctors had tried to save her, but she had been without oxygen to her brain for too long. There was nothing that could be done to bring her back from where she had gone to. A nurse brought the sisters some water and tissues and then backed out of the room and closed the door. There were no words of comfort to be found. A mother had lost her child and grandchild in one terrible act and there would be no consoling her. The grief was suffocating, and the guilt was crushing her from the inside. She felt like her heart was being ripped out.

Marion held her sister and tried to breathe but her chest was constricted. Abi was gone and with her, all her hopes and dreams for her had gone too. She had nurtured her daughter from the cradle and now she would see her to her grave. It was an abomination, something that should never happen to a mother. For the few hours she had spent, knowing she was going to be a grandmother, she hadn't taken the opportunity to tell Abi that she was proud of her, that she would stand by her and help her become a mother, no matter how young she was. She had been angry, and bitter and disappointed and Abi had committed suicide because she saw death as the better option to life with her angry mother. Marion collapsed into a ball on the floor and screamed until she thought she would choke.

Liz tried to comfort her, but it was impossible, she simply did not know what to do. Her husband Mitch knocked gently and poked his head around the door.

'Not now, Mitch,' Liz whispered.

'You need to know there are detectives here and they want to speak to Marion,' he said.

'What do they want?' Liz hissed. 'Her daughter has died!'

'I've told them that, but they said other people's children have died too,' Mitch said, shrugging. 'They're going to wait.'

Chapter 32. Phil/ Leo.

How can I just let you walk away, just let you leave without a trace, when I stand here taking every breath, with you?

LEO WAS PROCESSED AND it was deemed he was the victim of child exploitation, rather than a key player in the Madern OCG. Phil Molt was with him in the custody suite when he retrieved his belongings. Leo went straight for his phone and checked to see if he had any messages.

'Abi still hasn't replied,' Leo said to Phil. Phil shrugged and ruffled his hair. 'I reckon her mum has taken her phone or she's dropped it down the toilet and it's broken.'

'Let's get you out of here,' Phil said, ignoring the issue.

'What do you think?' Leo asked.

'I think if she could message you, she would,' Phil said.

They walked to the release exit and a uniformed officer let them out.

'I can't believe they're letting me out,' Leo said, smiling. 'They believed me for a change.'

They walked to the car and Phil opened the doors.

'Did Simon Tickle really try to assault you?' Phil asked.

'No,' Leo said, blushing. 'I just wanted people to think he's a paedophile.'

'You might see him again one day,' Phil said. 'You need to be careful how many bridges your burn. Life has a way of creeping up on you when you least expect it.'

'I hate him,' Leo said. 'I hate them all.'

'Get in the car, trouble,' Phil said. Leo climbed into the front seat and fastened his belt.

'Where are we going?' Leo asked. He looked at Phil and Phil looked away. He seemed distracted.

'We need to go to the office and have a chat with my boss, Jo,' Phil said.

'Oh no,' Leo said, shaking his head. 'I like Jo but she's so bossy. She always gives me a bollocking when she sees me.'

'That's our Jo Lilly,' Phil said. 'She tells it how it is and if she gives you a bollocking, it's because you deserve one.'

'Great,' Leo said. 'I'm knackered.'

'Get your head down while we drive,' Phil said. 'A power nap will do you good.'

Leo closed his eyes and sleep took him quickly.

Chapter 33. Jo.

I see your mouth moving, but there's a circus coming out, always busy proving what the world is all about...

JO WAS SITTING AT HER desk, trying to catch up. The Deacon children had given samples of DNA to be tested against their older sibling, Tom. It was the best way to see if they were related to Barry Madern without asking him for a sample. The furthest they could keep him from proceedings, the better. If the children were full siblings, she would have her answer. It would take a few weeks for the results to come back but the judge had given temporary PR to the service, which was the best start. Madern had failed to get the paperwork to court on time and judges don't delay for anyone, no matter how much they're paying their solicitor. The job of finding them a forever home could begin.

'Can I have a word with you, Jo?' Becca Lewis asked, approaching the desk. Becca was the youngest social worker in the assessment team. She had worked her placement in Knowsley during her degree and then applied for a position in the assessment teams as an ASYE. 'I know you've been busy with the Deacon case. I heard that the mother died, how terribly sad.'

'It is,' Jo said, patting the seat next to her. 'I haven't seen you all week. Sit down and tell me what's up?'

'I wanted to check with you about unborn Ahmed,' Becca said.

'What's the problem?'

'She's twelve weeks in and I'm not sure this mum has capacity to understand what we're asking her.'

'Tell me what makes you think that?' Jo said.

'We've just had a meeting and she's completely withdrawn,' Becca said. 'She put her fingers in her ears and closed her eyes and sang Whitney songs for the entire meeting.'

'That's not a good sign,' Jo said. 'Whitney is very yesterday.' She smiled. 'Seriously, if she's not got the capacity to engage in meetings, she's not going to cope with a newborn.' Jo opened the case on her screen. 'What is dad's capacity?' Jo asked.

'He's keen and wants to engage but I don't see either of them coping with a newborn baby without a lot of support.'

'Mum had her first child removed right?' Jo asked.

'Yes. That was two years ago. There was risk of significant harm,' Becca said. 'She's with paternal grandmother and they have supervised contact, but she can't take another baby. She's in her sixties.'

'Have we explored all other family members?' Jo asked.

'There's one maternal aunt who hasn't replied yet, but otherwise, yes,' Becca said. 'Dad has no family to speak of, so there's no support from that direction.'

'Let's get a cognitive assessment on mum and dad. Have you sent me the C and F report?'

'It should be in your tray,' Becca said.

'Have you included the EDD?'

'Yes.'

'We need to assume the aunt isn't going to be an option,' Jo said. 'You said mum and dad are definitely not communicating with each other?'

'No. There was DV in the relationship through lockdown,' Becca said. 'They barely look at each other in meetings.'

'Makes me wonder how they got pregnant twelve weeks ago unless it was the immaculate conception,' Jo said. Her phone rang and she checked the screen. It was a switchboard. 'I need to take this. Double check the C and F and let me see it when it's done. We need a Head of Service case discussion on this with Hayley. We need to find a way for this mum to keep her baby.'

'Absolutely. Okay, thanks,' Becca said, standing up.

'Hello, Jo speaking,' she answered.

'Jo, it's Jane Bennet.'

'Hello Jane. I was hoping you would call. How did it go with Leo Tomkins?'

'It's CE all day long,' Jane said. 'We've released him on tag, and I'll discuss it with Matrix. They will still want to talk to him but I'm trying to deflect them. The Madern case is red hot at the moment. He's enemy number one and they want people from within the OCG giving evidence against him. I'm assuming Leo doesn't know about Abi Barker yet?'

'Phil is bringing him in so we can sit him down and tell him,' Jo said. 'That is not a conversation that I'm looking forward to.'

'There's another twist in this tale,' Jane said. 'Are you sitting down?'

'I am as it happens,' Jo said.

'Marion Barker has been arrested at the hospital,' Jane said.

'Are you joking?' Jo said, shocked. 'What for?'

'There's a contaminated batch of cocaine in the city and four people have died so far,' Jane said. 'Apparently, anyone with a severe nut allergy is in big trouble if they inhale it.'

'Wow, that's not something your local dealer is going to ask before he sells you some Charlie, any allergies at all?' Jo said. 'What has it got to do with Marion Barker?'

'She has a cleaning company in the Woolton area and two of her clients died after inhaling a wrap of cocaine in their home gymnasium,' Jane explained.

'What on Earth is going on, they have a gymnasium in their home?' Jo asked. 'And they took cocaine there?'

'Yes. David died in the house and Rebecca Goodstone died in hospital forty minutes later. They had problems with cocaine use and the father was obsessed with keeping them away from it. Anyway, he was convinced the drugs had been brought into the house and called the police. They weren't expecting to stumble across anything to be honest, until the security guard told a detective that he had taken an unusual call from Marion Barker at the security gate, trying to get back into house. He said she was behaving oddly.'

'They have a security guard?' Jo said, listening intently.

'It's a big house and they've had problems with theft from the grounds.'

'Sounds like he's a switched on guard,' Jo said.

'He's an ex-copper from Coppice Hill and he said that Marion had expressed concerns about the cleaning cupboards being locked in the swimming pool area and he thought it was a bit odd to be bothered about that, considering what had happened, so he told the detective on the scene,' Jane explained. 'The dogs were brought in, and they found a container in a cleaning cupboard with a few thousand pounds worth of cocaine in it.'

'That is shocking. The poor man lost his children because of a few wraps of cocaine,' Jo said. 'And they connected it to Marion straight away?'

'They spoke to her at the hospital, and she coughed to it immediately. She was distraught and held up her hands,' Jane said. 'She was never going to get away with it. Her prints are on the container. Apparently, she sold drugs to David Goodstone every month. There's a money trail.'

'Well, it's not often that I'm lost for words but I'm speechless,' Jo said.

'No one would have found out but for the contaminated batch.'

'You said other people have died as well?' Jo asked.

'Four so far and a number of seriously ill in hospital. We're expecting that number to rise,' Jane said.

'How does cocaine get contaminated like that?' Jo said. 'It must have been cut with something toxic.'

'It will all come out in the wash,' Jane said. 'Will you tell Leo about Marion?'

'I don't think he needs to know that right now,' Jo said, shaking her head. 'It's too much to process in one sitting. Telling him about Abi is going to be hard enough.' Jo spotted Phil walking up the stairs with Leo. 'Speak of the devil,' Jo said. 'He's here now. I'll talk to you soon.'

'Okay, bye.'

Jo stood up and waved to Phil. She pointed to a meeting room near the stairs. He nodded and took Leo into it. Jo got three tins of orange from the machine and walked across the office. There were only a handful of people in, but it would be bedlam in a few hours. She went into the meeting room and closed the door.

'Good morning, young man,' Jo said. 'Hello Phil. I bet it's been a long night for you, Leo?'

'Hello Jo,' Leo said, looking sheepish. 'I've got myself in trouble again. Big trouble this time.'

'Oh, yes. You can say that again,' Jo said, hand on hips. 'You've excelled yourself.'

'I can't help myself, can I?' Leo said.

'You try and try and then slip up. Why change the habits of a lifetime, eh?' Jo said, smiling. 'What are we going to do with you?'

'Throw me in the bin,' Leo said. 'I'm rubbish at everything.'

'We don't throw people in the bin here,' Jo said. 'It's our job to make sure you don't end up in the bin, Leo. We've done a pretty good job of it so far, considering your addiction.' She handed him a drink. Leo opened it and sipped from it.

'I need help getting off the ket,' Leo said.

'Then we'll look at doing that and see what's available. How did your interview with PVPU go?'

'Okay, I think,' Leo said, shrugging. 'They know I was made to do it.'

'Okay,' Jo said. 'They think Matrix will want to speak to you, but we'd expect that. Just tell them what you told PVPU, and you'll be fine.'

'Abi will go mad when she finds out Matrix want to talk to me. She knows they're the big boys,' Leo said, nodding. 'Her mum already hates me. This will give her something else to moan about.'

'We need to talk to you about Abi,' Jo said.

'Why, what's she said?' Leo asked, sitting up at the mention of her name.

'She hasn't said anything. What I'm going to tell you now is very bad news,' Jo said. 'I want you to stay calm and we'll discuss it together, okay?'

'Oh no,' Leo said, turning to Phil. 'Has she finished with me?'

'Abi committed suicide yesterday,' Jo said, softly.

'Fucking hell,' Leo said. 'Is she going to be okay, will she lose the baby?'

'She's dead, Leo,' Jo said. 'She committed suicide and was taken to hospital, but they couldn't revive her.'

'Fuck off,' Leo said, shaking his head. 'This is a wind up.' He looked at Phil. 'Tell me this is a wind up, Phil.'

'It's true, Leo,' Phil said. 'Abi is dead, mate.'

Leo looked from one to the other and his eyes filled up. His mouth opened but no words came out. Jo could see the anguish in his eyes and her heart went out to him. The colour drained from his face.

'Take as long as you need to process what's happened,' Phil said. 'If you have any questions, just ask and we can talk about it.'

'Where is she?' Leo asked, sobbing now. 'I want to see her.'

'That won't be possible,' Jo said. 'She'll be looked after, Leo but you're not family. They won't let anyone see her but her mother.'

'I am her family,' Leo snapped. 'She was having my baby!' He broke down and banged his head on the table. 'Why has she killed herself?' He asked no one in particular. He banged his head again and Phil pulled him away from the table. Blood ran from a cut on his forehead. 'Why has she killed herself, Phil?'

'I don't know, mate,' Phil said. 'No one ever knows the real reasons.'

'I don't understand,' Leo said. 'Why has she left me here like this?'

'We may never know exactly why, Leo,' Jo said. 'Sometimes it's an accumulation of things. Not one reason.'

'It's because of me,' Leo sniffled. He nodded and wiped the blood from his face with his sleeve. 'It's because she was pregnant with my baby, and she didn't want to be with me anymore. No one I love stays around. They all fuck off and leave me.'

'I know it must feel like that,' Jo said. 'But what someone else does is beyond your control, Leo. Abi was just overwhelmed by her situation and people don't think straight when they're stressed.'

'Stressed,' Leo repeated. 'Her mother is to blame for this. She stressed Abi out all the time. I bet she blames me for this, the horrible cow. I hate her and she hates me, and Abi was stuck in the middle.'

'No one is to blame,' Jo said. 'Especially not you, Leo. You are going to experience a whole raft of emotions, guilt, rage, loss and they're all perfectly natural but you'll get through this. We'll be with you.'

'Why has she killed herself?' Leo shouted. He threw his tin across the room, and it bounced against the window, spraying orange down the wall. He jumped up onto the table and jumped down on the other side. Jo tried to stop him, but he had opened the door and bolted before she could reach him. Phil tried to follow him, but he was down the stairs and out of the building in a flash.

Chapter 34. PVPU.

*I*t was not your fault but mine...

DI LAURA LUNT WAS WALKING through the station when she spotted Jane Bennet sitting at a desk. She made a beeline for her and grabbed an empty chair, plonking it next to her.

'Hey, I need a word with you,' Laura said sitting down. Smoothing her faded jeans. 'I'm glad I've found you. We need to have a little chat about Leo Tompkins.'

'We released him on tag this morning,' Jane said. 'It's CE all day long. He's been bullied into picking up the rucksack from the Deacon house. Ged Tickle went to his flat with Les Smith and coerced him into doing it. He wasn't asked to do it; he was told to do it.'

'That is the biggest load of namby-pamby bullshit, I've heard this week,' Laura said, shaking her head. Her black hair was short at the sides and spiked on the top. Her eyes were dark and intense.

'I beg your pardon,' Jane said, shocked. 'I don't talk bullshit, thank you very much.'

'I said, namby-pamby bullshit and that's even worse,' Laura said, shaking her head. 'Leo Tompkins is involved in this, and he's pulled the wool over your eyes good and proper.'

'He has not pulled the wool over my eyes,' Jane argued.

'How can you be so soft on this little villain?' Laura asked. 'It's absolutely obvious that he's lying to you.'

'I disagree with you,' Jane said, frowning. 'We interviewed him and spoke with his social workers, and we all know what we're doing, thank you!'

'His social workers think the sun shines out of his backside because he's had a hard time growing up,' Laura said. 'Plenty of people have a hard upbringing but they don't all run with the Madern OCG. I'm telling you right now that kid is a bad apple and he's taking orders from the top.'

'What on Earth are you talking about?' Jane asked, shaking her head. 'You can't know that.'

'What was in the wall, Jane?' Laura asked. She sat back and waited for an answer.

'What?'

'You heard me,' Laura said. 'What was in the wall?'

'I'm not sure I know what you're talking about,' Jane said, confused.

'The floorboards were lifted, and the drugs were removed, and a hole was knocked in the wall,' Laura said. 'A hole no bigger than my fist, which tells me something was removed from it.' Jane blushed. 'So, what was in the wall, Jane?'

'I don't know.'

'No. You don't know but I'm betting Leo Tomkins does,' Laura said, lowering her voice. 'Les Smith removed something from that wall and he's dead. He was a habitual heroin addict and he overdosed on a job to recover something from that house, which has disappeared now.' Laura let it sink in. 'Don't you find it odd that a heroin addict, who has been injecting for donkey's years suddenly overdoses when he's doing a job for an OCG?'

'I'm not sure where you're going with this,' Jane said. 'Are you saying Les Smith was murdered?'

'Oh, come on, Jane,' Laura said. 'Wake up and smell the coffee. Leo Tompkins collected the rucksack from the Deacon house. We recovered the drugs and the rucksack from his flat but there was nothing else in it. What was in the wall and where is it?'

'I don't know.'

'You don't know because you didn't ask him the question. You lot have gone soft in here,' Laura said. 'You listened to him telling you how he's been bullied into this and let him go without putting the vital question to him. What was in the wall and where is it?'

'What exactly do you think he's done?' Jane asked, blushing again.

'I think he was given instructions by someone at the top of the tree and told to remove something from the bag,' Laura said.

'Why from the top of the tree?' Jane asked.

'Because the Tickle brothers were there,' Laura said. 'Leo Tompkins is the only one who could have taken anything out of the bag without anyone else seeing him do it. He was the only person apart from Les Smith, who had the opportunity to be alone with the bag.'

'What about the Tickle brothers?' Jane asked. 'They were at the flat and had access to the bag.'

'The Tickle brothers were searched at the scene and had nothing on them and they're saying nothing to anyone.' Laura lowered her voice again. 'I think Leo Tompkins has whatever was in the wall and, whatever it is, it's important enough to kill for.'

'I'm not convinced,' Jane said, shaking her head. 'Leo is a good kid, he's just mixed up. He does as he's told and nothing more.'

'I'm not saying he's a criminal mastermind, but he is capable of removing something from a rucksack and hiding it,' Laura said. 'I'm telling you that Les Smith was smoked because he knew what he put into that bag.'

'Which means Leo is the only person who knows where it is now?' Jane asked.

'Exactly.'

'Then he's in grave danger,' Jane said.

'Absolutely, he is,' Laura said. 'Where is he?'

'With social services,' Jane said.

'You need to go and get him and bring him in but this time, we'll be interviewing him,' Laura said, nodding. 'He knows exactly what he's doing and he's laughing at you. He won't get off the hook so lightly this time.'

Chapter 35. Leo.

T*ake me home, country roads, to a place, I belong...*

LEO RAN AND KEPT RUNNING until he couldn't run anymore. Nothing made any sense. Abi was in a hospital in the city centre, but he wasn't sure which one. She would be lying on a slab, cold and alone and he wanted to be next to her. He didn't know where he was running to. He had to get away from everyone. The police and social services and the Tickle brothers and their muppets could all fuck off. He just wanted to go home to get some money for bus fare into town. Maybe he could see Abi if he could find her.

Jo Lilly said they wouldn't let him see Abi, but he would find her and sneak in, even it was only for a minute. He wanted to see her even if she was dead.

His Abi, his little starling was gone.

His head was spinning, and he felt numb. Numb like he had felt when they told him his mum was dead all those years ago. There was nothing like that feeling of complete loss. It was the worst pain he had felt, and it was here again. The emptiness was devastating. He felt like his heart was being ripped out of his chest and crushed.

There was nothing he could do, nowhere he could go, no one he could talk to that would help with the debilitating grief. Nothing could stop the intense pain he was suffering. He thought about throwing himself from a motorway bridge, because he could hear the traffic in the distance. The sound of lorries thundering by drifted to him. They weren't far away. He looked around to try and work out where he was. There were fields and woods, no houses, nothing but grass until the far distance. On the horizon, he could see the water tower at Speke. He got his bearings.

Leo realised he had run from Huyton Village, along Wilson Road, through the industrial estate, over Tarbock Island and onto the farmland, which led to Tarbock Green, a green belt between Netherley and Hough Green. He used to go there when he was still at school, bunking off with his mates from the home. They would roam the fields and farm tracks for hours on end, enjoying the space and peace of the woodlands. There were ponds and streams to throw stones in and splash around. They built a raft from discarded pallets and an oil drum, but it was a death trap and sank on her maiden voyage. Jackie Ellis lost her shoes in the mud and had to walk home in her bare feet. Once they had stolen a tractor and driven it across the fields until they reached Tarbock Road, where they left it behind a hedge and walked home. He was expecting the police to come to the home for weeks, but no one ever did. Those days seemed so far away now.

He was heading in the wrong direction, so he turned around and began walking towards his flat. It was a half an hour walk, probably. There was a burning sensation in his guts, not from withdrawal but from grief.

Abi and his baby were dead.

She was the only good thing in his life, and she was gone. If she had told him she wanted to die, he would have gone with her, and they could be together. But she had gone alone and left him behind. He wondered if she just wanted to be away from him forever. There were so many questions and no answers. He hadn't asked any questions and now he wished he had. The shock had overwhelmed him, and he couldn't sit and listen to them any longer. He wanted to know how she died. What did she do?

He didn't know why it mattered but it did. It mattered lots. Abi was squeamish and frightened easily. She couldn't even watch a scary movie. She didn't like blood so she wouldn't have slashed her wrists, he could eliminate that one. Maybe she took pills. Marion had a cabinet full of pills. She could have taken a bottle of vodka to her room and swallowed the lot. That would be the easiest and most painless way to die, Leo thought.

He hoped she hadn't felt any pain although that was all she had left behind. What did she think killing herself would do to him? Didn't she know that it would destroy him? It would destroy her mother too. Marion would be devastated. Abi was everything to her. Leo hated her but he knew that she would be broken. He wanted to blame her for what Abi had done. If she hadn't stuck her big nose in their business, Abi might still be alive. He wanted to despise her and put all the blame at her feet but there was guilt and self-loathing seeping into his being, casting doubt on her guilt. Marion was protecting her daughter, from him as any mother would. He knew that it was him Abi had run from because his life was shit and he had made her life shit too. Everything he did was shit.

He had sent Abi to get him drugs because they had no money, because he was an addict. Their mattress smelled of piss, because he was an addict. There was no food in the kitchen and no money for electric in the meter, because he was an addict. He was travelling across North Wales with class-A drugs up his arse, because he was an addict. Their life was a struggle, and everything was shit, because he was an addict. Was it any wonder she didn't want to be with him and have a child together?

Leo walked back through the village, avoiding the social services' building. There were no more tears to cry for now. He skirted the shopping centre and reached his block of flats, in a zombie like state. Nothing mattered anymore. The communal front door was flapping in the wind, which meant the lock was broken again. They had only just fixed it. It was broken every few weeks and was nothing new. He opened it and noticed deep scratches on the frame. They were shiny and fresh. The door had been forced with a metal tool, but it didn't register. His brain was numb, his senses dulled, his awareness disarmed. The hallway was wet with multiple footprints, which led up the stairwell. He didn't question who had climbed the stairs or why. He was oblivious to his surroundings.

Leo trudged up the stairs, exhausted by a night in the cells and running for miles. Grief was sapping his energy like a vampire sucking his lifeforce from him. Every step was a mammoth effort. He reached the top landing and saw his door was ajar. The sound of breaking crockery drifted to him. Someone was in his flat, breaking his stuff. Stuff he had struggled to pay for. Stuff him and Abi had saved up to buy. Fuck that for a game of soldiers, he thought. They're not getting away with breaking his stuff.

The rage he felt at losing Abi bubbled to the surface and numbed any fear he had left. He knew that whoever was in his flat was looking for Barry Madern's memory stick. Why else would anyone be there? He had nothing worth stealing. They wouldn't find it, but they were trashing his home looking for it. He could turn around and run away and wait for them to leave but he was sick of running. He was sick of living.

Leo walked to his door and opened it without pausing. He looked around and saw the carnage caused inside. The settee was upside down and the material had been slashed open, the stuffing scattered all over the flat, like a cottonwool explosion. The armchair had suffered a similar fate. His shelves were torn from the walls and his television was broken in two and the back removed. He could hear someone in his bedroom, tearing the mattress and someone else in the kitchen, emptying his cupboards onto the floor. He thought about leaving for a second and then walked into the chaos and headed for the kitchen.

'Have you found what you're looking for?' Leo asked. His voice sounded flat, different. The intruder turned around; a black bandana wrapped around his face and dark beanie hat pulled low to his eyes. 'Look at the fucking mess you have made.' Leo bent down and picked up a carving knife from the floor. 'Get out of my flat.'

The intruder paused for a moment and looked beyond Leo. Someone was behind him. Leo felt a blow to the back of his head and bright lights flashed in his brain. Arms grabbed him from behind and held him fast, his arms pinned to his side. The intruder in front of him approached and punched him in the nose. Leo was blinded by the pain for a second. Blood ran from both nostrils.

'Where is it?' the man asked.

'Fuck you.'

The man punched him again and snapped Leo's head back. 'Where is it, Leo?'

'Up your mum's arsehole,' Leo said, spitting blood into his face. The man punched him again, splitting his lips, top and bottom.

'Where is it, you little gobshite?' the man growled. 'I can play this game all day.'

'Better ask your mum to bend over then, eh?' Leo said. Another punch to the nose sent sparks flying through his brain. 'Is that the best you've got?' A blow to the midriff knocked the wind from his lungs and his knees buckled.

'Where is it, Leo?' the man holding him asked. Leo felt the carving knife in his hand and jerked it behind him. He wrestled enough room to stab it six inches into the man's thigh. His grip released and Leo was free. Leo stabbed him again in the leg. He screamed and staggered into the living room, clutching the wound.

A punch to his jaw, shook Leo to the core. His brain switched off for a split second. Leo dropped to his knees. He looked up and saw the man aiming a kick. He slashed at him, the blade cut through his tracksuit, slicing the skin above his knees. Blood sprayed into the air.

'Fucking hell!' the man shouted. Leo stabbed the knife into his right foot, the blade bit into the floorboards. He screamed again and tried to move but his foot was pinned to the floor. Leo pulled the knife out and stuck it into the man's guts. He screamed and staggered out of the kitchen, holding the wound. 'You're dead, you little bastard!'

Leo pushed him over and ran back into the kitchen. He searched the debris on the floor. There were jars and bottles everywhere. He found the tub of strawberry milkshake, opened it and poured out the contents. The pink powder flowed into his hand. The memory stick was still there. Leo slid it into his boxer shorts and ran into the living room. It was time to escape.

One of the intruders jumped on his back and flattened Leo. He crashed onto the floor face first. The pain in his broken nose was sickening. He felt blows raining down on the back of his head, each one driving his skull against the floor. The weight of the man was crushing the air from his lungs, and he couldn't breathe. He thought he was going to die right there on his living room floor, and he didn't care anymore.

There was a clatter and chorus of loud voices shouting as four uniformed officers burst in. He saw Jane Bennet following them and he watched as the two intruders tried to escape but they were overwhelmed quickly, cuffed and dragged down the stairs. Leo closed his eyes and let the pain wash over him. He wished he could sink into the eternal darkness, right then, and go and find Abi.

A paramedic came to him and turned him onto his back. Leo watched and listened, but nothing really sank in. Jane Bennet repeated the same question over and over.

'What where they looking for, Leo?' she repeated. Leo didn't reply. The paramedics wiped the blood from his nose and mouth. They told him his nose was broken but he didn't care. It hurt when they packed his nostrils with cottonwool.

'We know you took something from the rucksack, Leo,' Jane said but her voice was like an echo. He watched her lips moving but didn't want to answer. He didn't want to speak, or see, or hear. He wanted silence. Peace. 'What did you take out of the bag, Leo?'

Leo still didn't speak. He let them ask their questions but chose to disassociate himself from the scene. He drifted above it all.

'Matrix want to speak to you, Leo. I can't help you if you don't help me,' Jane whittered on and on. 'If they think you're hiding something for Barry Madern, they'll crucify you,' she said. Leo didn't care. He had what they were all looking for and he was going to keep it until he was ready to give it up. No one was going to make him do anything that he didn't want to do. Not anymore.

Chapter 36. One week later.

P*our me a drink, and I'll tell you some lies...*

DI JANE BENNET WALKED up the path to Anthony Head's house. The surname had made her smile when she first saw it. Angela Deacon had told the kids he was Tony Knobhead and now it made sense. They were going to talk to him about Rohypnol and having sex with Angela on the day she died. There was no warrant as there was no crime, yet. If he coughed to committing one, that would be a different matter. They knew what time his wife left for work and waited until she drove away. DS Gill Alan knocked on the door. It opened and Anthony Head was standing in a pair of shorts and a tee shirt, a confused look on his face.

'If you're selling anything, I'm skint,' he said. His eyes scanned the detectives up and down. They were both pleasing on the eye.

'I'm DI Jane Bennet and this is DS Gill Alan,' Jane said. 'Can we have a word with you, please.'

'Yes. What's the problem?' Tony asked, folding his arms.

'Inside would be better,' Jane said. They had arrived in a marked police car and two youths on bikes had spotted it. They stopped and watched them.

'What is this about?'

'Hey Tony, why are the pigs there?' one of the youths shouted.

'Trust me, it would be better if we went inside,' Jane said. Tony stepped back and opened the door for the detectives to enter.

'Nosey fuckers around here,' Tony joked, nervously. 'You can't fart on this estate without everyone knowing.'

'Have a seat,' Gill said.

'What is this about?' Tony asked, sitting on the settee. The detectives remained standing.

'Angela Deacon,' Jane said. Tony blushed.

'That was a shame what happened to her,' Tony said. 'At such a young age too. You would never expect it to happen, would you?'

'We know you had sex with her on the day she died,' Jane said. 'Your DNA is in the system.'

'I see,' Tony said, nodding. He blushed red. 'You've caught me with my pants down, so to speak.' He shrugged. 'We had a thing every now and again. I'm married. My missus doesn't need to know about this, does she?'

'So, you were having an affair with Angela?' Gill asked, frowning.

'Sort of,' Tony said, stuttering. 'It was just a casual thing, you know. I wouldn't call it an affair.'

'No,' Jane said. 'I wouldn't call it an affair, either.'

'You wouldn't?'

'No.'

'That's good then,' Tony said, nodding.

'I wouldn't call it an affair because if the sex was consensual, you wouldn't need to drug her, would you?' Jane said. Tony went pale. 'With Rohypnol.'

'She was badly bruised,' Gill said. 'Her ribs were broken.' Tony didn't answer. 'You raped her, Tony.'

'You drugged her wine and then you took her to her bedroom, buggered her and raped her, didn't you?'

'That's not what happened,' Tony said, shaking his head. 'She liked it rough.'

'Oh, bullshit Tony,' Jane said. 'No woman wants her ribs broken. It was rape.'

'Are you arresting me?' Tony asked. He stood up. 'Because if you're not, I want you to leave my house.'

'We can come back later when your wife is home,' Jane said.

'Get out,' Tony said. 'If you go near my wife, I'll sue you. We were having an affair, we often had sex and you can't prove any different.'

'Okay,' Jane said. 'We'll go, for now but you know that you raped her. We know that you raped her, and we'll be watching you. If you breathe the wrong way and we'll come down on you like a ton of bricks.'

'Get out,' Tony said, pointing to the door.

The detectives left the house and walked down the path. There were four youths on bikes now. One of them was circling their vehicle.

'Hey pigs, why are you talking to Tony?' he shouted. 'What's he done?'

They looked at each other and got into the car. It was tempting to leak the fact that Anthony Head was a rapist, but they couldn't. Jane felt as if they were expected to fight the criminals with their hands were tied behind their backs.

'I'm not sure what I expected but I can't help but feel disappointed,' Jane said. Her phone rang and she answered it. 'DI Bennet.'

'Jane, you put a flag on an address in Dovecot, belonging to William Hughes?'

'Yes,' Jane said. 'What's happened?'

'Uniform are there, and they've reported a fatality at the scene,' the desk sergeant said.

'Oh shit,' Jane said. 'We're ten minutes away. We'll go there now.'

She ended the call and started the engine. 'Did you get that?' she asked her DS.

'Yes,' Gill said.

They headed through the Bluebell estate to Prescot Road and headed towards the city centre. The traffic was light as they approached Dovecot. William Hughes lived in a bungalow on the edge of a sheltered housing estate. It was a cul-de-sac, and the road was narrow. There was an ambulance at the far end of the street and several marked police vehicles. Jane parked the car half on the kerb.

'I don't want to do this,' she said. 'My stomach is twisted.'

'We put a marker on the address, we couldn't have done anything else,' Gill said.

They walked quickly towards the bungalow at the end of the street. Uniformed officers had cordoned off the road. A forensic tent had been erected on a small patch of lawn in front of the bungalow. The sign that a dead body was being processed. A detective from MIT saw them approaching and waved a hand. She recognised him as Gavin Stokes.

'Hello Jane,' he said, a stern expression on his face. 'I'm told you put a marker on this address?'

'Yes,' Jane said. 'The occupant is a seventy-nine-year-old man, who reported being cuckooed by some local thugs. They were terrorising him.' She gestured to the tent. 'What's happened?'

'Mr Hughes has a son, Eddie,' Gavin said, he ran his hand over his bald head and removed his rimless glasses. 'He's a kickboxing instructor from Chester, apparently and his father had told him what was going on. A group of teenagers knocked on the door expecting the old man to answer but his son opened it. There was an altercation and one of the youths pulled a knife.'

'Oh no,' Jane said, fearing the worst.

'The deceased is seventeen. Eliot Cann,' Gavin said. Jane and Gill exchanged glances. 'Do you know him?'

'We know the name,' Jane said. 'He was mentioned as the ringleader.'

'I see. Eddie Hughes has been arrested and taken in. It looks like self-defence on the face of it. Cann fell onto the knife in the struggle.'

'These kids are out of control,' Jane said, shaking her head. 'Do his parents know?'

'Uniform are on their way now,' Gavin said. 'Unfortunately, some of them are becoming very experienced at breaking bad news to families.'

Chapter 37. Matrix.

*O*h mother, tell your children, not to do what I have done, spend your lives in sin and misery, in the House of the Rising Sun...

DC JOHNSON WAS SITTING at her desk, chewing on a wine gum. It was raining and the rain was trickling down the window, blurring everything outside. Her phone rang. It reflected the mood in the building at the moment. Everyone was on edge, waiting for the go ahead to smash the Madern OCG once and for all.

'DC Johnson, speaking.'

'Hello, this is Rob Wilkinson from forensics, Warrington.'

'Hello Rob. What can I do for you?'

'I have the results back on a firearm recovered from the address of an Angela Deacon,' he said. 'Good news on two fronts.'

'I like the sound of this.'

'The gun matches three bullets recovered from the murder of Rasim Ahman in Liverpool 8 last year,' Rob said. 'The rifling is an exact match.

'That is great news.'

'Better still,' he said. 'We have DNA on the handle and the trigger, and we have a match. Simon Tickle.'

'That's the best news I've heard all day,' Johnson said.

Chapter 38. Kenny Fulshaw.

C razy skies all wild above me now, winter howling at my face, and everything I held so dear, disappeared without a trace...

KENNY WALKED AROUND the Albert Dock, trying to clear his head. He couldn't see any way out of his predicament. The contaminated cocaine had started a series of events which had snowballed. The police would be looking for him, which meant he couldn't go home. Barry Madern would have eyes trying to find him, which meant he couldn't stay in the city. He had money, lots of money. Selling cocaine for Madern had been very profitable. He was paid well, and he'd skimmed hundreds of thousands from the top. All good things must come to an end, but he hadn't expected it to end like this.

Barry had told him to disappear, or he would make him disappear. One way or the other, he had said. Fall on your sword, he had said too. What the fuck did that mean? Kill himself. That wasn't going to happen. He was in desperate trouble, but suicide wasn't on the cards. Absolutely not. Madern could go and swivel on it. His days were numbered anyway. It was time to cut free from him and set up somewhere else. He had money and he had a passport. The world was his to explore. He decided to book a night in one of the waterfront hotels while he made a concrete plan. Dublin was the obvious place to go. He could take a ferry from Liverpool and stay a night in Dublin before taking a flight to New York. America had always fascinated him, but he had never been. Maybe this was an opportunity to broaden his horizons and see a bit of the world before he decided where he wanted to stay.

Kenny went into the Pumphouse and ordered a pint of Stella. It was busy with tourists and locals alike. There were a lot of shorts being worn and just as many business suits. He took his pint and walked to an empty table next to a window. He slid into the bench seat and looked out over part of the dock. The water was dark, almost green in parts. He looked up at Canning Place, the police headquarters and wondered if his mugshot was being sent out to the uniformed officers on the streets. If it wasn't already, it would be soon. There was nowhere to hide.

'Kenny Fulshaw,' a voice said. Kenny jumped and looked around. He was looking into the dark eyes of a man he vaguely recognised. 'What the fuck are you doing in this part of town?'

'Do I know you?' Kenny asked. Behind the man, he could see three others leaning against a steel column, staring. They were all Asian males, with Cuban hairlines and sculptured stubble. One of them was familiar but he wasn't sure why.

'You know my cousin, Rasim Ahman,' the man said, glaring into his eyes.

'I've never heard of him,' Kenny said, lying. 'Rasim who?'

'Ahman.'

'The trouble with you lot is your names are all the same,' Kenny said. 'You should think up some new ones to save any confusion.'

'Funny fucker, eh?' the man said, anger in his eyes. 'The big guy over there is Rasim's brother and he knows that it was one of your crew who shot his brother.'

'Okay,' Kenny said, waving to the man he was talking about. The group of men were incensed. 'Firstly, I don't have a crew. Secondly, I don't know Rasim Ahman and thirdly, if you don't get out of my face, I'm going to blow your fucking head off, right here and now.' Kenny had his right hand in his pocket. The man looked down and backed away. Kenny slid out of the bench seat and stood up. 'I'm going to walk out of here and if any of you follow me, I'll send you where we sent your cousin.'

'You're a dead man, Fulshaw,' one of the men shouted.

Kenny walked out into the gloomy daylight of the afternoon and the wind gusted, making him wrap his coat tighter. Rain hammered down and bounced off the cobbled streets. He jogged around the Pumphouse and headed for the museum, taking the footbridge to the Pier Head. The wind blew harder. Kenny put his head down and walked beneath the Liver Building, past the bronze statue of the Beatles. He could see the Crown Plaza ahead and thought it was the closest hotel and he could try to get a room. If they didn't have one, they had a decent bar where he could wait until the rain went off.

Kenny stopped at a zebra crossing; half a dozen other people were waiting. The lights changed and he crossed the road, head down, battling against the wind and rain. A motorbike pulled up on the pavement and stopped behind him. The pillion rider aimed a Glock and fired three times before it roared off into the traffic. Kenny was dead before he hit the puddle he fell into.

Chapter 39. Sam.

I can't get there on my own, you can't leave me here alone, I'm just trying to do what's right, a man ain't a man unless he's fought the fight...

SAM WAS DRIVING A FORKLIFT truck between two huge storage racks, loading a delivery of engine oil. It was trickier lifting liquids than solids and not all the drivers were qualified to do it. He would get paid extra for staying on to shift the pallets. Work was a welcome distraction at the moment. Losing Angela was really biting hard, especially as her house was across the road. He missed her and he missed the kids. They would see each other most days, at least once. He had phoned social services and left messages, but no one had called him back. He wanted to see them, but he wasn't their father, and he wasn't related to them, so he didn't matter.

His mobile vibrated and he unloaded the pallet from the forks and stopped the truck. It was a text message. His pulse rate increased, and he had to take a deep breath to read the message. It was from the number they had messaged him from before. Shotgun Degsy or whatever the silly fucker was called. He was reluctant to open it but didn't want petrol pouring through his letterbox. He opened it.

Our sources have told us the Dibble have interviewed Tony Head across the road from you. They believe he drugged Angela, buggered her, broke her ribs and raped her. They have DNA but can't do anything about it. Someone should.

The message was like a punch in the guts. He felt physically sick. Angela couldn't stand Tony. Tony Knobhead was the politest thing she called him. Wanker was common and pervert was standard when she spoke about him. She said he was a creep, always making innuendos and lude comments. His wife was always rude to Angela but that was probably because he used to stare at her with his tongue hanging out. The bastard had drugged his Angela and violated her in the vilest way he could imagine, and the police had cast iron proof but couldn't do anything. Anger coursed through his veins. Shotgun Degsy was right. Someone should do something about it.

Chapter 40. Lenny.

One by one I've seen em fall, some just don't show up at all, I'm just here to fight the fire, a man ain't a man 'less he has desire...

LENNY PULLED UP AT the address he had been given and turned off the engine. He was driving the F-type Jaguar that he had bought the week before, just because he could. He was hoping no one would buy it, so that he could keep it for as long as possible. It was one of the joys of being a car dealer. He was about to look at a Porsche Boxster, which was another of his favourite cars. This one was a 2002 and sought after because of the V6 engine. They were rare in good condition. He had seen pictures of it, and it was a beauty in dark blue, and it would be snapped up quickly. The owner had contacted him via his website and was very keen to sell as he was going away travelling for a few years. It sounded like he would take a reasonable offer on the spot just to liquidise the asset. The Boxster was in a lockup in St Helens, which was a fifteen-minute drive away. He checked his phone and Google maps said the lockups were on the left behind the petrol station, which was across the road.

Lenny got out of the Jag and walked to the petrol station. It was busy and all the pumps were in operation. He went into the shop and bought a bottle of water to take with him to the meeting. When he walked outside, he spotted a path which led between the garage and a playing field, where a game of football was being played between two teams of adults. He watched them kicking the ball and shouting to each other as if it was a cup final being played at Wembley. Their enthusiasm made him smile.

When he reached the end of the path, he could see the lockups to his right and a cinder driveway leading to them. A single male was standing next to a black BMW, smoking a cigarette. Lenny approached and the man nodded a greeting.

'You must be Lenny Ray,' the man said. The man was wearing a black leather jacket and a baseball cap. His complexion was ruddy, and he had a drinker's nose.

'I am. Are you Fred?' Lenny asked. Lenny saw the man eyeing him up. He was wearing a tee-shirt with a padded gillet over it, leaving his arms bare. He was used to people staring because of the ink on his arms and hands. People still judged tattoos but there was something else. Something wrong. He sensed the man was gauging his size. Lenny went to the gym every day. He was a strong man. There was no handshake offered, which Lenny found odd.

'I am, Fred, yes. The Boxster is in this lockup over here,' Fred said, walking away from the BMW. Lenny stepped around the car and followed him, a few paces behind. The rear doors opened, and two men climbed out. Lenny sensed something was wrong, but it was too late. One of the men held a silver revolver in his right hand and pointed it low at his abdomen.

'Stay still and don't try to run or I'll put one in the back of your head, understand?'

'Okay,' Lenny said. 'I haven't got any cash on me. I don't bring cash to car deals.'

'We're not after your money,' Fred said. 'My boss is Barry Madern, you've heard of him?'

'Yes,' Lenny said, feeling scared, now. He thought they were looking for cash, but this was much worse. 'I've heard of him.'

'Your missus has snatched Barry's children and he's not a happy man,' Fred said.

'I don't suppose he is, but I don't know anything about his children,' Lenny said. He looked around to see if they could be seen from the road or the playing fields, but they were hidden from view. They had picked a good spot for an ambush.

'Where are they?' one of the men said stepping closer. Lenny could see he was wearing a knuckleduster on his right hand.

'Where are who?' Lenny stalled.

'His kids.'

'I don't know anything about her work,' Lenny said. 'She doesn't tell me anything like that. It's all confidential. We don't talk work at home.'

'They took the kids from a house in Huyton at teatime and moved them somewhere, so she was probably late home that night,' Fred said. 'Surely, she told you where she had been. Have a good think about where she went with them. Trust me, it's in your interest to remember.'

'I don't ask her where she's been,' Lenny said, shrugging. 'You're wasting your time.'

'I'm going to give you one more chance to tell me where the kids are,' Fred said, frowning.

'Like I said, she doesn't tell me the details,' Lenny said. He was pumped with fear and adrenalin. Fight or flight mode engaged. 'And if the truth be told, even if I did know, I wouldn't tell you anyway.'

'This guy is a prick,' knuckleduster man said.

'I'm not the one wearing knuckles,' Lenny said. 'I think that makes you the prick.'

'Tough guy, are you?' Fred asked. But he didn't look as confident as he had earlier.

'I've had my moments,' Lenny said, backing away.

'Can you stop a bullet?'

'No,' Lenny said, shaking his head. 'But plenty of people will hear one being fired.'

'He's not going to tell us, so we'll have to ask your missus, won't we,' Fred said. He nodded to the men. 'Let's give her some encouragement to tell us, shall we.'

Lenny saw the first punch coming and dodged it. The knuckleduster whizzed past his ear. Lenny launched himself forward and headbutted the attacker, cracking his nose. He felt the tiny bones crack. The second man punched Lenny in the side of his head, but it was knuckle on bone and he shook it off. Lenny kneed him in the testicles and the man collapsed to his knees, gasping for breath. Lenny threw a left hook, and it was a thunderous blow. The man crumpled to the cinders.

Lenny thought he had given himself enough space to turn and run but felt the sledgehammer blow to his guts a millisecond before he heard the gunshot. It crushed the air from his lungs. His knees gave way and he clutched at his stomach, feeling his blood pumping out of the bullet wound. He fell onto his back and the men began kicking him in the head and body. Stars flashed in his head and an agonising ache came from his abdomen. A kick to his face numbed his jaw and cheekbone and he could feel blood filling his mouth. He vomited and thought he was going to choke to death. A heavy kick to the temple stunned him. Kick after kick thudded against his skull. The pain and trauma were too much, and darkness cloaked him as he lost consciousness.

Chapter 41. Sam.

I *'m the flame, short of fire, I'm the dark in need of light...*

SAM FOLLOWED TONY HEAD from his house, walking a hundred yards behind him. He was heading towards the Bluebell Arms, and he looked like he was on a mission. There was a spring in his step because he thought he was going to meet an eighteen-year-old girl called Chelsea, that he'd been grooming online. The girl had been chatting to him and sexting for a few days, but she didn't exist. Sam had set up the profile and catfished him to lure him to the car park at the cricket club, where Tony had arranged to meet the girl before going for a drink in the Bluebell. What Tony didn't know was that Barry Madern was incensed that the mother of his children had been drugged and raped and he wanted revenge. Sam was more than happy to help set him up.

Tony reached the entrance to the cricket club, which was closed and in darkness and jogged down the path to the car park. The girl, Chelsea had told him she would be waiting under the shelter by the smoking area. A single security light cast a dull glow across the car park.

As Tony turned the corner, a smile on his face, he walked straight into a baseball bat, which took him off his feet. Sam slid into some bushes and watched from a distance as Tony was bundled into the back of a transit van by two gorillas. What they had planned for him, he didn't know and didn't care. That was their business. His job was done.

Sam went back to his flat and opened a tin of beer, raising it to Angela's empty house, in cheers that her rapist was probably more scared than she ever was. He scrolled through Netflix and found a war film to take his mind away for a while. He was unsure how he felt about what he had done. His phone vibrated.

Well done, lad. This twat has got ruffies in his pocket, he just doesn't learn. Delete this number, you won't hear from us again. He won't be going home.

Chapter 42. Leo.

When the walls come down, you tore out my heart, you threw it away...

LEO HAD BEEN SUCKED up into the Madern investigation, interviewed under caution, bullied and coaxed in equal amounts. He had agreed to give Matrix information in return for going into witness protection, which meant he couldn't talk to anyone outside of the investigation. Social Services had enquired where he was and what was happening and they had been told, he was no longer their problem.

He had been very useful to the investigation. So, far he had given them the addresses of three houses that the OCG used to store weapons and drugs, none of them were previously on the police radar. The raids had yielded over eighty kilos of class-A drugs and a number of firearms.

Coping with the death of Abi was impossible and he cried himself to sleep most nights. Each day brought the same desperate yearning to see her again, in this world or the next. There was nothing left in this world for him. Everything he loved was gone. They had told him about Marion being arrested, and he had a strange sense of sadness for her. The hate was waning. She had lost Abi and her grandchild and now she was in prison, her business down the pan, staring at a long sentence. What more could she lose? There was a sense of empathy there. Leo was functioning and not much more, but he had a plan. He was trying to hang on by taking one day at a time.

He was holding vital information back and drip feeding them, remembering new details here and there. Prolonging the disclosure was in his interest. They were also helping him get off the ket. He was seeing a specialist, who prescribed him the drugs he required to get straight, and he was sleeping in a halfway house, while they processed him and set up his new identity. It was warm and he could eat whatever he wanted, and watch films; the bed was comfortable and didn't stink of piss. For the first time in his life, he felt in control.

The detectives were ready for the next round of interviews. Leo was sitting with a cup of tea with three sugars. It reminded him of Phil, and he wondered how he was.

'Good morning, Leo,' Laura Lunt said, sitting down. She brought a whiff of Armani Diamonds with her. Leo thought she was quite fit for a copper, in a female punky type of way. 'How are you today?'

'Living the dream,' Leo said. 'Have you arrested Barry Madern yet?'

'No. Not yet.'

'What are you waiting for?'

'We've been making sure we've got him, and he can't squirm out. The addresses you have given us have helped enormously.' She paused. 'You know Jo Lilly from child protection, don't you?'

'Yes,' Leo said. 'We go way back. She was a social worker when I was in care before she became the big boss. She's a top lady in my book, although I've had a few bollockings from her in my time.'

'I can imagine she doesn't take any shit.' Laura paused. 'Her husband was shot yesterday,' Laura said. 'Barry Madern had him set up and attacked.'

'Why?'

'Because Jo took Angela's children into care,' Laura said. 'Madern is their father.'

'What the fuck,' Leo whispered. 'Is her husband dead?'

'He's in intensive care and he's fifty, fifty,' Laura said. 'It's prompted us to move quicker than we wanted to, so we're arresting Madern today. Leo, anything you can give us today will help us keep the bastard locked up.'

'You need to lock him up forever. He's a monster,' Leo said. 'He ruins lives.'

'He is a monster,' Laura said. 'Can you think of anything else we could use against him?'

'Yes.'

'What?'

'I have a memory stick, which belongs to him,' Leo said. 'But I need to go to the toilet.'

'What did you say?'

'I have a memory stick that he hid at Angela's. I took it from the rucksack.' Leo stood up. 'I'll go to the loo.'

'Can't you wait a minute?' Laura said.

'Not if you want this memory stick,' Leo said. 'I've got it hidden, if you know what I mean.'

Chapter 43. Jo Lilly.

L ying close to you feeling your heart beating, and I'm wondering what you're dreaming, wondering if it's me you're seeing...

JO WAS SITTING NEXT to the door when they brought Lenny from theatre. The intensive care unit was quiet, and the trolley rattled and squeaked. Lenny looked like he had been run over by a train, both eyes were swollen shut, purple and deep blue. His nose was crooked, and his lips were blackened. He was attached to a respirator and was being kept alive; blood and saline were being fed into his arms. The nurses checked and double-checked that everything was where it should be. She watched his chest rise and fall in time with the machine and she felt a million miles away from him. The tears streamed down her face. He looked so vulnerable and broken. She wanted to hold him and tell him it was going to be alright.

'How is he?' her friend Jody from work asked. She had gone to get drinks and handed her a bottle of water.

'They've just wheeled him in. He's just come back from theatre,' Jo said. 'I haven't spoken to anyone yet. Look at his face,' she said, crying uncontrollably. 'Look what they did to his lovely face. It doesn't even look like him. How could anyone do such a thing to such a gentle soul as Lenny?'

'I don't know, Jo,' Jody said. 'I honestly don't know.'

'They're cowards, the cowardly bastards!' Jo sobbed. 'He was nothing to do with anything. It was me they should have come to.'

'Excuse me. Are you Lenny's partner?' a voice came from behind her. She turned to see a tall man, with black skin. He was wearing green scrubs. Jo nodded but couldn't find her voice. 'I'm Mr Ramoosh and I'm one of the surgeons that operated on him.'

'I'm Jo. Thank you, for what you've done,' Jo said. 'Is he going to die, Mr Ramoosh?'

'It's hanging in the balance, Jo,' Mr Ramoosh said, shaking his head. 'We've removed the bullet from his abdomen and the good news is that none of his major organs were damaged.'

'That's good news, isn't it?' Jo said.

'Yes. He was shot at close range, but the bullet hit his belt buckle, which took some of the impact.'

'I always tell him that belt is shit,' Jo said, sniffling. 'I've been trying to get him to wear a different one for years.'

'It probably saved his life,' Mr Ramoosh said, nodding. 'His internal injuries are manageable but it's the damage to his brain that we're concerned about.' He touched Jo's shoulder. 'Let's take a seat.' They sat down. 'I'll explain his condition to you.'

'Okay,' Jo said.

'His skull is fractured in three places and his brain is swelling. If it keeps swelling, it will be fatal.'

'Oh no!' Jo said, shaking her head. 'Don't say that. What can you do?' Jo asked. 'I don't want him to die. I can't live without my Lenny.'

'We have done everything we can, now all we can do is wait and hope the swelling subsides. If he makes it through tonight, he has a chance but only time will tell.' Mr Ramoosh removed his glasses and cleaned them on his tunic. 'He's a strong man and he's made it this far. Are you a religious person?'

'Not really,' Jo said, sobbing. 'But I'll say some prayers tonight.'

'So, will I,' Mr Ramoosh said. 'I've got to see some other patients, but I'll be back in a few hours to see how he's doing. The neurologist is looking at the scans and he will be along shortly. He'll give you an update when he can.'

'Can I see him, please?' Jo said.

'Yes. I'll get a nurse to give you a mask and gown and you can sit with him for a while,' Dr Ramoosh said. 'Talk to him, he will be able to hear you even if he can't respond.'

An alarm went off and the surgeon stood up and looked through the glass.

'Code blue, room one, code blue, room one.'

Jo stood up and watched as doctors and nurses flocked to Lenny's room.

'What is a code blue?' she asked, panicking. 'Tell me what is going on!'

'His heart has stopped beating,' Mr Ramoosh said.

Chapter 44. Twelve months later.

S itting on the dock of the bay, wasting time...

LEO WAS SITTING ON a trailer, drinking coffee from a flask. Next to him were fifty bales of hay that he was scattering across the field where the younger pigs were kept. They were snorting and snuffling and running around for no reason except to run. He loved the pigs, especially the young ones. Working on the farm had put him off eating bacon, even though the smell of bacon cooking still appealed, he couldn't eat it.

The sun was shining, and he could feel the rays, warming his skin. His face and arms were tanned from working outside and he was filling out. Manual work and eating well agreed with him. He hadn't had any drugs for five months and his body was recovering slowly. So was his brain. The urge to take ket crept up on him every now and again but he was fifty miles from the nearest town, and he had no access to drugs. The temptation to use was minimal and he felt like he had been set free from a horrendous curse. He had been given a second chance at life.

Living near the south coast was like living in a different world. The sea was nearby, and it calmed him and enthralled him in equal measure. There was nothing for him in Liverpool, although it would always be in his heart. He followed the advice given to him by his councillors and things were better than he could have expected.

Abi was a constant on his mind and there was still a gaping hole where she had once been. He didn't think he would ever get over her death but the need to join her on the other side wasn't there anymore. He wanted to live. His memories of being a mule and an addict were painful and would be engrained in his brain and he would never sink to those depths again. As a child, he had never really had a chance. He had one now and he had grabbed it with both hands.

Chapter 45. Jo Lilly.

I *can't live, if living is without you...*

PHIL MOLT CHECKED HIS pigeonhole and sorted the important post from the junk. There was the usual stack of memos that were sent via email and also in the internal post just to make sure they were read. A handwritten envelope caught his eye. He took it back to his desk. Jo had arrived in the office and was sitting at the desk next to his.

'Morning Jo,' he said, sitting down.

'Hello, lovely,' Jo said. She looked up and smiled. 'What are you doing today?'

'I've got a strat on the Wilkes case to complete and pre preceding's on the Lancaster children,' he said.

'Let me see the strat before it goes to Hayley,' Jo said. 'She's got a thing about commas at the moment.'

'I struggle with commas, to be honest,' Phil said.

'You all do, that's why she's on one about them.' Jo smiled. 'I get reports sent back to me marked in red pen. I feel like a naughty schoolgirl because you lot don't use a grammar check.'

'Are you telling me off?'

'Yes. Use a spelling and grammar check,' Jo said, nodding. 'It's not rocket fuel.'

'Science,' Phil said.

'That's what I said.'

'Fair enough.' He laughed. 'How's Lenny?'

'Angry, bored, sore, pissed off and constantly watching the local news, looking for information on the Madern investigation,' Jo said. 'Physically, he's getting stronger, day by day. He's going to the gym and progressing slowly but surely. Mentally, he's struggling to occupy his mind. I've told him to read more, and he's bought a kindle.'

'It's good he's getting better,' Phil said. 'He's lucky he survived.'

'He doesn't know the half of it. He was just lying there snoring for weeks while I had to sit there, wondering if he was going to live or die. He was Mr Oblivious through the entire thing,' Jo said, smiling. 'Sometimes, we don't know what we have until it's nearly taken away from us. We just never know, do we?'

'True. I remember my dad going to work and never coming home,' Phil said. 'He was a bricky. Dropped dead with his trowel in his hand.'

'How old was he?'

'Forty-five.'

'That's no age.'

'Is Lenny still reading up about wines?' Phil asked, frowning.

'Yes. He's been ordering some belters, lately. He said it's only money and he can't take it with him,' Jo said, smiling. 'I suppose every cloud has a silver lining.'

'I've been to check my post and I'm a bit worried. Take a look at this,' Phil said, handing Jo the envelope. She looked at the postmark. 'Do you recognise the handwriting?'

'I think so,' Jo said. She mouthed Leo and Phil nodded.

'He shouldn't be contacting anyone,' Phil said. 'I don't want to be breaking any protocols.'

'He's a little bugger,' Jo said. 'He always was. Do you want me to open it?'

'Yes please,' Phil said.

Jo opened the letter. There was a twenty-pound note inside. She took it out with a handwritten note, which read.

I hope you're well, mate. Here's the twenty quid I owe you for the chippy.

'He hasn't signed it but it's from Leo,' Jo said, smiling. 'He must be doing okay.'

'That's his way of telling us he's alright?' Phil said, nodding. 'Looks like lunch is on me.'

Chapter 46. Barry Madern.

H*e didn't even say goodbye, he didn't take the time to lie...*

BARRY WAS FOLDING TOWELS in the laundry with two other inmates. He was driving himself insane with anger. Leo Tompkins had handed the memory stick to Matrix. The little shit. He didn't think he had the balls to do such a thing. Everything had been in hand, and he would have walked on the conspiracy charges but the information in those files would send him away for life. And not just him. There had been a wave of arrests following the forensic investigation into the files.

Judges, barristers, lawyers, police officers, detectives, journalists, gangsters, couriers, money launderers and hitmen were all documented in the files. Times, dates, amounts of cash, transactions, voice recordings, video recordings and digital images were stored on it. They were supposed to be his lifeboat if anything went wrong. He could have used the information stored to blackmail himself to anywhere in the world. Instead, it was the weapon that would finish him and half of the criminals in the city.

All because of a little baghead, Leo Tompkins.

Barry took his stack of towels and carried it into laundry room. He put them on the shelf and went back to the machines, which whirred monotonously. Something rattled inside, metal on metal. He realised that the other inmates had gone.

Barry looked around for them, but he couldn't see them. Were they having a cheeky joint in the toilets, without him?

He hardly felt the arm slipping around his neck, but he felt the sharp sting of the razor blade that sliced through his jugular and windpipe. His blood sprayed into the air in a fan shape, and he tried to stem the jet of claret with his fingers, but it was impossible. Darkness and pain engulfed him within seconds and the day turned into night.

Epilogue;

Everyone has to find their own way, and I'm sure things will work out okay, all we know is the sun will rise, thank your lucky stars that you're alive, It's a beautiful life...

CALVIN LISTENED TO Coco snoring gently. It was a soothing sound, comforting and familiar. Their beds were warm, Calvin on the top bunk and Coco below. She loved the bed and played pirate ships on it. Calvin was always the captain and Coco was everybody else, usually a mermaid with magic powers. They were safe and happy in their forever home. Their new parents were a childless couple with good jobs and all the love in their hearts to give. Coco loved both of them and Calvin loved her. They were lovely people, and he was growing attached. Their kindness knew no boundaries and he knew they would be safe.

At night when Coco had gone to sleep, he would talk to his mum in his head. He missed her terribly but talking to her made him feel close to her again. He knew she was there because she pulled at his heart strings to let him know, that she was right there beside him. The ache in his chest was her sign to him that she would never leave his side. Not ever.

The End

Author's notes

Thank you for reading my latest novel. I hope you enjoyed it. Each one is a nervous adventure for me as the author, hoping you, the reader will want to read more. As the 30th novel, it's a milestone and venture into new places. The research has been spread across multiple boroughs and gathered from talking to many social work practitioners. My partner works in child protection and so do some of the people I went to school with. They have been invaluable in creating this novel. I grew up in Knowsley and went to school there for a while, so I chose it as the setting for the book. Huyton Village is familiar to me from my early teens. I used to cycle from home to Huyton Lane to see my friends, and I had family in, Huyton, Dovecot, and St Helens. I like to write about the places that I know, so I set some of the story there.

As a teenager at Prescot Comp, I used to bunk off school on a Friday and get the number 10 bus into Liverpool city centre and watch bands in Eric's on Mathew Street, the Mountford Hall and the Empire. I bought records from Pete Burns (Dead or Alive) when he worked in Probe records, and he scared me to death with his black contact lenses. Liverpool and music go hand in hand for me. Those streets and venues have special memories for me, hence I set scenes there. I remember my parents getting a letter from the school pointing out that I was absent quite a lot on Fridays and there was a pattern forming. I explained to them that some of the bands I wanted to see, played on a Friday and it was double maths at school, which made me want to throw myself under a bus. They went apeshit and my adventures into Liverpool were shifted to Saturdays. I couldn't see what the problem was. I hated maths and loved music. At no point in my adult life have I needed to use cosines, tangents or formulas, but I listen to tunes all day, every day.

The Bluebell pub was a landmark on Prescot Road but is demolished now. This is a work of total fiction, created from years of researching Child Exploitation by drug gangs across the planet. CE and cuckooing are daily occurrences across the UK and are not unique to Liverpool and we're struggling in the battle against drugs. Social services are struggling with aftermath. To anyone considering it as a career, it's a vocation not a job. It takes very special people to carry out the work that the child protection teams do daily. Thankfully, there are special people around. Thank you so much for reading my books, I'm very grateful.

The cheapest way to read my other books are to download the box sets. They're all on Amazon and here are the links.

The Anglesey Murders 1-6

https://www.amazon.co.uk/dp/B08122Z9RQ

The Anglesey Murders 7-10

https://amzn.eu/d/8fVLNzy

The Detective Alec Ramsay Series

https://amzn.eu/d/29B6Rw4

The Inspector Braddick Series

https://amzn.eu/d/ck2TLaV

The Soft Target Series

https://amzn.eu/d/4WNJEH4

The Journey Series

https://amzn.eu/d/6onSAZz

Printed in Great Britain
by Amazon